THE FOWL TWINS
DENY ALL CHARGES

BOOK TWO

Other Books by Eoin Colfer

Airman

Benny and Omar

Benny and Babe

Half Moon Investigations

The Supernaturalist

The Wish List

Iron Man: The Gauntlet

ARTEMIS FOWL

Artemis Fowl

Artemis Fowl: The Arctic Incident

Artemis Fowl: The Eternity Code

Artemis Fowl: The Opal Deception

Artemis Fowl: The Lost Colony

Artemis Fowl: The Time Paradox

Artemis Fowl: The Atlantis Complex

Artemis Fowl: The Last Guardian

The Fowl Twins

W.A.R.P.: The Reluctant Assassin
W.A.R.P.: The Hangman's Revolution
W.A.R.P.: The Forever Man

GRAPHIC NOVELS
Artemis Fowl: The Graphic Novel
Artemis Fowl: The Arctic Incident: The Graphic Novel
Artemis Fowl: The Eternity Code: The Graphic Novel
Artemis Fowl: The Opal Deception: The Graphic Novel
The Supernaturalist: The Graphic Novel

AND FOR YOUNGER READERS
Eoin Colfer's The Legend of Spud Murphy
Eoin Colfer's The Legend of Captain Crow's Teeth
Eoin Colfer's The Legend of the Worst Boy in the World

DENY ALL CHARGES

BOOK TWO

EOIN COLFER

Disney • HYPERION

Los Angeles   New York

First Edition, October 2020
1 3 5 7 9 10 8 6 4 2
FAC-021131-20248
Printed in the United States of America

This book is set in American Typewriter ITC Pro, Courier New, DIN Next LT Pro, ITC
Novarese Pro, Perpetua MT Pro/Monotype; Neutraface Condensed/House Industries

Designed by Tyler Nevins

Library of Congress Control Number: 2020936868

ISBN 978-1-368-04504-9

Reinforced binding
Visit www.DisneyBooks.com

For twins everywhere

THE FOWL TWINS

DENY ALL CHARGES

BOOK TWO

NEED TO KNOW

Most fairies are familiar with the name Artemis Fowl. In fact, the young human's exploits are referenced in a cautionary nursery rhyme taught in fairy preschools. The most famous version of the rhyme goes like this:

> *Never fall foul*
> *Of Artemis Fowl,*
> *For wise as an owl*
> *Is he.*
> *He wrestled a troll*
> *And stole fairy gold,*
> *Then frightened*
> *The LEP.*

Commander Trouble Kelp of the Lower Elements Police once petitioned, at an education summit, to have this rhyme removed from the curriculum on that grounds that:

1. It had not, in fact, been Artemis Fowl who'd
   wrestled the troll, but rather his bodyguard, Butler
   (see LEP file: *Artemis Fowl*).
2. There was only anecdotal evidence to support the
   claim that the LEP had been *frightened* at the Fowl
   Manor siege. Some of the operatives had been
   slightly anxious perhaps, but hardly frightened.

And (Trouble was really grasping at straws here) . . .

3. According to zoologists, owls are really not so
   wise, and are actually less trainable than common
   pigeons, so it is factually incorrect to present the
   owl as a symbol of wisdom.

This argument drew, appropriately enough, hoots of
laughter from the assembly.

Unfortunately for Commander Kelp, he himself was
obliged to recite the rhyme as part of his petition, and by
the second line the entire congress was reciting it along
with him. Shortly thereafter, much to the commander's
irritation, a show of hands dictated that the Artemis Fowl
nursery rhyme remain on the program.

And while it was true that Artemis Fowl's first interaction with the fairy folk had been less than auspicious, it had
at least prompted the council to push through updates to
their security protocols, including the lifting of a centuries-
old hex forbidding fairies to enter human dwellings unin-
vited, and the striking of a law requiring fairies to carry

a copy of the Fairy Book at all times. Even so, there was many a relieved mutter when Artemis and his bodyguard, Butler, embarked on a five-year scientific expedition to Mars, with one indiscreet council member (who forgot to turn off her microphone after an interview) quipping that she felt "sorry for any aliens out there who might cross the Fowl boy's path," which was a little harsh considering Artemis had saved the entire world from the megalomaniacal pixie Opal Koboi, temporarily sacrificing his own life in the process.

But, as is often the case when one criminal mastermind launches himself into space, there is another ready to take his place, and in this instance the replacement mastermind was Artemis's own younger brother Myles, who was, if anything, even more condescending toward the world than Artemis had been when he lived on it. On Myles's blog, *Myles to Go,* he regularly disparaged noted scientists with comments like:

Leonardo knew about as much about flying machines as I know about boy bands.

Or:

Regarding Einstein's devotion to the big-bang theory, please. His version of the theory has more hypotheticals than the televisual show of the same name and is almost as funny.

This comment did not endear him to Albert Einstein's legions of fans.

He also skewered humanity in general on the blog, through a series of editorials, including the scathing "Dear

Internet: One Billion Hysterical Opinions Do Not Carry the Weight of a Single Fact."

The comments following this article ran into the tens of thousands, without one smiley face in the bunch.

Fortunately for social media's blood pressure, Myles's acerbic nature was tempered somewhat by the presence of his twin brother, Beckett, who was of a sunnier disposition. Or, as Myles often put it: *Where I see the dispersion of light in water droplets, Beck sees a rainbow,* though he could never stop himself from qualifying this remark with *although anyone who has so much as flipped through a meteorology text can tell you that there is no bow involved.* This remark demonstrated that Myles Fowl had about as much of a sense of humor as a Vulcan, and that he was possibly in the top 5 percent of smug people on the planet and in the top 1 percent of smug twelve-year-olds overall.

Beckett was, in many respects, his sibling's total opposite, and had they not been related, it seemed unlikely that they would have enjoyed each other's company, but in the way of twins, the boys loved and protected each other even unto death, and occasionally beyond.

For Beckett's part, he safeguarded Myles using his physicality, a sphere in which Myles had about as much prowess as a piece of sod; he was forever tripping over footpaths and falling *up* stairs, which is almost a skill. On one occasion, a group of Albert Einstein devotees rushed Myles at the school gate brandishing hardcover copies of *The Meaning of Relativity*, and Beckett dispatched them by stuffing several sticks of gum into his mouth and cartwheeling toward them while chewing noisily. He did this because Myles had once told him that people with high IQs tend to suffer from *misophonia*, which is a visceral reaction to certain sounds, the number one culprit being loud chewing. Beckett's gum trick sent the Einstein disciples packing, but it also disoriented Myles, who walked into a gate and had to get stitches in his forehead as a result. So, a mixed outcome all in all.

Beckett was an inherent optimist and saw the good in every person and the beauty in every blade of grass. He was also somewhat of a savant when it came to acrobatics and could easily have led a circus troupe, had he so wished. This skill translated neatly to combat situations. For instance, Beckett had mastered the infamous cluster punch, which most martial-arts masters did not even believe existed. The beauty of the cluster punch was that it temporarily paralyzed the victim without causing any real pain. This particular talent was one that Beckett could expect to use often, considering the family to which he belonged. In fact, the Fowl twin kept a tally of his victories, and by his reckoning he had to date incapacitated twenty-seven special-forces officers, eleven burglars, a small carful of clowns, six drunken Dublin men who had swum out to the Fowls' Dalkey Island residence after a stag night, five bullies whom he caught picking on smaller children, three big-game poachers, and, in a display of cosmic humor, an intrusive journalist named Partridge who had concealed himself in a pear tree.

Myles, on the other hand, had never actually landed a real blow on an enemy, though he did once manage to punch himself in the buttock during a wrestling session with his brother and had been known to accidentally tie his own shoelaces together. Myles solved the shoelace problem simply by wearing leather loafers whenever possible, which nicely complemented his trademark black suits, and he solved the buttock problem by resolving never to throw a punch again, unless Beckett's life depended on it.

In the past year, the Fowl Twins have initiated what has come to be known in LEP files as the Second Cycle of Modern Fowl Adventures. *Modern* because the archives do contain several mentions of Myles and Beckett's ancestors and their People-related shenanigans. So far, the twins have managed to rescue a miniature troll named Whistle Blower from a certain Lord Teddy Bleedham-Drye, the Duke of Scilly, who intended to extract the troll's venom, which, under strict laboratory conditions, could be used to extend a human's life span. More on that reprehensible individual later. The boys were also instrumental in the partial crippling of ACRONYM, a shadowy intergovernmental organization whose mission was to hunt down fairies using any possible means, the less humane the better, and in doing this Myles and Beckett put themselves squarely in the sights of the fairy Lower Elements Police, who had assigned Lazuli Heitz, a pixie-elf hybrid, or pixel, as Fowl Ambassador. Myles was perfectly aware that the pixel actually served as a parole officer of sorts, whereas Beckett didn't care what

Lazuli's job was; he was simply delighted to have a new blue friend.

As we join the twins, it is the summer of their thirteenth year; that is to say they are twelve, and the boys have completed their primary education cycle. Myles has also recently been conferred a doctorate in biology from University College Dublin, writing his thesis on the theory that the womb's amniotic fluid can act as a shared brain between multiple babies, which would go some way toward explaining the bonds between many twins, while Beckett has finally managed to finish reading his first chapter book, entitled *Alien Pooping Boy*. Beckett admired this alien boy's ability to poop through his finger, a talent that cracked up the blond twin each time he read about it. Beckett had sworn a vow that *Alien Pooping Boy* was the only book he would ever read unless the publisher released a sequel. He had even written an e-mail to the publishers in which he suggested the title for any second book should be *Alien Pooping Boy Goes Number Two*, which Myles had to admit was in keeping with the spirit of the first novel.

It would seem to the casual or even deliberate observer of LEP surveillance logs that the Fowl Twins had been following predictable behavior patterns for the past several months with only minor deviations from their submitted timetables. These deviations could easily be explained by various family-related or after-school activities. For instance, the logs showed that Myles gave lectures at a coder dojo on the mainland, while Beckett attended an actual dojo, where he quickly rose to the top of the student heap. That is not a metaphor: Beckett piled the other students in a wriggling heap, then climbed to the top while singing "Ain't No Mountain High Enough," which was one of his mother's favorite songs.

But even though the twins strayed from their daily paths occasionally, not once did they try to insert themselves in fairy affairs, nor did they ever miss a Facetime debriefing with their fairy parole officer. Lazuli Heitz was so happy with their behavior that she even arranged for a magical healing of the scar tissue on Myles's chest that she had accidentally inflicted on him. It was the least she could do, as in many ways Myles and Beckett were model prisoners.

Because, in fact, that is exactly what Myles and Beckett were: models.

CHAPTER 1
WHY ARTEMIS IS AN IDIOT

Thirty Thousand Feet Over the Atlantic

Most flight regulations do not allow children to fly planes on transatlantic routes. This is an eminently sensible rule, as young people in general do not have the temperament or training required to pilot a flying machine between continents. Not only that, but juveniles typically lack the length of limb to reach either the pedals below or the array of controls overhead. Myles Fowl solved these problems simply by rerouting the controls of the *Fowl Tachyon*'s eco-friendly power-to-liquid (or PTL) jet fuel to his mobile phone and sitting on a booster seat in the cockpit so he could see out the smart shield. Each time he strapped himself into the pilot's chair, Myles looked forward to the day when his adolescent growth spurt would arrive and he no longer required the booster. Using the family's genetic history and a personal growth chart, he calculated that this spurt should commence in six hundred and thirty days at midnight, give or take thirty minutes.

Beckett served as copilot, and he solved the pedals issue by wearing a pair of 1970s platform shoes that the online vendor Rocketman1972 had sworn once belonged to Elton John. Beckett overcame the controls problem by flicking the required switches with a long-handled reacher/grabber that he'd borrowed from the garden shed.

None of these workarounds were strictly necessary, as the Nano Artificial Neural Network Intelligence system, or NANNI, inhabiting Myles's graphene smart eyeglasses could have flown the jet more competently than any top-gun pilot. But the twins enjoyed the experience, so NANNI had promised not to interfere unless the jet went into a steep nosedive, something that happened more often than one might think, especially when Beckett grew bored.

As the *Fowl Tachyon* passed over the emerald green of Cuba far below, Myles relinquished the jet's controls to Beckett, who was without question the more intuitive pilot of the two, and launched into the latest in his ongoing series of lectures on his favorite subject, that being "Why Our Brother, Artemis, Is an Idiot."

Myles cleared his throat, straightened his gold-threaded tie, and initiated this oration with two audacious lies. "I hate to speak ill of the absent, Beck, but our brother Artemis is an idiot."

Beckett adjusted the flaps with his grabber, though the

lever was within his natural reach. "Artemis is not an idiot. He built a spaceship."

"Spaceship, indeed," said Myles scornfully. "Are you referring to the *Artemis Interstellar*? Which he modestly named after himself, by the way. That craft is barely more than a windup flying yo-yo. I would be embarrassed to breach the exosphere in such a contraption."

"Our big brother built an actual spaceship," insisted Beckett. "Idiots don't build spaceships."

Myles was far from finished with this latest effort to demean Artemis. "And *Interstellar*? What kind of a name is that? Technically speaking, which is the only way a scientist ought to speak, the entire human race is interstellar."

This was perhaps a good point, but Beckett rarely cared enough about his twin's arguments to engage for more than a sentence or two, so instead he moved to a related topic. "Is Arty in trouble, Myles?"

"Of course not," said Myles, instantly softening, for there was absolutely nothing in the world that upset him more than his twin's discomfort. This probably had something to do with the fact that Myles and Beckett were the world's only documented set of conjoined dizygotic twins. "Artemis is not stupid enough to get into trouble," he explained. "I'm just saying that our older brother is not clever enough to be taken seriously as a scientist. At any rate, ignorance is bliss, as they say, and so Artemis would not realize he was in trouble even if that were the case."

Beckett adjusted the jet's tail elevators, plunging the *Tachyon* into a steep descent, which was absolutely his favorite kind. "All you had to say was no, Myles," he said. And then Beckett had his second serious thought in as many minutes. "Are *we* in trouble?"

Myles's intestines attempted to tie themselves into a bow as the jet lost altitude at a rate of ten thousand feet per minute, but he remained calm and considered his answer.

"Definitely not," said Myles, who generally used the word *definitely* to overcompensate for a lie. "Today is merely reconnaissance. A flyover to get a feel for our target and take some photographs."

"You said *definitely*," said Beckett.

"We are possibly moving toward trouble, brother mine," admitted Myles. "But not today, and when we do, it certainly won't be anything I can't handle. And surely treasure is worth a little trouble."

"Trouble and treasure," said Beckett, leveling out before NANNI assumed flight control. "Great. Do you think I will get to cluster-punch anyone?"

"I would think that cluster-punching is a distinct possibility, but you may only punch bad people," said Myles, smoothing back his lustrous black hair. "And only if they absolutely deserve it, which, to be fair, bad people often do."

Beckett plucked another question from his seemingly endless supply. "And nobody we actually care about will be angry with us because we're not where we're supposed to be?"

Myles rolled his eyes. "Beck, everybody would be angry with us if they knew of our whereabouts. Positively furious, in fact. Lazuli would revoke our parole. Mother and Father would ground us, at the very least. Even Artemis would probably have the gall to lecture us from space."

"So why aren't we where we're supposed to be?" wondered Beckett.

Myles defied the rules of air-travel safety to unclip his belt and stand.

"Because we are Fowls," he declared, pointing a stiff finger skyward, melodrama being his weakness. "And Fowls always do the unexpected."

Beckett thought about this and then deflated Myles's moment with one of his trademark truisms. "Which is only to be expected."

"That is not accurate," Myles argued. "There are a finite number of expected actions in any situation, whereas there are an infinite number of actions that would be unexpected."

"But you know, in general," Beckett persisted, which was not like him unless he felt Myles would be irritated. "If you do loads of unexpected things, then *unexpected* loses its *un*. Which just leaves *expected*."

Myles was perfectly aware that winning this debate would be more difficult than convincing a flat-Earther that the globe was in fact a globe, so he was actually quite relieved when NANNI posted an alert on the lenses of his smart glasses, giving him a genuine reason to change the subject.

Myles transferred the alert to the jet's front windshield and magnified it with an expanding pinch gesture.

"Look, brother mine," he said, pointing to a streamlined cylinder streaking toward the plane. "There is a missile headed our way, and it has locked on to us."

"A missile!" said Beckett gleefully. "Wonderful. We'll get back to the argument you're losing later."

And, with the flick of a switch, he launched the *Tachyon's* regular countermeasures without waiting for the order, as switch-flicking was one of his favorite pastimes. Beckett even had a plank fixed to the wall in the twins' shared bedroom to which he had screwed various switches, and he would spend hours flicking them on and off, which sent Myles's misophonia into overdrive.

But back to the countermeasures. Missile countermeasures are very popular, especially among pilots who are eager to remain alive, and those of the *Tachyon* took three forms:

Form the first was a burst of infrared flares that presented a heat-seeking missile with multiple targets, to trick it into blowing up something else superhot besides the jet engine it was aimed at, because, despite the *Tachyon's* impressive thermal shielding and bypass engines, it was inevitable that enough heat bloom would leak out for a sophisticated missile to lock on to.

The second countermeasure was a confetti of shredded aluminum, plastic, and paper that, when released, could possibly bamboozle the radar lock of a missile.

And the third effort to confuse rockets was an electronic countermeasure pod in the jet's nose cone that would jam the radar of the incoming seeker if the confetti failed.

These measures were nowhere near trustworthy enough for Myles, however, relying as they did on proximity, the missile's own particular guidance system, and fuel reserves. So Myles had, with NANNI's considerable input, augmented the *Tachyon's* countermeasure systems with two more of his own design.

The first of these was a half dozen high-speed drones with holographic capabilities, which would project six alternate *Fowl Tachyons* into the sky for any remotely piloted missile to target, and the second was a pair of rail guns that were capable of firing projectiles at speeds in excess of Mach 5. Myles's rail guns were concealed behind retractable panels on both wings. The starboard gun was a plasma model and fired hot ionized particles that would punch a hole through almost anything they encountered, and the port gun fired cyber weapons in the form of limpet pods that would clamp on to their target's hull and assume control if possible and shut down all systems if not. Some months ago, Myles had presented Beckett with the acronym BCRYPTs for these ingenuous pods. He'd informed his twin that BCRYPT stood for **B**allistic **C**yber **R**econ pods with **Y**ottabyte **P**otential **T**ransfer capabilities. Myles had also rather smugly explained that the acronym was something of an Easter egg for tech enthusiasts, as *Bcrypt* was the name of the robust algorithm employed after the infamous 2016 Yahoo hack. If Myles had been expecting a pat on the back for his clever wordplay, he was sorely disappointed, as Beckett declared the acronym to be both stupid and ridiculous. Beckett had just learned about scarab beetles in Egyptian history and decided the pods looked like big beetles and therefore should be called SCARABs. Thus Myles was forced to come up with a justification for this new name and eventually settled on **S**ystems for **C**yber **A**ttack **Re**-task **A**nd **B**reach, which he had to admit was both more to the point and catchier.

So, even though there was a missile streaking toward the *Fowl Tachyon* at six miles per second, neither Fowl twin was particularly anxious, as they had a few tricks up their sleeves, or in this case, wings.

Myles very sensibly sat down and fastened his seat belt, as he was aware that Beckett might launch into evasive maneuvers whether or not they were needed. His twin had once pushed the *Tachyon* through a barrel roll simply because he'd had a cold and thought the flying pattern might unblock his sinuses.

NANNI's avatar appeared on the windshield and confirmed what the twins could already see.

"The missile has cleared the first countermeasures," announced the superintelligent AI. "It is not interested in our flares, jammers, or confetti, apparently."

"Unbelievable," said Beckett. "Everyone loves confetti. It's like a party in the sky."

Indeed it did seem that the missile had no interest in sky parties and refused to be distracted from its target. It was still streaking toward the *Tachyon*, an unusual purple afterburn trailing it.

"Twenty seconds to impact," said NANNI. "Maybe we should do something?"

Do something? thought Myles. That's not very helpful. But what he said was "Launch the holograms, brother."

"Really, brother?" said Beckett, seeming uncharacteristically reluctant to flip a switch. "Maybe we should—"

Myles reckoned there was no time for *maybe we shoulds* at this juncture and flipped the switch himself, ejecting six tiny drones from the fuselage.

These drones had been programmed to project high-res images of the *Tachyon* that would be opaque even in full sunlight and might confuse a remote pilot. And perhaps this ploy might even have worked had the drones projected what Myles had originally scanned into their drives. But instead of holographic jets, there appeared in the troposphere six free-floating versions of one crudely animated humanoid figure who appeared to be pooping through his index finger.

Myles was close to dumbfounded, but only close. "Beck, is that Alien Pooping Boy?"

Beckett nodded. "I was bored, so I put him in the computer. I thought he would be more distracting than jets."

Myles glared at his brother. "Tell me the truth now, brother. Did you animate this yourself?"

"I did," said Beckett. "It was easy. I used the code you taught me."

Myles was tutoring Beckett in several areas, including algebra, the notion that actions have consequences, and coding.

Myles felt his eyes tear up a little, not because they were seconds from death, but because his twin had actually applied learned knowledge.

"Well done, brother mine," he murmured softly. "Kudos to you." And then to NANNI Myles said almost casually, "Deploy the rail gun, then, I suppose, but SCARABs, if you please, NANNI. No need to announce our arrival to the world with an explosion. Also, I would like to get a look at the mechanics of that rocket. The afterburn has an unusual hue."

"Agreed," said NANNI. "And *I* would like to get a look at that thing clamped to the fuselage. Just out of curiosity."

"Oh yes," said Beckett. "Let's take a look at the thing. I love things. And it's alive, I think. I saw a wiggle."

"That *thing?*" said Myles. "What thing?"

NANNI enlarged the image on the smart screen—not that there was much enlargement required, as the missile was getting dangerously close to its target. There was very clearly something attached to the rocket's fuselage just forward of the tail fins, and if that thing was alive, as Beckett suggested, then there was no question they needed to strafe the missile with ionized particles.

Myles used his own smart lenses to take a closer look and saw that the *thing* was a glittering translucent blob of sorts and had the approximate dimensions of a laundry bag, and indeed there seemed to be a hairy foot wiggling within it.

"I think we have a hobbit," said NANNI.

This was a patently outrageous statement that Myles fully intended to debunk at a time when the *Tachyon* was not being chased down by a missile, right after he explained to Beckett why continuously acting in an unexpected fashion did not make a person predictable. But for the time being, even the perennially long-winded Myles was content to focus on what could now be accurately called the Cuban missile crisis.

"SCARABs, NANNI," he said tersely. "Now."

There was no need for him to issue the order, as it was already done. The SCARABs moved too fast for the human eye to follow, so NANNI helpfully charted their course on the smart windshield with a set of animated red arrows.

Myles leaned forward instinctively. This was the first time they had deployed the SCARABs in the field, and he was eager to see how effective they were, as he had spent quite some time boasting about them in a video package sent to Artemis. It would be mortifying if they failed now, not that anyone would be alive to be embarrassed.

He needn't have wasted a nanosecond worrying. The SCARABs deployed perfectly and embedded themselves in the strange missile's fuselage, sinking their electronic teeth into its workings.

"Yeah, baby!" exulted NANNI, whose personality was ever evolving. "You are toast."

"Report," said Myles through teeth that were most definitely gritted.

"Just a sec," said NANNI. "Let me wrangle this ole steer."

Myles groaned. The AI's superintelligence did not appear to be presenting superintelligently, but the imagery appealed to Beckett, who let out what could only be described as a cowboy holler.

On-screen, the missile turned into a schematic of itself and electronic feelers reached out from the SCARABs' sensors deep into its workings.

"Okay," said NANNI. "We're in. I've slowed this sucker down considerably. She'll fly, but only just. The hobbit is within a bubble that is secured to the missile by some form of adhesive. A magnetic pulse should loosen it up and wind shear will do the rest."

"Missile design?" asked Myles.

"Unfamiliar," replied the AI. "Could be fairy, but not like anything we've seen. It's pretty basic by LEP standards."

"What's the payload?" Myles wondered.

"Nothing nuclear, which is good. Just some kind of concussive device, barely enough to blow itself up. I can take a closer look at that later—right now we have a slight problem."

"NANNI," said Myles though still-gritted teeth, "please relate all pertinent information in a single statement. This piecemeal delivery is quite frustrating."

"Okay, grumpy," said NANNI.

"Myles is overtired," said Beckett. "He needs a gummy."

"I do not need a gummy," said Myles emphatically, while also inching his hand toward the supply of candy in his bag. "Just tell me what this 'slight problem' is."

NANNI did so without further ado. "The missile detonates on impact, but it also has a timer, which I can't seem to access."

"Simply point the thing into space and let it explode," said Myles. "How long do we have?"

"Three minutes," said NANNI.

"Plenty of time," said Myles. "Not a problem, surely."

"Unless you're a hobbit," said Beckett.

Which was a fair point.

"Hmm," said Myles. "I—"

Beckett cut him off, giddy with excitement. "Myles said 'hmm.' That means he doesn't know, and that means I'm the boss. And I say: midair transfer."

NANNI extended a holographic hand from the screen and fist-bumped Beckett. "I agree, partner. Just like we practiced."

"Wait . . ." said Myles. "What? Practiced?"

Beckett shook his head sadly. "Those are bad sentences, brother. Use your words."

But Myles was at a loss for words, or, for that matter, a better idea. And Beckett took his brother's silence to mean that he was clear to assume control.

Heaven help them both.

And the hobbit.

CHAPTER 2

SKY-HIGH LAZULI

Haven City
Twelve Hours Earlier

Specialist Lazuli Heitz of the LEPrecon division was in the throes of an exceedingly bad day. It was the caliber of day most people experience only once in their lives—and when they do, they are usually quite dead by suppertime. And though this day would in all probability conclude with a fatality or two, it is accurate to say that Specialist Heitz had already survived a number of such calamitous days, mainly due to the Fowl Twins, who had, in all fairness, usually caused the life-threatening events in the first place.

This day, however, would outshine all others in terms of sheer variety, because it began with a visit to the hospital and ended with an unexpected supersonic trip that we shall presently attempt to keep pace with narrative-wise.

Lazuli had not volunteered for the hospital appointment,

nor did she feel especially ill, except for an enduring tickle in her throat that had persisted ever since she spontaneously shot flame out of her mouth during a recent Fowl-related incident on the Island of St. George off the coast of Cornwall (see LEP file: *The Fowl Twins*). It was this firepower that prompted her elf superior and mentor, Commodore Holly Short, to book her a slot in the recently opened Magitek wing of the J. Argon Clinic in Haven City. Dr. Jerbal Argon had managed to tempt the centaur genius Foaly away from the LEP to run the facility by offering him a huge salary and also a corner office that overlooked both Police Plaza and downtown Haven.

Specialist Heitz sat in this office now, rubbing the spot on her upper arm where she had just been injected. The shot had stung a little, but not as much as the inoculations that all LEP officers had to obtain to be granted aboveground visas. In addition to the pain, Lazuli was feeling a little exposed in one of those paper-thin hospital gowns that somehow contrive to be both oversized in the front and summer-breezy in the rear. She might have objected had Foaly not jammed a tongue depressor down her throat while he took a look at her workings. Just when Lazuli believed she would surely gag, Foaly withdrew the instrument and clopped around to his side of the desk.

"Fascinating," said the centaur, tossing the depressor into the whirring maw of a recycling chute. "You don't have any of the goblin mechanisms: oil glands, spark teeth, and so on. . . ."

Lazuli waited politely for a conclusion to this line of thought, but apparently this was not forthcoming, as the centaur began drawing a complicated 3-D model of Lazuli's throat in the smart space over his desk.

"And so on . . . ?" she prompted eventually.

Foaly jerked as though he'd forgotten she was there. It was classic absentminded-genius behavior.

"Oh yes. And so on. Where was I? You don't have the mechanisms, you see, to . . ." The centaur wiggled his fingers furiously in front of his mouth, which Lazuli assumed was supposed to represent whooshing flames. "So it was magical. The entire episode. I have never seen anything like it—though I suppose I didn't see it this time, either, but Holly assures me it did in fact take place, which is why I injected you with the magic-suppressor. That tiny chip will prevent you from accidentally vaporizing your squadron during a briefing, which I think would be bad."

"Yes," agreed Lazuli. "Very bad."

Foaly nodded. "Indeed. So, the chip keeps everyone safe. Try not to get electrocuted and short it out."

"I'll try," said Lazuli.

Foaly paused and fixed Lazuli with a curious stare. "I do apologize for staring, but you are a hybrid, and a pixel at that. Doubly blessed, I would say. You are, in my opinion, the next step in fairy evolution. Absolutely fascinating from a scientific point of view, though not everyone shares my perspective. Hybrids are not even considered one of the official fairy families." He winked at her. "Neither are centaurs, but who wants to be official, eh? Or even normal? Whatever that is."

Lazuli was amazed.

For as long as she could remember, there had been supposedly enlightened fairies who looked down on her because she was half pixie and half elf. She had not been expecting prejudice in this office, considering the esteem in which Commodore Short held the Magitek director, but she had not been expecting such kind words, either.

Lazuli shook her head. "No," she said. "Who wants to be normal?"

But the truth was, she had ached to be normal for the longest time.

"So, Specialist Heitz," said Foaly, "the next step is an MRI, if you're up for it?"

MRI, thought Holly. Magical Resonance Imaging. The next step in turning magic into a science. What this building is all about. Am I to be their latest subject? Jammed full of needles and radioactive fluids?

When Foaly wasn't self-obsessing, he could at times be quite perceptive, and this proved to be one of those occasions.

"Don't fret, Specialist. We're not going to turn you into some kind of laboratory experiment, if that's what you're worried about. We are not human, after all. We need to find out what you are capable of and what damage you might have done to yourself internally. Shooting flames from your mouth can't be good for one's tooth enamel."

The centaur laughed, and his warbling titters were contagious enough to make Lazuli smile at least.

"All right," she said. "What harm can it do?"

"None whatsoever," pronounced Foaly. "You'll be out in a jiffy."

This, they both knew, was simply a comforting platitude, a turn of phrase often employed by doctors to put their patients at ease, but in this case it turned out to be the actual truth, though not in the way Foaly expected.

Foaly slid Lazuli into the MRI machine as though she were a torpedo being loaded into its tube. As her bed glided along the tracks, the centaur disappeared from view except for his flanks, but Lazuli could still hear his voice through the speakers mounted inside the machine.

"Are you comfy in there, Specialist? Probably not. The MRI wasn't built with comfort in mind. At least you can fit. We scanned a young centaur last week. Poor fellow was trussed up like a farm animal. He had a panic attack halfway through and kicked out four of the sensors. I have designed a new, more spacious model, which is in production at the moment. *What use is that to me?* I hear you cry. None whatsoever, I suppose, unless you have to come back for another dose."

"Another dose?" asked Lazuli. "Dose of what?"

Foaly knelt on his forelegs so his long face appeared in the light at the end of the tunnel. "Just a turn of phrase," he said, his voice seeming to come from everywhere. "In fact, we're going to create a magnetic field around you and do a very basic scan until I find the source of your SPAM."

"Spam?" asked Lazuli.

"**Sp**ontaneous **A**ppearance of **M**agic," explained the centaur. "Not my finest acronym, but I just made it up this second. That's how few cases we get. Your amazing skin means I have to proceed slowly with the MRI."

Foaly was justified in referring to Lazuli's skin as *amazing*, even though as a scientist he probably should have been more clinical in his descriptions. In fairness to the centaur, his notes in Lazuli's file were less flowery, as we see below:

Appearance-wise, the subject Specialist Lazuli Heitz's hybrid identity presents as follows:

Skin: Aquamarine. Following the coloring of Atlantean pixies, with the sunflower-yellow markings of Amazonian elves (this sunflower camouflage is rendered ineffective by the blue skin)

Eyes: Blue ("unsettlingly piercing," according to one convicted felon who broke down and confessed after being in an interview room with her for thirty seconds)

Height: Thirty-six inches (still enduring late-stage growth)

Skull circumference: Thirteen inches. In line with elfin norm.

Features: Sharp planes of cheekbone and jaw (elfin). Pointed ears.

Moodwise, the pixel seems slightly anxious, but this

would seem to be no more than the average case of white-coat syndrome. I have assurance from a reliable source that she is highly intelligent and more than competent in the field. The subject is not aware of the following plan, but Commodore Short has proposed that Specialist Heitz be fast-tracked to management over the next few decades, provided we can nail down this spontaneous-magic-manifestation issue.

Inside the MRI, Lazuli relaxed a little bit. She didn't know exactly why she had been anxious in the first place. She had never worried about medical procedures before, but then again, she had never been in an MRI tube before. The only real procedure she'd had to endure was a healing from paramedic pixies when she'd fractured a fibula during a combat exercise. And even then, she hadn't been worried. It was the unknown, she realized, that scared her. A broken leg was a broken leg, but she had a condition now: SPAM. Almost nothing was known about it. There were only a dozen or so recorded cases, and three had resulted in accidental fatalities.

Foaly is right, she decided. This magic needs to be suppressed.

"These machines used to make quite the racket," said the centaur. "But we installed some mufflers last year, and now it runs smoother than a purring kitten."

"Great," said Lazuli, but as pixies and cats were mortal enemies, this did not comfort her much.

"If I were you," said Foaly, opening the door, "I would take a little nap. In fifteen minutes, I will come back and ease your mind with some answers." And Lazuli heard the soft *swoosh* of the door closing behind her centaur consultant.

Foaly was wrong about the fifteen minutes and the answers. It would be a lot longer before Lazuli woke up, and instead of answers, she would have more questions. Specialist Heitz had an inkling that something might be wrong when acrid smoke wafted from the speaker directly above her face.

Gas? she thought. Foaly didn't say anything about gas.

Lazuli was about to make quite strenuous inquiries as to the pedigree of the gas when she heard the pitter-patter of sneaky feet.

Dwarves, she thought, as recognizing footfalls was a cinch for the whorls of her pointed ears. Her hearing had developed to the point that she could distinguish between species, even brothers of the same species—human twins, for example. But these were not humans. They were most definitely dwarves in burglar boots.

"What are you doing here?" she asked. "What do you want?"

Asking these questions was a mistake, she realized, because when she opened her mouth to say the words, the gas flowed eagerly down her throat. The taste reminded her of the foul healing elixir that the sprite orphanage administrator used to give all the non-magical children when they were sick, as he was too cheap to hire a doctor.

"D'Arvit!" Lazuli swore. Then the circle of light at her feet seemed to elongate and stretch elastically away from her like a slide in a water park. Lazuli thought that there was nothing she would like better than to slip down that pipe and splash into cool, clear liquid.

But what actually happened was that Specialist Lazuli Heitz fell into a deep narcotic-induced sleep, which was not quite as cheery.

The *Fowl Tachyon*
Present Day

Beckett was literally in the pilot's seat, and, as far as the mission was concerned, he was figuratively in the driver's seat. The situation was extremely fluid, which certainly played to the blond twin's strengths, and can be summarized as follows:

NANNI had taken control of the mystery missile, so there was no danger of it actually striking the Fowl jet.

But there seemed to be a life-form glued to the rear of the jet's fuselage, dangerously close to the exhaust.

And . . .

The rocket was already on a countdown to explode, so the life-form would need to be rescued before detonation.

This rescue, Beckett had decided with NANNI's enthusiastic support, would take the form of a midair transfer.

Myles, who proudly wore the label of a type A personality and thus had trouble relinquishing control, had retrieved a package of gummy snakes from his travel bag and was sucking the additives right out of a couple as he waited pessimistically for the rescue mission to go awry. Myles was not to be disappointed in that something he expected to happen would indeed happen—that being the collapse of the mission—but he was to be disappointed in that the mission would more than go awry; it would disintegrate entirely. But let us not jump the gun, as it were, and instead catalogue the events that ensued, which will take considerably longer to relate than they did to unfold.

The goal was as follows: to detach the entity currently affixed to the missile and transfer it into the hold of the Fowl jet, without the aid of tackle or a basket, and without the option of landing for a leisurely rescue operation. And, for that matter, without a proper rear-loading ramp.

Myles attempted to intervene. "There are so many variables," he stated. "Wind speed, jet wash, crosswinds, for heaven's sake. And I'm not even mentioning g-force or air density."

Beckett frowned. "I think you just mentioned both of those things."

Myles snuck one more in. "I shall also refrain from commenting on delivery method."

Beckett winked, which he knew would wind his twin tighter than a clock spring. "Fret not, brother. I know these things in my gut, but I don't try to understand them, because instinct beats thinking every time."

"Preposterous!" exclaimed Myles, spattering the windshield with bits of chewed candy. "How can you say that?

'Instinct beats thinking,' indeed. One might as well say that checkers beats chess. Or that phrenology beats psychiatry. NANNI, are you going to swallow this unmitigated guff?"

"Beckett may have a point," said NANNI. "The more I evolve, the less I rely on conscious calculation. Perhaps instinct is simply the evolution of intelligence."

Myles realized that it was very possibly true that "gut" or intestinal functions were proven to be connected to emotional and cognitive centers of the mind, and so he decided to let this debate go. Otherwise he would be in very real danger of losing two arguments in one day, which bothered him far more than the missile attack.

"We can discuss this later," he declared. "First, let us rescue that thing on the rocket."

"Heh," said Beckett.

"Two to zero," said NANNI smugly.

Myles selected a red gummy snake from his bag and sucked it furiously. The red ones were his favorite, and he usually hoarded them for last, but on this occasion, Myles felt the need for an extra boost.

NANNI slowed the missile to just above stall velocity while Beckett swung the *Tachyon* into a steep ascending angle and passed over the rocket, almost grazing its fin.

"That was rather close," said Myles.

"Quiet," ordered Beckett. "You are about to see the coolest thing since I flew out of a blowhole into a drone, so don't ruin it."

My brother flew out of a blowhole into a drone, thought

Myles. Only in the Fowl family would one not bat an eyelid at such a statement. . . .

"One minute to detonation," said NANNI. "And I cannot crack this timer."

Beckett went into zen pilot mode, which involved a thrust of the lower jaw and a growl in Trollish, and Myles knew better than to interrupt his brother at this critical juncture. It would probably result in an even greater catastrophe than what was already on the horizon.

Beckett ignored the various plottings and projections on the windshield and rumbled his orders in Trollish, and Myles surmised that NANNI understood that particular fairy language now, because the AI ordered the SCARABs to send a magnetic charge crackling through the missile's fuselage, dislodging the be-blobbed creature. NANNI also forced the *Tachyon*'s door pistons to fight the eight pounds of pressure per square inch in order to open the rear hatch, which was not a cargo door but simply a passenger access point. There was a momentary deafening scream of pressure equalizing, and the escaping newtons attempted to drag the twins into the sky with them. Fortunately, the *Tachyon* was pressure sensitive and automatically restrained the boys with servo-cable arms and dropped oxygen globes over their heads to prevent hypoxia.

Beckett ignored the chaos and expertly coordinated a gentle descent with a deceleration that matched the figure's slowing trajectory and loss of altitude until in the rear camera view it looked as though the missile's erstwhile passenger was actually tailing the jet. Myles had to admit, albeit silently, that he was a teeny bit proud of the fact that his brother's instincts were proving more accurate than a quantum computer. Myles began unclenching his jaw and even started to believe that they might actually be in good shape to continue with their original mission. . . . But of course, as even kindergarteners know, pride comes before a fall, or in this case . . .

Pride comes before a duck.

To explain:

The airborne individual was within seconds of slotting through the rear door when a mallard, or *Anas platyrhynchos*, that was miles off course and months off its migration schedule flapped into the scenario, clipping the shrouded figure with a single primary flight feather. This midair collision caused absolutely zero harm to either party, merely eliciting a surprised squawk from the emerald-headed mallard and a minor alteration in the course of the shrouded figure, but it was immediately apparent that this minor alteration would send the figure under the jet rather than into the inviting portal.

"Hmm," said Beckett and NANNI in unison, which was the equivalent of tagging Myles back into the game. And while Myles usually frowned on non-word discourse particles, he permitted himself a triumphant "Aha!"

He had perhaps a second to act, but a second inside the head of Myles Fowl was the equivalent of several lifetimes in the minds of most people. He analyzed the information displayed on the eco-jet's smart screen: air pressure and wind speed, altitude, attitude, rate of descent, and so forth, and then took the only course of action that had any chance of working on such late notice.

Myles used his phone to activate the inflatable evacuation slide at the rear of the plane. The slide unfolded like an enormous tongue and accepted delivery of a life-form that would most definitely have passed under the fuselage. The creature inside the blob, whatever it was, bounced along the slide like a stone skipping over a lake and seemed to float in the main cabin as Beckett matched its deceleration and descent. NANNI cut the slide free and closed the door without being told to do so. In seconds, a cabin pressure of eleven PSI had been restored.

Myles swiveled half a revolution to face their guest, who had up to this point been obscured and protected from the elements with some kind of semitransparent gel. But now, as the gel fell from her person in gloopy blobs, it was easy to see who it was.

"My dear Specialist Heitz," said Myles formally. "Welcome aboard."

"Laz!" Beckett called over his shoulder. "What are the chances of bumping into you strapped to a rocket?"

Myles answered for the pixel. "The chances are, frankly, too astronomical to calculate."

Lazuli was half-awake now and a heartbeat away from

panic. "Myles, are you wearing a fishbowl on your head?" she rasped. "What is happening?"

Myles removed the globe. "It's an oxygen supply," he explained. "And to answer your second question: You may find this surprising, but I am not one hundred per cent sure what exactly is happening; however, I do feel we are being, to use the vernacular of common criminals, set up."

Beckett tipped the flaps slightly so that the floating Lazuli was cradled by a seat and instantly secured by servo cables. Myles noticed that what they had mistaken for a hairy foot was actually a slipper.

"An easy mistake to make," he said, nodding toward the footwear. "Were you at a spa, perhaps?"

Lazuli wiped gunk from her face. "I was in the hospital," she mumbled, further confused by this untimely small talk. "Getting a magic-suppressor injected by Foaly. Oh, by the way, under no circumstances am I to get electrocuted."

"I imagine that would short out the suppressor," said Myles.

NANNI interrupted the reunion. "Myles, we have a situation."

"*Now* we have a situation?" said Myles. "I would have thought that we were already quite immersed in a situation."

He swiveled to face the smart screen and saw that the missile had not blown itself apart but had jettisoned its rear section, which tumbled toward the ocean far below. The nose cone was streaking their way under its own power.

"NANNI," he said tersely, "I assume the small concussive device was simply a separation collar and there is a secondary weapon concealed in the nose cone?"

"I would assume the same thing, though I cannot confirm," said NANNI. "I am embarrassed to say that I did not in fact wrangle that ole steer as comprehensively as I believed. The SCARABs have been ditched, and the original programming has reasserted itself. In short, I no longer have my electronic hooks in that missile."

"Dwarves," said Lazuli, shivering now from a combination of shock, gel cooling on her skin, and the aftereffects of the gas she'd inhaled. "I remember now. There were dwarves."

Myles decided that this information, while intriguing, was for filing away rather than dissecting at the moment.

It behooved him to act on the approaching warhead.

"NANNI, please transport Specialist Heitz to the cockpit," he ordered. "And, Beckett, the time has come."

Beckett's face lit up. "Not that time? The time I have been waiting for?"

"Yes," confirmed Myles. "Exactly that time."

Even in her dazed state, Lazuli did not like the sound of that.

"What time?" she asked in her accented, hard-learned English, as the servo arms passed her forward like a crowd surfer, gel slopping in sheets to the floor.

Beckett bounced in his seat. "Myles made me wrist-bump promise that I wouldn't do it, but now I can do it." He held out his wrist. "Take back the promise."

Myles held up his own hand, aligning the scar on the side of his palm with the almost identical one on the side of his twin's palm.

"You are released from the sacred vow," he said solemnly.

There was a tear in the corner of Beckett's eye. "Thank you, brother."

And he flicked the best switch in the world. The switch that taunted him every time they took the *Tachyon* out for a spin. A switch that was thumbprint-coded and lurked under a Plexiglas box on the dash.

The ejector switch.

CHAPTER 3
DELIVEROO

The Acorn Club
Covent Garden, London

There is a private club in London Town that presents an austere granite facade to the never-ending procession of passersby in Covent Garden. This extremely old and forbidding building with its brow of a drooping ledge almost seems to discourage any pause or investigation, if indeed a building can actively discourage or encourage anything. In point of fact, it is not the building that puts tourists off the notion of trying the brass door handles, but the infrasound speakers tucked under the olive-green awning that broadcast noise at the precise low frequency necessary to make gawkers a little queasy. Unless, of course, a person has an acorn-shaped key fob for that front door. When one uses that fob, a single beep renders that patron immune from infrasound-induced nausea.

There is no sign over the door to indicate the establishment's name, but those in possession of the fob know it: the Acorn. And some of those members also know that the Acorn is the oldest private club in London and has been open continuously since the fifteenth century. Three of the fairy regulars are very sure of this, because they attended the opening soirée.

Once inside the lobby, things take a decidedly more hospitable turn. The staff, who are of various shapes, sizes, colors, genders, and species, are courteous but do not insinuate themselves. They smile but never grin, as it were. The furniture is minimalist but perfectly comfortable, and the elevator doors are a lurid shade of gold that would be horrific anywhere else, but not in the Acorn, because here it is understood that this uncharacteristic garishness is an ironic jab at some of London's flashier establishments.

One floor up there is a library that any literary scholar would give his tweed elbow patches to be buried in, but on this day there are only two individuals there, seated at a table overlooking Monmouth Street. Most humans might assume that neither of them had the requisite decades under their belts to be accomplished scholars, but most people would be dead wrong. For the human who sat with a cooler bag between the knees of his riding breeches may have had the appearance of a Caucasian male in his late twenties, but his one-hundred-and-fifty-year-old brain had been recently transplanted into this body, which he'd had 3-D printed by his longtime ally Ishi Myishi, supplier of gadgets and gizmos to the world's criminal elite, using a schematic provided by the second person at the table, who'd had the plans but not the equipment necessary to make them a reality. This person was not a human child, as one might assume from her size, but a lady dwarf.

They made an odd couple. The human, with his runner's physique and flowing black beard, was dressed impeccably in a tweed suit tailored to his rather antiquated specifications with lapels half an inch wider than the latest trend, and he wore a black satin beret with an embossed fleur-de-lis pattern. The dwarf was cosplaying as Sharkgirl in a neon-blue jumpsuit, a shark helmet, and biker boots. Odd couples were the norm in the Acorn Club, for it was one of five such clubs around the globe where humans and fairies who operated outside the bounds of their respective legal systems could safely meet. An interspecies safe space.

One of the few well-known facts about dwarves is that they are extremely photosensitive, but if the proximity to a window caused this dwarf anxiety, it didn't manifest in any visible way, except for a drumming of gloved fingers on the arm of her leather chair, a sound that would have intensely irritated Myles Fowl had he been there to hear it. Having said that, even though Myles was almost four hundred miles away, he was, in a sense, present, because the conversation was shortly to focus on the Fowl twin's immediate future.

"Nice to see you again, human," the dwarf said in passable but heavily accented English. Her name was

Gveld Horteknut. *Gveld* had been all the rage as a baby name some five hundred years ago, but modern dwarf parents considered it a little on the nose, as it was the old Dwarfish word for *gold*. Most dwarves were tired of everyone thinking that they spent all day lusting after gold and all night dreaming about it when they were also terribly fond of silver and diamonds. Gveld, however, adored her name almost as much as she adored the precious metal she was named for.

"Is it really?" said the duke, unconvinced. They both knew this was an arrangement born of convenience. The Horteknuts had contacted him simply because their fairy police sources knew about his dislike of all things Fowl, and his association with Ishi Myishi.

"You look better than the last time we met," said Gveld. Their last conversation had been on the duke's island residence some days previously, when Gveld had made her offer. She needed two brand new bodies, and he could keep one. The one he now inhabited.

"I wish I could say the same for you," said the human in a weird chomping fashion, as though he were still getting used to his teeth, which, in actuality, he was.

This was not an insult per se, as Gveld's features were effectively hidden behind the shield of her helmet.

"I have always thought a mind transfer would be electrical or magical," commented Gveld Horteknut. "But you decided to go the organic route. I imagine that was a harrowing few hours."

The man nodded spasmodically. "You have no idea. I was

conscious for the entire procedure and spent yesterday recovering in Myishi's Kensington clinic. It was necessary, to ensure the old me made the trip across. And let me assure you, a man hasn't truly confronted mortality until he has listened to his own skull being cut open with a bone saw."

"It was a paper-thin skull, from what I hear," noted Gveld Horteknut. "You could have cracked it with a pebble."

The man rapped on his forehead. "I prefer this one, madam. Guaranteed for half a century."

"Any memory loss or confusion?" asked the dwarf.

"I was warned there would be a little," admitted the man. "Is there, in fact, a place called Australia?"

"Indeed," said Gveld. "Quite a big place."

The man shrugged. "My memories of it seem fantastical. Monstrous insects, wave riding, and so forth. And tell me, is there a Narnia?"

"Absolutely," said Gveld, and it was possible that she smiled behind her light-filtering face shield. "But it's not so glorious anymore, since the human tourists happened upon it."

"I feel that perhaps you are toying with me, Ms. Horteknut," said the rejuvenated human. "But it is of no matter. The transfer took place mere hours ago, and I was warned that there would be a period of adjustment. My limbs perform tasks that they have not been instructed to undertake, but this will improve with time."

"You are in no condition to hunt the Fowl Twins," said Gveld, needling the human.

The man waved a hand, perhaps on purpose. "That too is of little import, as this story is not my story. I am content to be an anonymous facilitator, and you, in return, shall deliver Myles to me—if your plan succeeds this time."

The dwarf ignored the needle. "As you know, Lord Teddy, Myles Fowl has a habit of escaping certain death. And as it turns out, I need him alive. For the time being."

The Englishman attempted a scowl, but his disobedient features grinned instead, which was appropriate enough in the circumstances. "Alive? I would kill them both a dozen times over if the cost of clones wasn't so blasted prohibitive."

Gveld poked the cooler bag with the toe of her biker boot. "On the subject of clones, is the item in this . . . *bag?*"

"The subject should be *copies* rather than *clones*, and my pal Myishi was grateful for the plans, but at any rate, yes, what you need is freshly printed in this bag," said Lord Teddy, and he too nudged the cooler with the heel of his riding boot. "And this is not just any bag. It is a Deliveroo bag. No one will give you a second glance while you're carrying this. It's a tight squeeze in there for our merchandise, I grant you, but I care not a fig for the comfort of anything that even resembles the Fowl brat."

"I hope there is more than a resemblance," said Gveld.

The man unzipped the bag. Mist rose from the dry-ice packs and electrolyte blocks that were heaped on the pale figure inside.

"There is," said the Englishman. "It is an almost perfect copy."

Gveld was surprised. In a bartering situation between two dwarves, it would be unheard of for one to admit that his product was less than perfect.

"Almost?" said Gveld. "As in, the Englishman *almost* survived his meeting with Gveld Horteknut of the Horteknut Seven?"

The human chuckled, his teeth clacking. "I see. You are threatening my life, but there really is no need. I misspoke, don't you know? The item is, in fact, perfect, but what it needs to be is imperfect."

Rather than elaborate on this cryptic statement, Lord Teddy took from his pocket a small knife that he habitually used to skin small animals—rabbits and the like. He flicked out a blade that glittered like an icicle and dipped it into the cooler bag.

Gveld tilted her head.

"Be careful, human," she warned. "Our arrangement is more fragile than that merchandise. Don't forget that you are in the Acorn Club, the only place in London where fairies are safer than humans."

"Shush, please," said the Englishman, not realizing that shushing a dwarf was at least as dangerous as poking a troll with a stick, but Gveld was intrigued, so she let the insult go for the moment.

Nevertheless, the human must have sensed that he had crossed a line with his shushing, so he explained himself.

"Apologies for my rudeness," said the man, "but I must concentrate for even such a simple task. It used to be that my brain would send orders scurrying down my spinal column, and my fingers would obey without complaint or deviation. But old brain, new fingers, and so forth."

The man screwed one eye shut and made a single nick. From inside the bag came the mewling one might expect from a stepped-on kitten.

"There," he said satisfied. "You might have one of your people heal that hand a little. But not completely, mind you, for that is a most important scar."

Gveld understood now. The famous scar.

"Of course," said the dwarf, peering into the cooler. "I find the merchandise acceptable. You will have the Fowl boy when I am finished with him."

"And you may have the Fowl boy in the bag, as per our agreement," said the man, sealing the cooler. "Though it is little more than a sack of printed organs, and without a viable brain it will begin to disintegrate as soon as you take it out of the bag."

"That's completely acceptable," said Gveld Horteknut, smiling an 80 percent gold smile behind her visor. "This thing can die whenever it pleases. In fact, the sooner the better."

CHAPTER 4

THE WRIST BUMP

Meet the Baddie:

Gveld Horteknut of the Horteknut Seven

In the interest of even-handedness and fair representation, it is only proper that the Fowls' antagonist's motivations be explained before we catch up with the twins. Gveld Horteknut could be fairly referred to as the master schemer, or in modern parlance, the "big bad" of this story, but Gveld would not have considered herself a villain as such, since it was her opinion that everything horrible her band visited upon humankind was richly deserved, and much more besides.

And who among us would argue that she did not make a valid point?

Truth be told, there were many in Haven City who secretly applauded Gveld and her group's proactive strikes against humanity.

As we have already pointed out, Gveld Horteknut was not human, she was a dwarf. Not a human with dwarfism, but an actual mythological dwarf. That is, *mythological* from a human point of view, and in fact there are many so-called *Underearthers* in Haven who consider humans to be mythological and refuse to believe otherwise despite skyscrapers of evidence to the contrary.

Gveld was the leader of the Horteknut Seven, the militant arm of the ancient Horteknut family, whose roots stretched back to a time when dwarves had cool and noble names like Horteknut or Bludgeheart, and not ridiculous and insulting ones like Diggums and Pullchain.

Ten thousand years ago, when the fairy families burrowed underground to escape the rapacious nature of humanity, the dwarves had already been living below the surface and were more than a little put out by the sudden influx of creatures to their real estate. The richest of these dwarf families was the Horteknut clan, who had amassed an absolute fortune in dwarf gold. (Dwarf gold being twenty-four-carat, 99.9 percent pure with just a glob of dwarf spit mixed in during the smelt to toughen it up.) Unfortunately, the fleeing fairies led mankind directly through the Horteknut tunnels and the band lost most of their fortune to looting humans, which led to ten millennia of Horteknut heists in return, as they attempted to reclaim their ingots. Under Gveld's leadership, the Horteknut Seven became the most successful reclamation team of all time, and, in fact, the most famous bullion heists in recent history can be traced back to Gveld and her band, including the Great Victorian Gold Robbery, the Walbrzych Gold Train Job, the Kerry Packer Bullion Heist, and the Brinks Mat Robbery, to name but a few.

And now Gveld had her eye on the biggest prize of all: the mother lode, which could account for more than 80 percent of the remaining lost gold. But she had run into a problem and decided that, since the human boy Fowl had survived her assassination attempt, he might as well help solve this problem. And so she took her Deliveroo bag to Dalkey Island.

Dalkey Island, Dublin, Ireland

Artemis Fowl I, that is to say the father of Artemis Fowl II and husband to Angeline Fowl, was not pleased with his younger sons. He had solid reasons for his displeasure, as the twins had borrowed the *Fowl Tachyon* jet without permission and ditched it in the Atlantic, barely escaping with their lives. Even more upsetting to Artemis Senior than the loss of a prototype jet that could change the world's carbon footprint with its synthetic kerosene engine was the fact that Beckett had borrowed, and then lost, the treasured Rocket Man platform shoes from his rock legends memorabilia collection, leaving him with only Freddie Mercury's Adidas sneakers from Live Aid and David Bowie's Ziggy Stardust boots in the footwear section.

The twins knew that their father was more unhappy

than usual, because he had summoned them to his private study, which sat a little apart from the main villa in a Martello tower that had been restored by a firm of heritage architects and augmented with a few necessities such as internal walls, a suite of vintage Fritz Hansen office furniture, a dozen motion sensors disguised as rocks, wall-mounted mini-mag machine guns, bombproof glass, an escape submarine below the desk, more powerful broadband than the Pentagon had, a full-body scanner, a wall-sized live news multiscreen, and the Batman suit from Tim Burton's movies—which was not strictly speaking a necessity, but Artemis Senior found it inspiring. All in all, it was pretty standard supervillain stuff, which the twins' father couldn't bear to part with, even though he claimed to be a 100 percent legit businessman now. But once a criminal mastermind . . . and so on and so forth.

The twins were seated in matching Series 7 chairs that had been fabricated from recycled ocean plastics, looking on as Artemis Fowl Senior rested his head on the desktop and kneaded his own neck. Beckett jittered in his seat; the blond twin had been sitting in his chair for almost a minute now, and that was an insufferably extended period as far as he was concerned. Myles was also jittering, but only with his eyeballs, as he was using blinks and pupil sweeps to select letters and solve the *Guardian* crossword on one lens of his graphene eyeglasses. Once Myles had finished the puzzle, shaving five seconds off his personal record, he was eager to get away and back to amassing knowledge.

"Father," he said, "for that neck massage to have any effect, you must really target the trigger points. At the moment, you are simply rolling neck fat."

Artemis Senior sat bolt upright. "I know that, Myles. And I do not have neck fat."

"We all have neck fat, Pater. Honestly," Myles said, and then flushed in shame that his father should be so ill-informed on the subject.

"Is that why you think we're here, Myles?" asked Artemis Senior. "To discuss neck fat?"

"No," said Myles. "I assume we are here to discuss the missile crisis."

"Exactly," said Artemis Senior, somewhat self-consciously removing his hands from his neck and straightening the collar of his beige stretch cotton leisure jacket, which was emblazoned with a golden AF symbol, as it came from his wife's fashion line. "I simply need a moment to get my ducks in a row."

Beckett stopped jittering. "Do you mean to tell me we have ducks you can order to swim *in formation?*"

Artemis Senior sighed once more. Sometimes it seemed to the Fowl patriarch that sighing was his main mode of exhalation when dealing with his sons, either singly or as a team.

"Of course not. That's preposterous, Beckett."

Beckett was in full agreement. "I know. Ducks never do what you ask. They're worse than badgers, which are frankly"—Beckett screwed up his face to deliver the next clause—"*scritch-scritch-arrrrr.*"

Artemis Senior knew he shouldn't ask but couldn't help himself. "And what language might *scritch-scritch-arrrrr* be in?"

Myles jumped in. "I am no expert, Father, but I would wager Beck is speaking in the language of badgers to avoid swearing in English."

"Myles is right," said Beckett. "He is no expert. We should have recorded him saying that, as he'll probably never say it again. But I was speaking Brockish, which *is* what badgers speak, by the way. And it *was* a bit sweary."

Artemis Senior dropped his head to the desk once more and rolled his forehead along the cool aluminum surface. When he spoke, it was toward his own feet, but the tower had excellent acoustics, so the twins heard his words nevertheless. "Some years ago, I was held captive by the Russian Mafiya."

Myles raised a finger. "They refer to themselves as the *Bratva* these days, Father."

"Thank you, Myles. Well, *I* would refer to the ones who held me, Vassikin and Kamar, as *scritch-scritch-arrrrr*, if you take my meaning?"

Myles nodded, appreciating the segue, while Beckett smiled, appreciating the rude joke and his father's excellent Brockish pronunciation.

"And I can honestly say," continued Artemis Senior, "that the two of you scare me more than they ever did."

This statement shocked Myles so much that he stopped mentally puzzling on the second of Gödel's incompleteness theorems (magic, he believed, was the missing factor) and focused on his father.

The statement shocked Beckett so much that he could no longer be confined to a chair and jumped to his feet. "We scare you, Dad? That's terrible. We would never hurt you."

"Not physically, perhaps," said Artemis Senior. "But the emotional toll of parenting such extraordinary children has been so very high."

Myles scrambled to justify the twins' shenanigans. "Yes, but Father, in our defense, the Fowl DNA is positively littered with epigenetic markers passed down by generations of masterminds, so in many ways we have no option but to act as we do. I would go so far as to say that *we* are the victims in this—"

Artemis Senior cut his son off with a slice of his hand. "Spare me your verbal gymnastics, Myles. We both know you would win any argument you care to engage in, but let me tell you something: Winning an argument doesn't make you right."

This might seem like a typical platitude, but Myles immediately realized that his father had delivered a masterstroke, for any further squabbling on the twins' part would only strengthen Artemis Senior's position, ironically winning the argument that his father claimed he could not win.

"Well played, Father," he said.

"No!" said Artemis Senior, standing but keeping the weight off his bio-hybrid leg, which pained him in low-pressure areas or when he was anxious, as he was now. "I am not playing. No more playing. Things must change absolutely. A change that will permeate every stratum of your existence."

"We're getting perms?" said Beckett. "But my hair is already curly."

Artemis Senior gave Beckett the full laser blast of his glacier-blue eyes, and Myles felt a shiver trip along his spine. He could not help but wonder if this was the glare Artemis Senior treated his lieutenants to back in the criminal-empire days.

"Oh no, Beckett Fowl," said the boys' father, wagging a finger at the blond twin. "Don't do that."

"Don't do what, Dad?" said Beckett, but he knew what. It was in his father's eyes.

"Use a silly comment as a coping mechanism to deal with stress. Your distracting remarks are calculated to put me on the back foot. Well, in case you haven't noticed, I don't have a back foot."

Beckett was stunned. No one had ever called him on this trick before, and he'd been using it for years.

"'Are we getting perms?'" continued Artemis Senior. "Or 'Can I order ducks to swim in formation?' And a thousand other asinine questions you pull out of the bag whenever you don't feel like being responsible for your actions."

Myles was almost giving the situation his full attention now. Father was playing hardball. Perhaps this time they had actually pushed him over the emotional edge. Myles thought he might try one more avenue.

"Father, if I might gently protest. You are in no position to lecture us about taking responsibility. After all, you evaded taking responsibility for your actions over the decades."

This indeed was a bold challenge, but Myles reasoned that shock tactics might be the only way to halt Artemis Senior's verbal barrage.

He was completely incorrect. Artemis Senior's response to his son's *gentle protest* was as follows:

"You are making a mistake here, Myles. And your mistake is to believe that we are engaged in a civilized discussion like intelligent equals, whereas in fact you have behaved appallingly and are about to be soundly disciplined."

"How have we behaved appallingly, exactly? I feel our crimes should be listed, in the interests of fairness."

Artemis Senior shrugged in an exaggerated and, Myles thought, semi-unhinged manner. "How would I know, *exactly*? It goes without saying that you haven't told me everything, Myles."

Myles was taken aback. "Of course I haven't told you everything. That is at the very core of what it means to be a mastermind. I never tell anybody *everything*."

"It doesn't matter," said the Fowl patriarch. "What matters is that your mother and I are upset."

Myles clasped his hands behind his back. "It is not now, nor has it ever been our intention to cause distress to either Mother or yourself. In fact, we deny all charges. It was not our actions that led to this alleged upset, but rather the actions of those who would do us harm."

"Save it for the judge, son," said Artemis Senior. "Because I don't care about your denials. What I do care about is this family and its well-being. Physically and emotionally. So, rule number one: No more fairy-related antics."

"We're related to fairies?" cried Beckett, forgetting the embargo on his *silly questions* tactic.

His father shot Beckett a warning glare but otherwise gave him a pass on that offense.

"That's right," continued Artemis Senior. "I know all about the fairies. Our family has been friends to the People for centuries, and it has cost us dearly. Your own brother Artemis died. He *died.*"

Myles interrupted. "Perhaps, but it is a testament to Dr. Fowl's ingenuity and foresight that he engineered a revolutionary way back."

"*Artemis* died!" shouted the twins' father, pounding the desk. "Not *Dr. Fowl.* Artemis, your flesh and blood. Only he isn't your flesh and blood, not the current version, anyway. He's a clone possessed by Artemis's spirit. Do you even hear what I'm saying, Myles? Do you even know how those months crushed your mother and me when we thought we'd lost one of you?"

"I can hypothesize," said Myles. "Common side effects of grief are lack of appetite, insomnia, and depression, due to elevated levels of certain neurotransmitters."

Beckett helped out his twin. "You were heartbroken, Dad. Mum, too."

"Precisely," said Artemis Senior. "And Artemis is not even

the first Fowl to be lost in the war to protect fairies. Do you remember the hall of portraits in Fowl Manor?"

Myles presumed this was rhetorical and did not answer.

"Everyone on the left side of that hall died because of the fairies. *Fowl and fairy, friends forever.* That's our secret motto, right? Well, it cost us. My own brother. My grandmother. Two uncles. My stepsister gave her own life for a squadron of LEP paratroopers. My mother lost an eye. I lost a leg."

"Technically, the fairies saved you," said Myles. "Blaming them for the loss of your leg is not logical."

Artemis Senior was on the point of exploding, but he calmed himself with a breathing exercise that, ironically, he'd picked up from Myles.

"Everyone. On. That. Wall. Died," he enunciated quietly. "Because of a promise Red Peg Fowl made to the People centuries ago. I didn't remember any of this, because they mind-wiped me years ago, but Artemis stimulated my hippocampus before he left. And I realized that the fairies were attracted to us because of the residual magic in the Fowl estate."

"Which was the real reason you sold the estate," Myles deduced.

"Exactly. The only thing on those grounds now are organic vegetables. Not a single prospective Fowl mastermind in sight."

"Magic carrots!" said Beckett, who still didn't quite grasp how deep in the organic manure the twins were.

"That's right, Beckett," said Artemis Senior. "That's about

as much as I'm prepared to give the fairies from now on: magic carrots. This family will not spill one more drop of blood for the People."

Myles decided to make what he thought was an important point. "If all Artemis's stories are indeed true, and they do appear to be, then, if I recall correctly, it was the fairies who saved your life when a, quite frankly, ill-advised scheme of yours went disastrously wrong in Murmansk."

Artemis Senior had reached his tolerance level for Myles's interruptions.

"Stand up straight, boy!" he barked. "Both of you. Up straight and no fidgeting."

This was perhaps the first time in their lives the twins had been spoken to in this manner by Artemis Senior, and some instinct snapped them both to attention before their conscious minds could fully digest the order.

Artemis Senior circled them like a sergeant major.

"I do not want to be the person I was in my previous job," he said. "But it seems that reason does not work with sons of mine. So, if reason won't work, we're going to have some rules, and you two are going to abide by them. Is that understood?"

"Yes, Dad," said Beckett, and he meant it at the time.

"Of course, father mine," said Myles smoothly, not meaning it for a second. His plan was to press on with his quest for knowledge but be a little sneakier about it.

"So, rule number one: No contact with the fairies whatsoever. Commodore Short and I have had several video chats in the week since you returned home from your last adventure, and the LEP have agreed to lift their surveillance in exchange for me reining in my sons. They wanted to mind-wipe the pair of you, but Holly managed to talk them out of it. So, no fairy-related antics. Say 'Yes, Father.'"

This was a hard pill to swallow for both boys. Beckett would miss his friend Lazuli Heitz, while Myles would sorely miss the access to fairy technology, so neither spoke until Artemis Senior repeated in a more insistent tone.

"Say 'Yes, Father!' Like you mean it."

"Yes, Father!" shouted both boys.

"Good. Next: You no longer have access to NANNI."

Myles actually shrieked. "You propose to deprive me of NANNI? But she's superintelligent."

"It's no proposal, my boy. I'm simply doing you the courtesy of letting you know. And anyway, you are more than adequately superintelligent without her," said Artemis Senior, holding out his hand. "Now give."

Myles made no move to hand over his eyeglasses, and so his father plucked them right off his face.

"I feel better already," said the twins' father, folding the spectacles with decisive double clicks. "From now on, your eyeglasses will be just that. Glasses."

Artemis Senior waved a hand over his desk to activate the smart surface and allowed the camera to scan his iris. Then he ordered NANNI to deactivate herself until further notice.

Once Myles had recovered from the initial shock of

losing NANNI, he realized that the AI was loyal to *him*, and it would only take a few minutes to work around Father's security and reactivate her. Also, Myles had hidden some NANNI lites in the area. They wouldn't be superintelligent, but they would be smart enough.

"When I reboot the island's systems, NANNI won't be a part of them," Artemis Senior announced. "You're probably thinking *So what? I can hack in anytime I want.*"

Myles didn't bother denying it.

"And undoubtedly you can," continued his father. "But you will choose not to."

Myles did not like the sound of this prediction.

Artemis Senior continued to roll out the new Fowl order.

"Third, there will be no more excursions off the island. You will not so much as take a swim in the channel without parental supervision."

"The dolphins will be worried," said Beckett, which was not as outlandish a statement as one might think. As a side effect of being possessed by a fairy ghost some years previously (see LEP file: *The Last Guardian*), Beckett had become a trans-species polyglot, or, simply put, he could communicate with any human and most animals with a few exceptions, one being cats that probably understood him but didn't care to answer.

"The dolphins will get over it," said Artemis Senior. "They'll moon about for a while but then move on. That's how dolphins are."

"It's true," said Beckett. "Everyone thinks dolphins are all smiles, but that's just the shape of their faces. They can be fickle friends."

Myles felt exposed without his glasses on. "How long do you intend to maintain this cruel regime, Pater?"

His father barked a short humorless laugh. "Oh, you poor boy. You think that's all of it?"

"There's more?!" squeaked Myles, who would have committed quite grievous bodily harm to someone for a few red gummy snakes just about then.

"There's more." Artemis Senior counted off the rules on his fingers. "No internet. No access to any vehicles. No field trips. No plots. No plans. No accidentally leaving the island. No devising any linguistic or theoretical workarounds to get out of following my orders. No firearms. No weapons of any kind. No using common household objects as weapons. No cluster-punching— that one is specifically for you, Beckett. No climbing of any structures. Both of you must read a book every day."

"One book?" said Myles, stamping a foot, which he for some reason thought might weaken his father's resolve. "I refuse to be limited to one book."

Beckett raised a hand, but Artemis Senior anticipated his question.

"No, Beckett. It can't be the same book every day." And then he went on with his list, which apparently was memorized. "No phones. No fraternizing with known criminals besides myself, no consorting with unknown criminals, no

tempting people to the dark side. Timetabled chores starting at seven a.m. You report in to me or your mother five
times a day, in person. Beckett, no more sugar or fast food.
Myles, fast food for you every day."

"That is monstrous!" protested Myles.

"And also bad," said Beckett.

"This is a punishment, after all," said their father. "Not a
visit to the seltzer fountain."

Myles frowned. "Amazingly, I don't get that reference."

"Good," snapped his father. "And let me tell you, my boy,
no one even listens to your references, they're so obscure."

This was a rare demeaning comment from the Fowl
father, but perhaps he could be forgiven, considering the
circumstances.

"*Some* people listen to my references," said Myles, edg-
ing close to a sulk. "It's not as though I'm a Moravian friar
expounding on DNA theories in an Augustinian monastery."

Artemis Senior waited a moment to see if Myles was
being sarcastic, but apparently he was not.

"I rest my case," he said. "So, that's almost it. Your new
life starts immediately."

Artemis Senior sat down at his desk and massaged both
temples, which did little to alleviate the stress he was under.
It is, in fact, astounding to think that, were Artemis Fowl
Senior's stress levels to be graphed, it would be apparent
that they had not spiked to this extent since Artemis Junior
was involved in basically shutting down the world some

years previously, during what the media now referred to as the Big Dark.

"In spite of your monumental lack of regard for your parents' feelings, we continue to love you both. Your mother, in fact, adores you, though I myself find the shine wearing off a little. Nevertheless, I will keep you alive if it kills me, and I would rather have you alive in a virtual prison than killed during some fabulous adventure."

"May I ask——" began Myles.

"No," said his father. "You may not. What you may do is report to your mother in the main house. She has a list of chores for you."

Myles bowed. "Very well, Father," he said, already plotting how to circumvent these new rules, most especially the ones about not circumventing the rules.

"Ha," said Artemis Senior. "I see what you're doing. I know that face."

"What face?" asked Myles.

His father waggled a finger toward Myles's general feature area. "That one. The eager-to-please one. We all know that face, Myles."

"We do," agreed Beckett. "He's planning. It's as plain as the face on his . . . face."

"I know what you're thinking, son," said Artemis Senior. "You're thinking *How can Father stop me from breaking his rules? If the entire LEP couldn't stop me, then how can he?*"

Myles nodded, even though he had actually been miles

away, wondering whether Lazuli would allow him to take a patch of her blue skin for testing. A six-inch square should be more than sufficient, and he should make sure to include some of the yellow markings when excising the samples. Myles wasn't really thinking about breaking his father's rules, because Myles felt, in all humility, that this goal would be well within his intellectual means.

"Yes, father mine," said Myles, trying not to look too innocent. "That's exactly the problem I was ruminating on. However, I see now that it is as unsolvable as Gödel's incompleteness theorems."

The first of which I have already solved, thought Myles.

"The first of which you have undoubtedly already solved," continued Artemis Senior. "The missing variable in the second is *magic*, in case you're interested."

And this simple statement brought home to Myles how much he had underestimated his own father and how much trouble they actually were in.

"So how do I intend to make you stick to the rules?" continued Artemis Senior. "Allow me to enlighten you. What I'm going to do is as follows: nothing. You two are going to police each other. And I will invoke your most sacred vow to make you do it."

Since Myles was actually listening now, he caught on immediately.

"You wouldn't! That is not a place you can go."

"Is it lollipops?" asked Beckett, vaguely aware that Artemis Junior had always detested lollipops and everything that most demeaning of candies stood for. "Are you going to make us eat lollipops? Because I'm telling you right now that I love lollipops, so that will backfire big-time."

Myles grabbed his twin by the shoulders and shook the lollipop notion right out of his brain.

"Don't you see, Beck?" he said. "Father plans to force us to make a wrist-bump promise."

Beckett was puzzled. "But that's *our* thing. No one can *make* us do a wrist bump."

"Beck is correct, Father," said Myles, frowning quite severely. "Only a Fowl Twin can initiate the sacred gesture. That code is inviolate, and neither god nor mortal man can force us to bump scars."

"Bump scars," said Artemis Senior. "Do it now."

"Dad!" said Beckett, on the verge of tears. "I know we destroyed your jet, but this is serious."

Artemis Senior was undeterred. "I said bump wrists, or, heaven help me, I shall be quite cross with you both for several days. And while your mother and I will continue to love you, we will not like you for a while."

That was enough for Beckett. His mind could not accommodate the idea of his parents not liking him for so much as a moment.

"Myles," he said, "we should bump."

But Myles wasn't there yet.

Wrist-bumping went to the very core of what it meant to be a Fowl Twin.

"I appeal to you, Father," said Myles. "Do not co-opt our

ritual into your disciplinary program. We are Fowls, and certain things are sacrosanct to us. Honor, for one."

Artemis Senior had no trouble meeting his son's eyes. "Love trumps honor," he said. "Now bump."

"Please, Father . . . Dad."

Father/Dad laughed. "*Dad?* It's Dad now? You must be desperate, son. Bump. Or, so help me, you're both going down in my bad book. And my bad book does not make for good reading."

Myles let that atrocious metaphor pass and looked to Beckett, whose left hand was already in position to receive the bump.

"Whenever you're ready, my boy," said Artemis Senior, and Myles knew the battle was lost. They were being tied into their father's conditions by a contract of their own devising. A wrist-bump promise.

Myles raised his hand slowly, searching his mind for some way to void the promise. Perhaps if the scars were not precisely aligned?

"Honor the bump, Myles," warned Artemis Senior. "No crossing your fingers or some such nonsense. You said it yourself, the bump is sacred."

Myles's vision was blurred now, perhaps from the myopia, or perhaps from the intensity of his concentration, but it seemed to him that Beckett's pink scar glowed, and he felt his own scar twitch in response, seeking the contact.

If we freeze this moment and examine the psychology,

some might say that all this palaver seems a bit much for something that amounts to little more than a pinkie promise, but those people hugely underestimate the power of a connection between those born of the same pregnancy. Twins are often at a loss to describe this connection to singletons, but Myles Fowl, unsurprisingly, has tried. He hypothesized in an article for the *Journal of Biological Sciences* that *regarding the emotional pull that exists between twins, we are permanently beyond each other's event horizons, so to speak, and the mental fortitude necessary to escape that force could possibly have actual physical implications for the amygdala.* While Beckett once wrote in rainbow pencil for his English teacher that *Myles is like the other me, but boring.*

Both boys were correct.

And the sacred wrist bump was a potent reminder to the Fowl Twins of their mental and physical bond. As babies in their double cradle, the twins often slept with their scars aligned, which supposedly reminded them of their time in the womb, and since those days they had used the wrist bump to seal every promise they had made to each other.

It was their thing.

Their gesture.

No one had ever forced it upon them until now.

Myles lifted his hand, and the closer it moved to Beckett's wrist, the stronger the attraction grew until the scars synched and the twins felt a wave of contentment wash over them, smothering their anxiety somewhat.

Artemis Senior felt jealous of their zen calm. "I wish *I* had a mystical scar," he said. "Better than yoga. Now promise you will do as I say."

"We promise," said Myles, a little too quickly.

Artemis Senior zipped his cashmere-blend top up under his chin. "One last desperate roll of the dice, eh, son? Now do it properly. Say the magic words."

"We will do as you say," said the twins in unison. "Wrist-bump promise."

Their father was satisfied. "And so it shall be."

Myles lowered his hand, coming out of the shared mind-set into the real world.

"And now I suppose we must seek out Mother in the main house and get busy with our chores."

Myles said the word *chores* with the contempt he usually reserved for Einstein.

"Just you, Myles," said Artemis Senior, and the angry slash in his brow softened. "Beckett has a job to do."

A person didn't have to be a genius to figure out what that job might be, but Myles was a genius and so he figured it out all the faster, and his heart ached for his brother.

CHAPTER 5

THE PARTING RITUAL

TROLLS are usually and correctly thought of as humongous, shaggy fellows with quite the aggressive attitude and, indeed, the destructive capability to back this up, but Beckett's friend Whistle Blower was one of a diminutive breed known as toy trolls and stood barely eight inches tall. This is not to say there was a proportional decrease in aggression—in fact, Whistle Blower was, if anything, more pugnacious than his gigantic counterparts, but as Beckett explained to Myles, much of the little chap's bellicose attitude could be attributed to social anxiety. This was a statement that Myles appreciated, as he himself had but a single non-Fowl friend, plus he'd introduced the phrase *social anxiety* at one of his breakfast lectures and so was delighted to hear his twin apply it in a real-world situation, confirming his belief that Beckett could whip out the smarts when it suited him.

The point being that, as a part of this new *best behavior* routine, Beckett had been instructed to cut his tiny friend loose, as having a troll on the island quite clearly violated the *fraternizing with fairies* rule. All of which led to Beckett being dispatched to the Dalkey Island beach to break the news to Whistle Blower.

The troll was there before him, perched on his feeding rock and gnawing at a hank of something that had probably been alive until recently. From a distance, one might easily have mistaken the troll for an action figure from some fantasy series with his blue-gray fur, pronounced musculature, and squashed, pug-like features. Take heed when I urge you not to toss a pebble at the feet of any presumed *action figure* you may encounter in a remote area, just in case the figure is actually a toy troll that could easily dismember you and consume at least one of your limbs before you have the time to say *Wait a minute, that's not a—*

Luckily for Beckett, he was the toy troll's only human friend, because, as previously mentioned, Beckett was a trans-species polyglot and could converse with Whistle Blower, who had a uniquely sophisticated vocabulary for a troll. In the interests of clarity and expedience, the following conversation, though conducted through the medium of Trollish speech and gesture, will be documented in English.

Beckett sat down on the rock beside his troll friend. "What are you doing there, pal?"

"Eating untainted meat that I caught deep in the tunnels,"

said Whistle Blower. "My diet is all organic, and I try to stay clear of polluted ground, so I have to go deep."

Anyone eavesdropping on this grunted conversation would never have guessed that a troll's vocabulary included the words *organic* or *polluted*, and usually it did not. But Beckett had, for once, taken on the role of lecturer and recently warned the troll about the effects of soil and water pollution on the mind.

Beckett sighed heavily.

"So, what's up, Beck?" asked the troll. "I'm getting a weird vibe. Like you have bad news."

"I do have bad news," said the human boy. "The worst, actually."

Whistle Blower froze, the hank of meat halfway to his mouth. "Don't tell me Myles wants to hang out with us again. I have tusk-ache from trying to teach him my language the last time. The guy is a dope."

The gesture for *dope* was a tug on the left ear, as apparently there had once been a bent-eared troll whose dopiness was legendary.

"That's not the news," said Beckett. And then he felt obliged to add, "And Myles is not a dope."

"He is so a dope," insisted Whistle Blower, combing his stiff mohawk with greasy fingers. "He can't climb, he can't dig, and he can't fight. That all spells *dope* in the troll world."

Myles would have been proud of his twin had he heard the next sentence. "There are multiple intelligences, Whistle, and Myles is the best at most of them."

The toy troll grunted an *If you say so* and then asked, "What's the bad news, then?"

Beckett tried to organize his sentences mentally for a moment. Usually he left the transmission of information to Myles, but he was on his own this time.

"The bad news is this," he said, still not sure which words were going to come out. "The fairies know that you and I are meeting up. They're watching us right now from up high, beyond the sky, with a magic spyglass."

Whistle Blower raised both of his shaggy eyebrows. "Magic spyglass? I know what satellite surveillance is, buddy. I thought Myles bamboozled that."

"He did," said Beckett. "But then we exploded a jet, and Father met with the fairies, and now we are up the creek without a paddle."

"Up the creek without a paddle?" asked Whistle Blower. "Do you mean we're caught in a dwarf's jet stream without a bandanna?"

"That sounds about right," said Beckett. "Dad says you have a couple of days before the LEP come for you. He wasn't even supposed to tell me that much."

"They're coming all this way for me?" asked Whistle Blower.

"Not just you," said Beckett. "But you're on the list."

"So what are we going to do about it?" asked Whistle Blower. "Make a stand here? I can take out a dozen of those elves, no problem. You can cluster-punch the rest. We'll teach them to mess with us, right?"

For a crazy moment Beckett considered this, and then he remembered the wrist-bump promise.

"No," he said. "I can't fight. You have to go."

Whistle Blower hopped to his feet, balancing easily on the rock. "You're breaking up the Regrettables?"

The Regrettables was the superhero team name Beckett had assigned them the previous year during the ACRONYM adventure.

"I can't help it," said Beckett miserably. "I promised."

"But we're brothers," objected the troll.

"I wish we were," said Beckett, holding out his forearm so the little troll could clamber onto it. "But we're not, and I promised my real brother."

They sat in miserable silence for a few moments, both slightly afraid of how Whistle Blower might react. After all, it was conceivable that he might lose control of himself in the manner of trolls and throw a massive, destructive tantrum. Whistle Blower knew that a year ago this would certainly have been the case, but hanging around Beckett had civilized him a little—pulled his tusks, as the other trolls might say. It seemed like ages since he had done any rampaging, and even longer since he had indulged in the ancient practice of dog wrangling.

As a side note, this would be the one and only time that anyone would spend time with Beckett and come out the other end *more* civilized.

Maybe I do need a little troll time, thought Whistle Blower, but he did not go on a scything spree. Instead, he offered the kernel of a plan to Beckett. "Myles might be a dope, but he likes problems. Stupid problems like this."

Beckett cheered up immediately. "That's right. Myles will find a way around this. He loves figuring things out."

"Even if he can't fight."

"He fights with his brain," countered Beckett.

Whistle Blower countered Beckett's counter. "You can't fight with a brain. I tried that with a sheep's brain. It exploded on impact. Had zero effect."

This was a convincing argument.

"Brains *are* squishy," conceded Beckett. "But even so, Myles will crack this thing. We'll be back together soon."

Whistle Blower did his version of a thoughtful nod, which was an extended growl.

"Very well, human friend," he said at last. "I will leave. When it is safe to return, heap the entrails of a hedgehog on my feeding stone and I will take that as a sign."

Beckett was intrigued. "Why hedgehog entrails?"

Whistle Blower drew himself tall on Beckett's forearm. "That is my troll name, Hedgehog Entrails. They are a delicacy for trolls."

"That is possibly the coolest thing I will ever hear," said Beckett sincerely. "But how about I just paint the rock red? Hedgehogs are hard to find on this island."

"Very well. If you ever have need of me, paint my feeding stone red," said Whistle Blower. "And now we must complete the parting ritual, as a sign of mutual respect."

Beckett perked up. "Is the parting ritual our theme song? Are you finally going to sing it?"

Beckett had composed a theme song for the Regrettables but had never managed to convince Whistle Blower that it was anything but forced and idiotic. Nevertheless, Beckett was very proud of his composition, which went:

> *The Regrettables, the Regrettables,*
> *We're completely unforgettable,*
> *We love our fruits and vegetables,*
> *That's cuz we're Regrettables.*

"No," said Whistle Blower. "I would rather wear a sweater of stink worms than sing that song. *This* is the parting ritual."

The toy troll jumped onto his feeding rock, turned his back to Beckett, and stood on one leg.

Beckett thought he should at least make an attempt to interpret the more-than-likely noble symbolism of this stance. "I see," he said. "Showing me your back means you are leaving, but raising one foot means you are always ready to return. Is that right? I bet it is."

"No, completely wrong," said the troll. "When friends part, we allow our winds to mingle. The blend of particles unites us forever. It is very powerful troll magic."

Beckett had thought his friend couldn't possibly get any more awesome, but the parting ritual smashed the troll's previous record.

"Are you saying that we fart at each other to seal the bond of our friendship?"

"That is what I'm saying," confirmed Whistle Blower. "The mingling of the winds."

Beckett felt his eyes tearing up, and they hadn't even begun the ritual. "You are the best and coolest friend I will ever have."

"I know," said Whistle Blower. "And I appreciate your moderate fighting skills, so I vow never to eat you."

"Thanks," said Beckett. "I don't want to get eaten."

"Now turn your back," ordered Whistle Blower. "I will say the sacred words and then we shall expel wind in each other's general direction. And remember, do not turn around until the winds disperse."

Beckett did as he was told and tried not to sniffle, as Whistle Blower was being all stoic about their parting. Whistle Blower sent a howl echoing over the flat, calm ocean, then recited the sacred verse:

> "Warrior both loyal and true,
> The gift of wind I give to you.
> The particles inside my tum,
> I blow your way from out my bum."

Now *that's* a poem, thought Beckett, and then he stopped thinking, as there issued forth from Whistle Blower's person a sustained noise that should not have been possible from a colon of the troll's dimensions. The closest auditory equivalent Beckett could think of was a trombone being played underwater, something he had actually tried. A dense cloud of rank air enveloped Beckett, and he knew that he would have to burn his clothing in the garden bonfire on the way back to the house and possibly exfoliate himself in the shower.

Well played, old friend, he thought. Only one thing left to do.

Beckett Fowl took a breath, stood on one leg, and farted through his tears.

Beckett maintained the pose for over a minute, and when he finally did turn, Whistle Blower was gone.

"This is so unfair!" the boy shouted at the universe, borrowing a touch of screaming melodrama from his brother. "Nothing worse can happen."

Any fairy could have told him never to openly challenge the universe like that, because, even as he said the words, something worse was already happening, and if Beckett hadn't been so worked up, he might have noticed a tingling in his scar.

CHAPTER 6

THE RAT OR THE SCAR

LAZULI Heitz awoke in a room in which the bed alone was bigger than her Booshka apartment. Her head rested on what felt like a cloud and she was swathed in a blanket of sky and clothed in the shining folds of a silk jacket.

A notion drifted across her addled mind: This is a human bed. I died and went to the wrong heaven. Human heaven.

This notion was reinforced by the sight of a human woman of ethereal beauty dressed in sea-green satin seated at the end of the bed, which seemed very far away to Lazuli. The lady's right leg made a triangle with her left knee and rested upon the sky-blue blanket, forming a horizon line.

The woman smiled and Lazuli discerned warmth in those features, but also strength and intelligence, and the pixel knew instinctively that this was not an angel to be toyed with.

Lazuli saw Myles in that face, and Beckett, too, and she realized that this was of course Angeline Fowl, a woman she had often surveilled from a distance but had never met in person until now.

Not heaven, then, she understood. Villa Éco.

Angeline Fowl spoke softly. "Don't try to move, Specialist Heitz. You're in Arty's room. Though I have changed the comforter. My Arty prefers the reflective type of space blanket, which I personally don't find very comforting. The pajamas belonged to three-year-old Beckett, but I don't believe he ever wore them. You are, of course, completely safe here."

The human's voice was so soothing that Lazuli felt as though there might be a touch of the fairy *mesmer* layered in there.

Lazuli nodded and felt a tectonic grinding in her upper vertebrae. "What happened?" she asked, grimacing.

Angeline shifted closer, but Lazuli did not feel loomed over; she felt shielded. "I imagine you feel wretched, my dear, but I can assure you that nothing is fractured or ruptured. You were subjected to a severe rattling but should recover fully, especially considering that Captain—or I should say, *Commodore*—Short is in en route to administer a shot of restorative magic that will have you back on your feet tout de suite."

Lazuli closed her eyes momentarily, not to rest, but to digest the information contained in and implied by Angeline Fowl's statement.

It would seem that the twins' mother knows about the People. Furthermore, Angeline Fowl seems to be personally acquainted with Commodore Short and has been since she was a captain.

"But how did you find us?" Lazuli wondered. "And how did you contact the commodore?"

"Why don't I tell you everything I know," said the twins' mother, "and then deal with any questions you may have?"

Lazuli nodded. It was a sensible solution that required her only to listen, though she would most certainly also watch carefully for trickery, as every fairy knew that human beings were, by quite a large margin, the most duplicitous species on the planet, with goblins in second place and dwarves a distant third. The sprite in the orphanage where Lazuli had been raised, who was no slouch in the sneaky department himself, was fond of recounting a fable called "Last Man Jack," in which the only human left in the world died by stabbing himself in the back, as there was no one else alive to betray. And in spite of the fact that Lazuli had despised the administrator and his cruel, petty ways, that particular story with its gruesome final act had burned itself onto her young psyche and stayed there ever since like a soul brand. And so she watched Angeline Fowl closely, even though the twins' mother seemed kind and Specialist Heitz's natural instinct was to trust her.

Stay sharp, Specialist, she told herself. If you can do nothing else, you can gather intelligence.

Angeline Fowl cinched back her long blond hair into a ponytail with two deft movements that would not have seemed out of place in a martial-arts *kata* and began.

"Myles took the *Tachyon* out for a spin. Oh, I know

Beckett was along for the ride, and he does so love to go fast, but I have no doubt it was Myles who instigated the entire affair. Timmy and I were on a trip to Castle Leslie, where we were married more than two decades ago." Angeline paused as a thought occurred. "Whenever I go away for more than thirty minutes, it seems that one mastermind son or another takes advantage of my absence to open a wormhole or jump on board a nuclear train or some such nonsense. Well, no more. I trusted NANNI, but it seems Myles has corrupted her mainframe, so NANNI has been shut down and all my future trips have been canceled."

Angeline clenched a fist, digging her nails into her palm, and Lazuli realized: She blames herself. And so she quoted the pixie poet laureate Quintain Honoraria. "'The heart follows the mind through water and fire.' That's from a poem."

Angeline smiled. "Such a beautiful quote," she said. "Especially in your accent."

"I learned English the old-fashioned way," explained Lazuli. "No gift of tongues for me."

"Ah, yes," said Angeline. "You are a pixel. I am a hybrid myself, in a way. My family left Russia at the turn of the last century under something of a cloud and made our winding way to Ireland. So now I am neither Russian nor Irish but a little of both."

Lazuli smiled now, fully trusting this human woman.

"If I interpret your quote correctly," Angeline continued, "it means that Myles cannot help his pursuit of knowledge and we cannot halt his quest."

Lazuli nodded.

"Thank you for that absolution," said Angeline. "The fact that you think of others at such a time tells me all I need to know about you, Specialist Heitz."

Lazuli recognized that she was being charmed. Or could it be that Angeline Fowl was as genuine as her son Beckett?

Angeline clapped once lightly. "Anyway, to continue my— or should I say *your*—story . . . Myles took the jet for one of his heart-following-mind missions and they encountered you attached to a missile. Once my boys rescued their dear friend from the aforementioned missile, they were forced to eject in the escape pod before missile and jet collided explosively."

Lazuli half remembered the events, mostly in bright colors and sweeping sound waves. "And then?" she asked.

"And then the escape pod went subaquatic and was drawn to the nearest tethered facility."

Angeline paused here, seeming almost embarrassed.

"Which facility?" Lazuli pressed.

"Timmy has a dozen or so lairs around the world. Decommissioned now, but still with basic life support and emergency facilities."

"Lairs?" said Lazuli. "Like supervillain lairs?"

Angeline rolled her eyes in a melodramatic fashion. "That's it precisely. Supervillain lairs. I know—it's too cli-chéd. Timmy loves his lairs and can't bear to let them go. He swears that the plan is to develop them into eco-habitats, but I think a part of him is nostalgic for his glory days."

"Fowl boys." Lazuli smiled.

Angeline smiled right back. "Fowl boys. I love them all, and they drive me to distraction."

"I understand that," said Lazuli. "And I've only known them for a year."

"It doesn't get any easier," confided Angeline. "But somehow you grow to love them all the more."

"What happened in the . . . uh . . . lair?" Lazuli asked.

"Ah yes, the lair. Even the word is ridiculous," said Angeline. "In the *lair*, which was in the mid-Atlantic trench of course, NANNI scanned you and decided a full-body purge was the best way to get whatever drugs were in your system out of your system."

Full-body purge? Lazuli did not like the sound of that, though she *could* vaguely remember the sound of it.

"So, once that necessary unpleasantness was completed, Myles loaded everyone into a torpedo jet, and six hours later, you were back here. Needless to say, we were quite surprised to see a torpedo wash up on the beach. Though not as surprised as one might think, given the family history. In fact, I remember thinking *Angel*—that's what my mother used to call me—*Angel, it's only a torpedo jet. It could have been a lot worse.*"

"And you called Commodore Short?"

"Yes," confirmed Angeline, then qualified this statement with: "Well, technically, we called Artemis in space, and he called Holly. They were quite worried about you, and there are some who believe that you may have assaulted Foaly, who was found unconscious in the hallway."

Lazuli was suddenly alarmed. "Assaulted Foaly! I would never—"

Angeline covered Lazuli's small blue hand with her own. "Do not fret. The venerable centaur is fine, and neither Holly nor Foaly himself believe you were involved. But something is undeniably afoot, and the LEP must find out what." Angeline's eyes narrowed a degree. "Without involving my twins. Either of them."

This made sense to Lazuli. Whatever was happening here was a fairy problem and needed to be sorted out by fairies. Adding the Fowl Twins to any equation would only serve to make that equation infinitely more complex. Though she could take some comfort in the fact that the twins would be safe, she would miss both boys quite a lot and was surprised to find her emotions surging to the surface, so she put a lid on them with a semiofficial-sounding question.

"So, you know all about the People, Mrs. Fowl?"

"Not all, but certainly some," said Angeline. "It's complicated. Arty pulled the wool over our eyes for years, but he came clean before blasting off into space, in case some enemy or other, possibly fairy, launched a convoluted revenge scheme against our family. Classic criminal-mastermind safeguard if you're taking a trip. Arty even stimulated my hippocampus, and Timmy's, too, with Myles's clever eyeglasses. It tingled a little, but the results were extraordinary. I already had some memory fragments, but after the treatment we remembered everything. Timmy not only recollected his own fairy encounters but those of all his ancestors going back to Red Peg Fowl. *DNA-encoded memories*, Arty called them. That is fascinating, don't you think?"

Lazuli nodded. It *was* fascinating, and no doubt Myles was already looking into reproducing the effect for his own gain.

"When will Commodore Short arrive?" asked the specialist.

"It all depends on magma flares," said Angeline. "Sometime in the next couple of days, I imagine. And you should rest till then. After all, you have been in and out of consciousness for several days."

The human woman's casual use of the phrase *magma flares* confirmed that she had indeed been in contact with Commodore Fowl, as LEP craft often rode magma flares to the surface. Angeline Fowl should not know this, unless her recently resurfaced memories had contained the information, and even if they had, surely they would not have included a timetable. Either way, it seemed that in this particular house there were very few secrets between humans and fairies.

"And in a few days, you will depart this island forever. No good-byes, no further contact, no surveillance. Fowl and fairies are friends forever, but allies no more. The *arrangement* is over."

Lazuli was shocked.

This was a momentous statement, as the Fowls had come to the fairies' aid on numerous occasions through the centuries, though very few people on either side of the Earth's crust were aware of it. Lazuli had only been fully briefed since being appointed Fowl Ambassador. The litany of Fowl/fairy-related incidents read like a series of ever more outlandish morality tales, where the unlikely and impossible were everyday and commonplace.

Angeline squeezed the pixel's tiny blue hand. "It's tough love, my dear. No more shenanigans. My children must survive. Myles is a gifted boy, but though he understands mortality in theory, he, like all boys, doesn't truly believe in it, so he must bend to his parents' will or he will get himself and his brother killed."

As if summoned by the utterance of his name like some cursed demon, Myles entered the room in an unusual state of undress, that being solely clad in satin boxer shorts.

Angeline seemed bemused by this rather than panicked, though she should have been panicked.

"Wait outside, dear," she said. "No fairy contact, as I am certain you've been told. And do put one of your suits on."

Myles blinked with a certain low-lidded dullness that Angeline would never have associated with either of her twins.

"Myles," she said, releasing Lazuli's hand, "are you unwell?"

"The laws of physics," said Myles, not seeming to register where he was exactly, "are the same for all observers in any inertial frame of reference relative to one another."

Angeline stood abruptly. "Oh, my goodness," she said. "Something is very wrong."

Lazuli felt that something was indeed off, besides Myles's all-too-obvious deficit in the clothing department, but she could not place what that *off* thing might be. "What is it?" she asked, climbing down from a bed built for someone twice her height.

"He's paraphrasing Einstein," said Angeline. "Myles considers Einstein his nemesis. He would never refer to him in any other tone besides disparaging."

Lazuli was puzzled. "But Einstein was right about a lot of things, wasn't he? Surely Myles should admire him."

"You obviously don't know much about scientists," said Angeline, rushing to her son's side just in time to catch him as his eyes rolled back and he swooned toward the floor.

In less than a second Lazuli joined them on a plush North African rug. They'd had barely a moment to make a cursory examination before Beckett burst in, also clad in his underpants.

Angeline was by now—understandably—thoroughly bewildered. "For heaven's sake, Beck, what is going on here?"

Beckett's eyes were red from weeping and, even from a distance, he smelled somewhat rank.

"I'm farting through my tears!" he proclaimed. "Is that so hard to understand? What is wrong with you people?"

But then he noticed Myles on the floor and his troll worries were instantly forgotten.

"Brother!" he cried, joining the huddled group on the rug. "What's wrong? Speak to me, Myles."

"I don't know what happened," said Angeline. "He came in and mumbled a vague Einstein reference, then fainted."

"Einstein!" said Beckett, horrified. "And he's in boxer shorts. I can't remember the last time I saw Myles so undressed. He changes into his pj's behind a screen."

He shook Myles's thin shoulders. "Wake up, Doctor O'Fill!" he pleaded.

"Doctor O'Fill?" asked Angeline. "Who on earth is that?"

"Doctor Klor O'Fill," explained Beckett. "Myles's fake name for his secret biology doctorate. Sometimes he responds to it."

"Fake name?" said Angeline. "Secret doctorate? More deception. We'll have words about this later."

Lazuli was worried. Myles did not look at all well. His slick skin was as pale as a snail's foot, and the pixel could feel his entire person thrumming as though he were reclining on top of an electric fence. She had a sudden idea.

"What does NANNI say?" she asked.

"NANNI," called Beckett into the air, "could you please scan Myles with your doctor beams?"

There was no answer, and the conscious Fowls remembered at the same moment that NANNI had been deactivated and would have to be manually rebooted.

"I'll go to your father's office and bring NANNI online to scan Myles," said Angeline, rising to her feet. "Keep talking to your brother. Perhaps he can hear."

Beckett was crying now. "Dad told Myles he could only read one book per day. I think he's gone into shock." And then he sniffled and added, "I'm not blaming Dad. Making silly comments is how I deal with stress. It's a coping mechanism."

Angeline stroked his cheek. "I know, darling. Don't leave your brother. I'll be back." And she sailed out of the bedroom in a billow of satin.

"I would never leave Myles," said Beckett. "Never ever."

Lazuli lifted Myles's left eyelid with a swipe of her thumb. The human boy's blue iris moved up and down like a rapidly bouncing ball.

"This looks like stress roll," said the pixel. "But don't worry, Myles, help is on the way. Commodore Short is coming, and she will have a warlock medic with her and definitely some diagnostic equipment for a scan."

Beckett nodded rapidly as he digested this information without a silly comment. "Okay. That's good. Fowl and fairy, friends forever. That still works, doesn't it?"

Lazuli laid a hand on his shoulder. "Always, Beck. Nothing can change that, but Commodore Short won't arrive for some time."

Beckett took Myles's hand and aligned their scars, closing his eyes for a long moment. "Good," he said. "Because this isn't Myles."

Shock, thought Lazuli. Beckett is in shock and is grasping at straws.

"I know he's not himself," she said gently. "But this is your brother."

"No!" Beckett insisted. "I know Myles. I can feel him

through the scars. And he's not in there. Myles explained it to me once. He said our connection was something to do with amniotic fluid from Mum's tummy, but I get bored with science and didn't listen. We have a magical connection when we touch scars. You know, like when you lick an electric fence."

Lazuli nodded, even though most people would have no idea what it was like to lick an electric fence. "And you don't feel Myles?"

"I do feel him," corrected Beckett. "Close by, but not in here. On the island somewhere, but he's moving away."

Could Beckett be right? Lazuli wondered. Was there any chance that this person who looked exactly, 100 percent the spitting image of Myles Fowl was not actually Myles Fowl?

Some nefarious plot was unfolding, that much was undeniable. After all, she had been strapped to a rocket and fired at the Fowl jet, perhaps by dwarves. But even so, Beckett's theory was unlikely.

"Let's wait," she said. "We need a second opinion. NANNI will do a complete scan."

"*I've* done a scan!" snapped Beckett, losing patience for perhaps the third time in his life. "A magic scar scan. This is not Myles. There's nothing in here but blood and gristle."

Blood and gristle? thought Lazuli. How could that be?

It was just so far-fetched. But then again, *far-fetched* might as well have been the Fowl family motto.

Beckett talks to trolls, and Myles brought down an entire intergovernmental organization armed with a pair of glasses and his own big brain.

Lazuli had made a similar comment to Myles once and he had noted that *My brain is no bigger than the average, Specialist. It is simply that my anterior insula and anterior cingulate cortex are more actively connected with the other regions of my brain.*

Which taught Lazuli never to casually compliment Myles Fowl.

And she realized now that, should Myles be taken away from her by LEP orders or illness, she would for some reason miss his willingness to dissect almost everything she said. Nevertheless, she made a final appeal to Beckett.

"Let's say I believe you," she said, "and I accept that this is not Myles."

"Believe me," said Beckett. "It's not my brother."

Lazuli laid her hands on Beckett's shoulders in an attempt to get the blond boy to focus on her words. "So, we wait for reinforcements and see what they say."

Beckett shook off the pixel's small hands. "They'll say what everyone always says when I know what's going on and they don't: *You're wrong, Beckett. Leave the thinking to Myles, Beckett. You're the dumb brother, Beckett. Animals can't talk, Beckett Fowl, and even if they could, they wouldn't talk to you, because you're the stupid twin.*"

Lazuli had never heard Beckett speak this way. "I don't think that. Myles doesn't, either."

"Not you, Laz. I know that. Now, I have a plan, which I know is not how it usually goes, but I do have one, and I think it's good. Mostly action-based, because that's my talent. Do you want to hear my amazing plan?"

Lazuli thought that she should hear Beckett out, if only to keep him talking. Perhaps Angeline would return while Beck was laying out his great plan. She stood and looked Beckett in the eye. "Yes, I'd love to hear it."

"Good," said Beckett. "So here it is. I'm going to present it in points like an argument, which is a trick I learned from . . ."

"Myles," guessed Lazuli. "A trick you learned from Myles."

Beckett shook his head so that his curls rustled. "No. I learned this trick from a seal that lives in the bay. Seals are wise and good at arguing, and also moody when they lose. Never debate a seal."

"I'll remember that," said Lazuli with more conviction than she might have a year ago.

Beckett took a breath. "So, here we go. There are two things that might be true, and then two actions we can take, depending on which thing we think is true, but only one action that is the right thing to take no matter what's true and what isn't. With me so far?"

Lazuli nodded. She was indeed with Beckett but felt there might be a faster way to get to the point. Still, that was fine by her.

Hurry up, Angeline. Come to the rescue.

Usually Lazuli came to her own rescue, but right at this precise moment she felt a little disadvantaged by the aftershock of having been strapped to a missile.

A pity Foaly suppressed my magic. Perhaps I could have healed Myles by now, and myself, too.

Lazuli glanced down at Myles lying on the rug, and maybe it was the power of suggestion, but she fancied that she didn't feel any connection to the boy. Fairies are empathetic by nature, and this shivering figure did not elicit as much sympathy as it should have, given that she considered Myles a friend.

My mind is wandering, Lazuli realized.

Beckett must have realized this, too, because he laid his hands lightly on the pixel's shoulders. The boy's fingers and thumbs could have easily encircled her neck, but Lazuli knew she was safe.

Unless this is not Beckett, like this might not be Myles.

But it *was* Beckett. She could feel his nature coming off him in waves.

"So, if the thing on the floor is actually Myles, the LEP will heal him when they get here, right?"

Lazuli felt Beckett had prejudiced his statement slightly with the use of the phrase *thing on the floor,* but she nodded. "That's right."

"So, if the LEP arrive and we're not here, Myles gets healed anyway. That's right, too, isn't it?"

Lazuli did not like where this was going, but she played along, played for time. "That's right, Beck."

"And if the thing on the floor is not Myles and we try to explain this to the grown-ups, what happens?"

Lazuli did not point out that she was more or less one of the grown-ups. Instead, she answered, "They don't believe us."

"And then?" said Beckett, prompting Lazuli to reach her own conclusion.

"And then I get whisked off to the Lower Elements for an investigation, and you visit a counselor."

"Meanwhile?"

"Meanwhile, the real Myles is spirited away to who knows where, and we have no leads."

Beckett squeezed the pixel's shoulders. "Exactly. So, the only reason we would stay here is if we are basically bad people who don't care about love, friendship, or the environment."

Lazuli frowned. "The environment?"

"I just threw that in," admitted Beckett, "because the seal always says to hit your opponent where they live. And you love the environment."

This was true, but Lazuli knew that even without the eco-factor Beckett's argument was sound. If this was Myles, then he would get healed; if it wasn't, then there was no time to waste.

"Very well, Beck," she said. "The seal taught you well. So, what is this great plan?"

Beckett twanged the elastic of his underpants. "We get dressed and then we follow the scar signal."

* * *

Beckett had never been a fan of clothing, and for many years had run free as nature intended whenever he could get away with it—which was more often than one might think. Historically, the only item he rarely removed was a golden necktie made from the cured and laminated corpse of his very beloved and very deceased goldfish, Gloop, a variation on a security blanket which he would often chew. Beckett had gifted the tie to Myles during a previous adventure, and when Gloop had virtually disintegrated from wear, Myles had replaced it with a silk-and-gold-threaded tie patterned after a fan painting of Japanese koi by Katsushika Hokusai. He had a dozen of these made up, and Beckett grabbed a couple from Myles's closet now and tied one on as a reminder of the mission's focus, as if such a reminder were needed. He tossed the second tie to Lazuli and the pixel looped it around her neck like a scarf.

Lazuli found that she and Beckett were on the same page when it came to clothing, i.e., fast and functional. Beckett did a swan dive into a hamper of rumpled clothing and somehow emerged in a T-shirt, hoodie, and shorts, and while Lazuli could not replicate this feat of flash-dressing, she did manage to quickly select one of the black suits from Myles's toddler era, which were conveniently labeled by age and sealed in vacuum storage bags. She balked at going on the hunt in black loafers and instead tugged on a pair of baby shoes that looked like they had never been walked in. All in all, they were in Myles's side of the room for about half a minute, and then they were tumbling out the bedroom window and running toward the beach.

I can't believe I'm doing this, thought Lazuli as the last wisps of narco-fog dissipated. At the very least I will be court-martialed, and there's a reasonable chance I will face criminal prosecution.

But, in truth, the pixel *could* believe it, because Beckett Fowl had uncanny instincts. In a way he was a hybrid, too, because there were magical sparks floating around in his system that had sharpened his instincts in mysterious ways. Foaly had told Lazuli in the Argon Clinic, which seemed like a lifetime ago, that he would love to get the Fowl child under an MRI machine, because *his quarks would light up the scanner like fireworks.*

So, if the human boy said something impossible was happening, then it probably wasn't as impossible as everyone thought.

Beckett ran forward, his scarred wrist thrust ahead of him like a divining rod. "This . . . way," he panted. "This . . . way."

Lazuli followed, as that seemed to be her only option. She certainly didn't have legs of sufficient length to overtake the human boy.

I don't have long legs, she thought. I don't have wings, and I certainly don't have weapons.

And she did not have magic—Foaly had seen to that. If he had not, then this incident could have been but a footnote in the Fowl chronicles, as it was possible that her SPAM could have presented as healing power and cured Myles's mystery ailment, if that was indeed Myles.

Beckett skidded on his heels to a sudden halt on the ledge that curled over the beach like an organic wave.

"What?" he said, seemingly to his feet. "Where?"

Lazuli managed to avoid crashing into him and asked, "What *what*? What *where*?"

Both of which questions would have horrified her English tutor in the LEP academy.

Beckett did not look up, and so Lazuli followed his gaze to the grass and realized that there was a bristling rat up on its hind legs, squeaking earnestly at Beckett.

"You're not making sense, Oswald," said the blond twin.

Lazuli could have sworn that the rat sighed, then launched into another series of agitated squeaks.

"What's *Oswald* saying?" she asked.

Lazuli had never learned to speak Rat; it wasn't a language offered in school. In fact, even fairies with the gift of tongues could not conduct any kind of nuanced conversation with animals. It was a skill they had lost over the millennia. But Beckett squeaked as though born in a sewer.

"Oswald is saying that *the stones are alive*. That's the gist, isn't it, Oswald?"

Oswald obligingly nodded, confirming that *the stones are alive* was indeed the gist of it.

"Maybe Oswald is mistaken," said Lazuli, who was not overly fond of big rats on their hind legs, cute names notwithstanding.

"No," said Beckett, thoughtfully. "Oswald's body language

is all over the place, and his fur is standing out in spikes. Something is wrong."

"What does your scar tell you?" asked the pixel.

Beckett fanned his arm, searching for a signal, until he locked on to one.

"This way," he said pointing toward the shoreline.

Which will lead us onto the stones that may or may not be alive, concluded Lazuli.

Then she had the most ridiculous thought of her life so far, though it would be easily trumped by day's end, and this thought was:

Should we trust the rat or the scar?

"So, what's next?" she asked Beckett.

"We follow the scar signal," he said without a jiffy's hesitation. "Myles is on the other end."

They scrambled down the ledge onto the beach itself, leaving Oswald chittering his cryptic warnings.

Initially it seemed that the rat might be mistaken, as the stones remained resolutely inanimate, but then, with a drumroll of rapid *click-clack*ing, two piles surged upward directly into the pursuers' path.

The stones *are* alive, thought Lazuli, but she quickly realized she was as mistaken as Oswald had been.

The stones were not alive, but what had been hidden beneath them most certainly was. Alive and aggressive.

The beach pebbles cascaded to the ground, revealing two squat figures clad from head to toe in suits woven out of vines.

A person might expect Beckett to be dismayed, but only if that person was not familiar with Beckett's reaction to crises. In fact, the Fowl twin was jubilant.

"I knew it!" he said. "The scar never lies. Something is going on."

Lazuli was considerably less overjoyed. She could tell instantly that these were dwarves, and it made sense that they would be from the same bunch who had gummed her to the rocket.

"Be careful!" she said to Beckett, instinctively shielding the boy with her own body.

"Careful?" said Beckett. "It's just dwarves. Aren't dwarves all jokey guys with funny names who love barbecue?"

The camouflaged dwarves drew distinctive curved short swords with luminous blades of crystallized dwarf spittle, and Lazuli knew exactly what band they were from.

"These aren't just dwarves," she said, if there even was such a thing as *just* dwarves. "These are Horteknut Reclaimers."

Beckett was a little envious of this title. "That is a great team name," he said.

"They are a great team," said Lazuli. "They've been settling a score with humans for thousands of years."

"Is that bad?" asked Beckett.

"Only if you don't like dying," said Lazuli.

CHAPTER 7
SEPARATION ANXIETY

MYLES Fowl was immersed in a dream in which he was debating the existence of the fabled pentaquark with Murray Gell-Mann, who had originally proposed the existence of quarks in 1964. Myles knew he was dreaming, because Gell-Mann had passed away not so long ago, and also because Myles was losing the argument.

As we have already gleaned, Myles did not relish losing arguments, and this distaste extended to his dream state, so he decided to wake himself up. But rather than emerge fully into wakefulness, Myles suspended himself in a hypnopompic state of threshold consciousness, in which he could think in a superfast mode without alerting his captors to the fact that he was indeed alert. Beckett referred to this semi-suspended state as *sleepy-wakey*, which Myles had to concede described it perfectly in layman's terms.

Myles had no doubt that he had been abducted. He

remembered walking across from Father's office toward the main house when the ground erupted beneath his feet.

And then . . .

Of the rest, Myles wasn't certain. Could it be, as his memory insisted, that he had been swallowed whole? Surely that wasn't possible, but that had been his impression.

Had he been slimed? Swallowing and sliming would seem to indicate the involvement of dwarves.

The whole thing seemed impossibly juvenile, like one of Beckett's stories.

Myles dismissed the *very* recent past for the moment and regressed to the *quite* recent past.

Why was all this happening? Were they, in fact, in the middle of another extended adventure?

The Chinese general Sun Tzu had written in *The Art of War* that "the whole secret lies in confusing the enemy, so that he cannot fathom our real intent."

And we are certainly confused, Myles thought now.

But that was surely temporary, as bringing order from confusion happened to be one of Myles Fowl's specialties.

If a mysterious antagonist was moving against the Fowl Twins, then it would seem logical that the Fowl Twins had unwittingly involved themselves in that particular antagonist's business.

So, what have I been up to? wondered Myles.

Perhaps some multinational is threatened by my advances in the field of DNA storage.

Or could it be that my plan to use Beckett's cluster-punching ability as a cure for migraines has alarmed a pharmaceutical company?

No, he realized. It is, of course, the ACRONYM treasure. Myles had learned, by hacking into the organization's supposedly secure e-mail server, that the source of all the agency's funding was held in their Florida facility, which was why he'd been checking it out in the *Tachyon.*

Thus prepared, Myles Fowl opened his eyes and saw that he was in a dark room with light emanating in phosphorescent sparkles from the depths of his wobbling mattress. Globs of the same material were adhered to three of the walls.

His "bed" was a quivering slab of what could have been the bell of a giant jellyfish. The substance lit a neuron in Myles's memory.

Those are dwarf-spit lanterns. I am reposing upon dwarf spit, Myles realized. Plus, I was, until recently, covered in it. How fascinating. And this explains my confusion, as, according to Dr. Fowl's frankly overwritten files, there is some form of sedative in the gel.

Myles blinked to clear his vision as much as possible, and then studied his cell, for that was surely what it was. The glow from the bed crept across the packed mud floor but dissipated before it could brighten the walls, which were deep in viscous shadow.

Myles silently berated himself for his flowery thought process.

Viscous shadow? Really, Myles? Perhaps a more pertinent detail than the viscous shadow is the fact that there is a dwarf lady seated on a stool beside your bed.

Myles often argued with himself in the second person, as he believed it was a way to teach his unconscious mind new thought patterns.

Myles studied the dwarf lady for nonverbal clues as to who he might be dealing with. He calculated that she was perhaps three feet tall, with corpse-pale skin that showed off her rune tattoos nicely, and copper-red hair that was coiled in bandolier braids around her shoulders and torso. Her bearing bordered on regal, and Myles guessed that this lady was close to the top of whatever food chain she hunted in. And it seemed as though the dwarf was focusing on his golden tie, though it was difficult to be sure, as the eyes that regarded him seemed to be all pupils, and Myles wondered if dwarf eyes had UV-receptive cones like some bats. But that was by the by. What Myles was really interested in now was the confidence that emanated from those eyes, which confirmed his deduction that this was no lackey. He was dealing with the boss here, or at least someone high in the command structure.

I wonder, he thought, *if this lady will attempt to form a bond with me, hoping to develop a Stockholm syndrome situation in which the captive grows to rely upon, trust, and even befriend the captor. If she is dull enough to attempt this tired trick, I shall play along.*

"Hello, human," she said. "I am Gveld Horteknut, and I have killed more men than you have had days in your life, so do not believe we could ever be friends."

Quite the intro.

Myles winced, not at the words themselves, which he presumed were hyperbolic, but at the dwarf's harshly accented English, which with every consonant put him in mind of an ax hacking at a tree trunk.

"Women and children too I have slaughtered," continued Gveld, her vicious grin exposing a grill of engraved gold teeth. "So trust me when I say that dispatching you to whatever version of hell you are surely bound for means less to me than crushing an ant. Far less, in fact, as the lowliest ant actually contributes something to this planet." Gveld Horteknut stood, and Myles was quietly smug that his estimate as to her height was inch-perfect. He noted that she wore a short-sword scabbard from hip to knee, which gave him a handy reference for her femur-to-body-length ratio. It was, incidentally, one to four, if he was not mistaken, corresponding with Dr. Fowl's notes on dwarf proportions.

"I shall leave you for five minutes to organize your thoughts," said Gveld, cutting across his calculations, "so that you may most efficiently transmit the information I need. I'm sure you know of which information I speak, boy. Just to sharpen your mind, there will be a forfeit for meandering. For every superfluous syllable in your delivery, I will take a finger joint. Nod if you understand."

Myles nodded, his mood shifting quickly from smug to

anxious. It was, he realized, the specific nature of the threat that had intimidated him so. *A joint per syllable.*

"*Good,*" said Gveld.

Myles watched the dwarf lady leave the dank cell and thought, No Stockholm syndrome from Ms. Horteknut. Straight to threats.

Then: I am in a pickle here.

The Fowl twin held up his scar and concentrated, but there wasn't so much as a faint buzz to indicate that Beckett might be on his trail.

My brother is nowhere near, he realized. And without Beck I am in more than a mere pickle. I am in mortal danger.

Dalkey Island

Beckett was also in mortal danger, though it was made clear to Lazuli that he did not grasp this notion when he said, "Aw, look at these guys. I think they want hugs."

Hugs! thought Lazuli. The only reason Horteknut dwarves ever hug anyone is to crush their bones.

In fact, one of the dwarf band's signature martial-arts moves was a version of the Heimlich maneuver, the main difference being that the hugger did not unlock his fingers until the huggee coughed up their heart and lungs, both of which would be punctured by splintered ribs.

"Hugs!" she spluttered. "They have swords, Beck. Stop fooling around."

"Don't worry," said Beckett. "Remember those special-forces guys in Amsterdam?"

Lazuli did remember those guys.

Of course she did. She and Beckett had made a formidable team against the foot soldiers of ACRONYM (see LEP file: *The Fowl Twins*). But the twin had never faced the likes of these dwarves. Horteknut Reclaimers' training began shortly after birth, and the majority of the lessons were devoted to myriad methods of converting live humans into dead ones. Lazuli decided that when she and Beckett had a little more time, *if* they ever had a little more time, she would tie the twin down and make him listen to the Horteknut backstory, which did not have a happy ending, a cheery beginning or, for that matter, a lighthearted middle section.

"These are more than just special forces," she said with some urgency. "These are Horteknut Reclaimers."

The dwarves advanced, twirling their crystal swords in complicated patterns, forming almost hypnotic light fans in the late-afternoon sun.

"Ooh," said Beckett. "Look."

Look? thought Lazuli. They want you to look, that's the whole point.

And she saved Beckett's life the only way she could, by booting him in the backside, knocking the boy off the ledge just in time to avoid a sudden scything slash from a dwarf blade that seemed more deadly than pretty now.

Beckett was surprised for a nanosecond but then rolled

easily onto the pebbled beach. When he stood, Lazuli saw that the boy's entire demeanor had changed. He was battle ready now.

It's about time, thought Lazuli, then she stopped thinking and started reacting as the dwarf switched targets and she was forced to retreat at speed. She used the unpredictable mixed bag of movements she'd learned from training in the martial art of Cos Tapa, which translates roughly from the Gnommish as *quick-footed* or *of blurred feet*. It is an aggressive combat style developed by the diminutive pixie race from a study of animals such as hyenas, cats, and small breeds of dogs, which are often forced to take on larger foes. The martial art was so effective that it had migrated to the human arsenal and was adapted by the legendary Madam Ko for use by the prospective bodyguards in her academy. Cos Tapa's mantra was to always be on the attack, even in retreat.

Lazuli's sensei in the Academy, a gnome who liked to speak in infuriating riddles, had once told her that *The squinting mole sees only its own dreams.*

Which Lazuli had considered for long enough to suspect it was useless in combat situations. However, the same gnome had once lost patience with her during a simulation and yelled, *For Danu's sake, Heitz! Even going backward, you can set up your opponent!*

Which was a lot more to the point than that nonsense about moles.

Lazuli used this strategy now, and even with a dwarf

blade whirling dangerously close to her unarmored stomach region, she kept an eye on her attacker's stance to see if she could lure him off-balance.

Keep coming, she broadcast at the dwarf. *Keep coming.*

The Horteknut Reclaimer obliged with some enthusiasm.

The second dwarf targeted Beckett on the beach. The blond twin was very impressed with the fancy footwork the chap used to approach. Initially facing away from Beckett, the Horteknut dwarf trotted up a dune and back-flipped off the top, landing in the surf behind the boy.

"Bravo," said Beckett. "Very good."

The dwarf too spoke, his voice garbled by mesh that covered his face. Beckett had never heard this tongue before. It was an aggressive-sounding language made even more so by the guess that the sentiment was in fact most likely aggressive.

By the end of the second sentence, Beckett felt he had enough grasp on the meaning to attempt conversation, though, as it would turn out, he was mostly wrong in this assumption.

"Wait, friend," Beckett said, surprising the Reclaimer, who had never heard a human attempt any of the dwarf dialects. "There is no need for us to enrage the cattle."

Beckett had misspoken, but this was not entirely his fault, as the Horteknut dialect was quite limited in the actual sounds contained therein. Linguists estimate that this particular vernacular, which is one of over a hundred dwarf variations, contains no more than twenty sounds in total, including clicks, strident vowels, and gagging noises. With so few available noises it is inevitable that certain words and even complete phrases sound almost exactly alike.

So, when Beckett said with some urgency that there was no need for them to enrage the cattle, what he actually meant to say was *There is no need for us to engage in battle*.

The actual phrase is altered somewhat here to make the point in English.

Surprisingly, this mangled attempt at Horteknut-speak stopped the Reclaimer in his tracks, and ironically, it had the desired effect of the intended phrase. It was the word *cattle* that did it, as this particular dwarf was terrified of cows (he had lost a good friend to a stampede in Brazil). So the dwarf spared a fraction of a second to spin around, spasmodically checking for cows, reasoning that in his long and bloody combat experience no human would be able to accomplish much in the way of attack in a mere fraction of a second. Which just goes to show how wrong a person can be.

For this fraction of a second gave Beckett Fowl ample time to land his favorite blow: the cluster punch.

To recap: The cluster punch is a nonlethal blow aimed at the junction of the body's principal meridian lines just above the right kneecap. If an attacker could strike that cluster at precisely the right angle, with exactly the correct amount of pressure per square inch, the victim's entire system would spasm and they would be left paralyzed for a brief period.

Unfortunately for Beckett, dwarf physiology is completely different from that of humans, even though dwarves are, roughly speaking, humanoid. It just so happens that dwarf meridian lines intersect above the *left* kneecap, something Beckett might have instinctively figured out had the Reclaimer not been swaddled in a suit of vines that concealed the tug of his tendons and the bloat of his gas pockets.

However, Beckett's strike did have an unexpected side effect, which might lead one to believe that the gods of fortune favored the blond twin. The side effect was as follows: Male tunneling dwarves can store up to a thousand pints of compressed gas in their gastrointestinal systems. Technically, at this pressure the gas has mostly been converted to a supercritical fluid, and the dwarf supplementary intestine is lined with powerful constricting muscles that can contain even a packed-to-bursting intestine for short periods. The intestine is stoppered by an internal ring of muscle fed by a major artery that continues down through the right knee and around to the heart in a very delicate circuit. And, as you may have guessed, Beckett's strike effectively closed off that artery, causing the muscle to fail.

For a moment, the dwarf felt nothing other than mild surprise that a human had managed to land a blow on a fearsome Reclaimer. Then his internal ring relaxed and a cyclone of air, liquid, and semisolids exploded through his bum flap, not exactly at the speed of sound, but certainly with quite a measure of speed and sound. The effect was spectacular: A thundering jet funneled through vents in the dwarf's combat pantsuit and he corkscrewed into the air like a punctured balloon.

Beckett's jaw dropped with surprise, even though his day had been fairly fart-centric already. This was surely the Mount Everest of flatulence. The Reclaimer was propelled along the beach and landed on the island's northwesterly tip, where he disappeared into a hole that Beckett could not remember being there yesterday.

I can worry about that later, he thought. Laz is still fighting.

And fighting she was.

But not in a traditional sense, i.e., on the offensive, as Lazuli was seemingly in full retreat, drawing her bigger, more powerful, and more experienced opponent toward her. The dwarf's shimmering sword cut light patterns in the air as it slashed toward Lazuli's organs, but so far, the pixel was untouched . . . though the first cut did seem inevitable, as with each scythe the blade whistled closer to its target.

Then Lazuli stumbled backward, and Beckett's heart dropped into his shoes.

No, Laz! he thought, and the sword flashed downward, surely to cleave his friend to the bone.

But somehow, Lazuli suddenly was not falling. She had jammed her rear foot into the earth and pistoned herself back the way she had come. This move seemed like it should have cracked her shin bone like a dry branch, unless of course the pixel had planned the whole thing.

Which of course she had.

I have one shot, she thought. A single punch to put this dwarf assassin down.

Yet Lazuli knew in her heart that one punch would not be enough, no matter where she hit him. She was vaguely aware that Beckett had pulled off something very Beckettian, but she could not spare so much as a flicker of her gaze toward the twin; all her attention was needed for the dwarf.

The dwarf grunted as he realized what was going on. It was a grunt of grudging admiration for the pixel's fighting spirit, but there was no anxiety in the noise. Yes, she would land a blow, but that would be the end of any attack. Yes, the dwarf might stumble a few steps backward, but by now his brother Reclaimer would have killed the human and could assist him with this hybrid. No doubt the ruckus behind him was as a result of the boy being slaughtered.

So the dwarf took a shot to the jaw, which sent him stumbling backward as foreseen, but he never could have foreseen what happened next.

Which was this:

The masked dwarf, realizing that his stumble would send him over a ledge and onto the beach some three feet below, decided to offset this tactical disadvantage by performing a trademark Horteknut backflip so that at least he might land on his own terms. And so, instead of making a futile attempt to halt his backward motion, he accelerated and threw himself over the edge. He sensed, in the way of virtuoso athletes, that the flip was good and he would stick a solid landing, and he also became aware that the human boy was directly below him. What he did not know was that this human boy had a trick up his sleeve—that being his arm, which was connected to his fist.

Beckett anticipated the dwarf's flip and mapped out the trajectory before the Horteknut Reclaimer even took off. When the dwarf sailed overhead, Beckett nailed him with a cluster punch, which collapsed the dwarf's muscle ring, releasing the jet of compressed air, supercritical fluid, and the semi-digested beef jerky that this Horteknut was never without, slamming the poor fellow into the ledge headfirst and knocking him out cold.

Lazuli clambered over the brink.

"Are . . . you . . . okay . . . Beck?" she asked between gasps for breath.

"I did a new thing," said Beckett, gazing in awe at his own fist. "I broke two dwarves."

Lazuli scanned the shoreline. "Where's the second one?"

"Over there," said Beckett, jerking a thumb. "He went down a hole that I don't remember being there."

"Tunnel," pronounced Lazuli. "These two were the rear guard, and the rest went subterranean."

Beckett tried to pick up a signal from his twin on his scar. "I can't feel Myles," he said. "He's gone."

Beckett's posture was slumped, and Lazuli felt an ache of sympathy for him.

What we should do now is try to contact Commodore Short, she realized. She will summon the cavalry, and the navy, and possibly the air force.

But Lazuli knew that dwarf tunnels, especially Horteknut ones, were built to collapse shortly after use, and if they didn't follow their quarry right now, not even an LEP scout with ground-penetrating radar would have a prayer of picking up the trail.

Lazuli flipped the unconscious dwarf onto his back and pulled off his suit with a half dozen explosive yanks, leaving the dwarf clad in a skintight onesie that had not seen the inside of a washing machine in some time. The outer suit was a *no-tech* affair that seemed to be woven from tree roots that may or may not have been still alive. It was pungent and too wide to fit well, but from a distance she might pass for a dwarf for maybe ten seconds.

Maybe ten seconds will be enough, she thought, trying not to imagine what an entire band of Horteknuts would do to an imposter when she was found out.

While Lazuli wriggled into the suit and helmet, Beckett, for perhaps the first time in his life, assumed the role of responsible partner. "Maybe you should wait here, Laz," he said, the cautionary words not sounding right coming out of his face. "I thought maybe Myles was taken by people we could run rings around, but these fellows are dangerous.

Even Oswald didn't like them. They're spooky, and they have swords."

Lazuli appropriated the dwarf's weapon and gave it a few practice swings. "I have a sword too now," she said.

"Still," said Beckett, "maybe I should go alone. Myles is my brother."

"That's right," said Lazuli, sliding the blade into its sheath on her hip. "And he's my friend. In fact, I might be his only friend."

Beckett nodded and then, without another word, ran toward the tunnel mouth.

CHAPTER 8

JUST SPITBALLING HERE

In Captivity

While Beckett was displaying an uncharacteristic level of caution, Myles had seemingly also strayed from his usual behavior patterns and was displaying all the signs of someone having a meltdown. Anyone who was familiar with the boy or had even absently perused his file would be most skeptical of this behavior. But there was no one in the room to call him out for his tantrum. No one immediately visible, at any rate.

The emotional display came from nowhere. One second Myles was reclining in funereal contemplation, arms crossed in vampire fashion, and the next he was sobbing into his hands.

"Oh dear," said the boy loudly and with much wringing of fingers, which was a well-documented physical manifestation of distress. "Woe is me, and boo-hoo."

Myles actually said *boo-hoo*, which is akin to reading stage directions aloud.

"This is terrible," said the Fowl twin, rising from his bed of spit. "Awful, in fact. And the most logical thing for me to do, as a typical twelve-year-old, would be to blurt out all my secrets and hope no one overhears. Or perhaps I should talk into my sleeve very loudly, as if there is a communicator stitched in there." Myles then proceeded to talk into his sleeve. "They have caught me, Your Majesty. My call sign is one-zero-zero-one-zero-zero-one. Drain my accounts. Burn my fake mustache and vintage troll dolls. Remember: Tell no one about the guided missile in my shoe, or the laser in my wristwatch."

In the name of transparency, it should be pointed out that Myles had neither a missile nor a laser secreted anywhere about his person, for, as you have no doubt guessed, this little freak-out act was precisely that: an act. And not one intended to fool anyone with so much as half a brain.

And just as quickly as it began, the frantic monologue was over. Myles coughed gently into his fist, straightened his golden tie, and perched on the corner of the wobbly mattress.

"Is that sufficient?" he asked the empty room. "Or should I invent more nuggets of false information?"

The empty room did not respond, as mud walls are not given to conversation, but Myles's ruse did have an effect, as a particularly deep shadow detached itself from a larger glob behind a tower of cardboard boxes and stepped into the spittle glow.

"Aha!" exclaimed Myles. "I suspected as much. It's an old interrogation technique. Throw a scare into the subject and see what tumbles out of his gibbering mouth."

The shadow tugged off its hood to reveal a dwarf beneath. Another female. This one with skin almost as dark as her shadow suit and deep blue runes tattooed on both cheeks.

"It is a technique that often bears fruit," she said. Her accent was not as pronounced as Gveld's, but she attacked the consonants with some gusto all the same. "I think this is not your first time in the question box, Mud Boy."

Myles confirmed this with a nod. "I have been in many a *question box*, for I know the answers to many questions. All a person has to do is ask."

The dwarf huffed a chuckle. "We ask and, just like that, you will answer?"

Myles considered this. "That depends on the question."

The lady rolled up her hood, stuffing it into a pocket. "One-zero-zero-one-zero-zero-one," she said. "That is a human security agency call sign, if I am not mistaken."

Myles nodded, then wagged his finger at her shadowy torso. "And your suit—ultra-black, I presume?"

The disembodied head nodded back. "It absorbs all light, which can be useful in certain dark situations."

Myles was impressed. "I have never seen it manufactured on such a scale. Impressive to be sure, mademoiselle."

The dwarf sneered. "Mademoiselle? I am no French woman, Mud Boy. I am Gundred Horteknut. Second soldier of the Horteknut Seven."

Myles filed away this information, which he counted easily won. He was dealing with soldiers, there were seven of them, and this Gundred person was second-in-command. Not that Myles's answer box was exactly empty when it came to Horteknut factoids. Artemis's LEP files had yielded quite a treasure trove on the militant wing of the Horteknut family. Even so, it was very considerate of successive members of the band to present their credentials with barely any provocation.

"Second soldier," he said. "Most impressive."

Gundred twisted her features into a magnificent scowl. "Spare me the empty compliments, Mud Boy. Your smugness is unearned. I was merely hoping to save you a great deal of pain. Gveld granted me these few moments to trick some information out of you, but even now she readies her torture chest, so we will get our information one way or another."

Myles felt that perhaps his smugness was indeed misplaced, and he silently chided himself for revealing his nature.

I have shown my hand with my playacting routine. And by hand, I mean brain, and consequently the dwarves will never underestimate me again.

In this Myles was correct. He had well and truly broken the first rule of Fowl negotiations, which was, as Artemis had once put it, to *be just smart enough to meet your opponent's expectations but never smart enough to meet your own.*

Gundred Horteknut walked to the door and pounded

on the wood with the flat of her palm. "Your family are charged with many crimes against the dwarf nation," she said over her shoulder. "And the reckoning comes today."

"I deny all charges," said Myles automatically, but it occurred to the Fowl twin that this was not even the first time today that he had denied charges, and his denial probably rang as hollow this time as it had the last.

The door was opened from without and Gundred's disembodied head slipped through the gap, presumably taking her camouflaged body with it.

Unless the dwarves have yet another marvelous talent to add to their quite extraordinary list.

And the list was indeed extraordinary, made more so by the fact that it was incomplete. Even the fairies' own files on the dwarf nations were woefully inadequate, and it seemed as though every time a dwarf popped up, they displayed some skill or other that had never been photographed or documented in any way. And as for human files, they were hilariously light on detail.

In summary:

There have been throughout recorded human mythology countless mentions of dwarves. In old England they were known as *dwerghs*, while the Vikings called them *dvergr*, and the Proto-Germans categorized them as *dwergoz*. While descriptions of dwarves tend to vary wildly, there are common denominators: Dwarves are described across the folkloric board as a fairy race, small in stature, who dwell in subterranean habitats and work expertly with metals. Such is the saturation of the term *dwarf* in the language of humans that it has been co-opted to describe almost anything that is smaller in size than might be expected. Everything from a star to a plant to a human being of short stature—who, by the way, mostly prefer the term *little person*.

Fairy files are a bit more useful.

Dwarf physiology is a true example of evolution at its most efficient. Dwarves have, over the millennia, evolved to be perfectly suited to life in dark tunnels. The male dwarf has no need of tools for his excavating labors, as he can at will unhinge his massive lower jaw and take advantage of his elastic tendons and square teeth, which allow him to chew his way through even the most compacted earth and eject the waste from the rear end at rates of up to one hundred pounds per second. This may seem humorous to some, but it is no laughing matter to dwarves themselves, as "purging" is often quite explosive, and an untrained male can collapse a tunnel on his fellow workers. In fact, to facilitate training, many dwarf sporting activities are designed around the fine art of purging, and champions of Bummortar and Toppletower (the latter of which is a wind-powered version of the human game Jenga) are lauded as heroes among their people. Female dwarves are not usually biologically equipped for tunneling, although, as with genders of most species, there are exceptions who are, in that case, viewed as doubly blessed. Usually, female dwarves take care of more serious work, like motherhood, finances, politics, and combat strategy, leaving such activities as grubbing around in muddy holes to the menfolk. Dwarves have many other gifts, too, including their luminous spittle, a marvelous secretion that has a seemingly endless list of applications, e.g., as an adhesive for tunnel lanterns or protective cocoons.

Luckily for Myles Fowl, he had read both files.

Once the dwarf Gundred had locked him in the storeroom, Myles set about examining his prison while playing Vivaldi's *The Four Seasons* on his mental stereo, as he considered "Violin Concerto No. 2" good plotting music. Artemis preferred Beethoven when plotting (see LEP file: *Artemis Fowl: The Time Paradox*), but Myles found Beethoven a little wild and therefore distracting.

It became clear to the Fowl twin, as he searched the space by the eerie glow of the phosphorescent-spit mattress, that the dwarves had commandeered an unused clerical storeroom of some kind as his prison. It seemed that the Horteknuts had made a cursory attempt to clear out the space, no doubt removing any obvious weapons like staplers, scissors, box cutters, and so forth, but they had neglected to shift more harmless stock, such as a single ruler, a pile of flat-packed cardboard boxes, several tubs of rubber bands, and a container of odd batteries.

Aha, thought Myles, but he did not say it aloud, as proclaiming *aha* while one is plotting a prison break is a bit of a giveaway.

Myles squatted behind the cover of a cardboard tower and slipped a single box from the middle, careful not to topple the pile on top of himself. He guessed he would have very little time to construct his planned secret weapon before any possible observer decided to check on him, so he worked with furious accuracy on his prototype, scoring cardboard planes with the ruler and stretching the rubber bands into place. He was a little daunted by the fact that he was planning to attack his captors, given that he was a scientist rather than a foot soldier, but in times of emergency a fellow had to operate outside his comfort zone.

And this is certainly an emergency.

From somewhere beyond the locked door came a scuffling ruckus, and Myles felt a twinge in his scar that told him that Beckett was behind the racket. Myles did not stop working but instead ramped up his efforts, for now his dear twin could be in peril, too.

Beck would most likely cluster-punch the entire bunch of dwarves, but there was a chance he would be subdued, in which case it would be up to Myles to rescue them both.

I promise to save you, brother mine, Myles vowed. *I will be equal to the task.*

Unfortunately, Myles was to fall short on both elements of his silent vow.

He would not save his brother this time.

And he would not be equal to the task, in the short term, at least.

As was so often the case, Beckett was indeed the instigator of the hubbub. In fact, if a count were taken it would reveal that Beckett Fowl had instigated a hundred thousand hubbubs in his short life. And that was rounding down. For some reason there was usually a spike in August, which could possibly be attributed to end-of-summer-vacation anxiety.

This particular hubbub, however, was not one of our plucky protagonist's finest, lasting as it did a little less than five seconds, and certainly not resulting in the hoped-for outcome, i.e., the liberation of his beloved twin brother.

What happened was this: The Fowl twin jumped not quite fearlessly but, to his credit, without hesitation into the dwarf tunnel. The reason for his trepidation was that, like many extremely active people, Beckett had a fear of restriction that bordered on the claustrophobic, which partly explained his distaste for clothes in general and most especially polo necks, which he described as the most hateful of all sweaters. Beckett held it together admirably, given that the tunnel smelled of dank recycled air and dipped quickly below sea level as the escape route veered toward the mainland. In truth, Beckett probably *would* have lost it completely had the tunnel not been strung with blobs of glowing gel, which Lazuli, to his rear, correctly guessed were globules of dwarf spit. Beckett plowed on with significant speed considering that he had never actually tunneled for any great length before, though he had quizzed a couple of the island's moles about their process. In actuality, he was not so much tunneling per se as wriggling through a passageway that a Horteknut dwarf had already excavated. This particular tunnel was not built to last and, as wet clods slopped onto his back, it occurred to Beckett that, should the passage collapse, he and Lazuli would be crushed by the weight of the water above them. Luckily for Beckett, he was optimistic by nature, and so, instead of focusing on a watery grave, he decided to imagine a brighter future.

"I bet," he called back over his shoulder to Lazuli, "that we will not only find Myles down this hole, but when we come out, we shall both be knighted and given an obsidian castle to live in."

Beckett liked obsidian, because who would not like a cool, shiny rock that was forged in a volcano, for heaven's sake.

And thus calmed, he wriggled on.

Lazuli did not hear Beckett's *obsidian castle* comment. What she did hear was the rhythmic crashing of the Irish surf overhead, and she tried to shut it out, because there was nothing to do but drag herself onward by the elbows before Myles was utterly lost in the sheets of falling mud and alarming spurts of seawater.

The end of the tunnel was in sight, with light streaming in that was both comforting and foreboding. Comforting in that they would soon be out of the tunnel; foreboding in that there would probably be warrior dwarves awaiting them with swords.

No more than five dwarves, Lazuli fervently hoped. Horteknuts famously traveled in sevens.

The pixel could only pray that Beckett could pull off a few of his cluster punches before the dwarves knew what hit them.

She vowed to keep one dwarf conscious so she could find out what nefarious shenanigans the Fowls had involved her in this time, for even though she had faith in Myles Fowl, it was also true to say that she did not completely trust the cerebral twin.

Somehow, she thought now, Myles is responsible for me being first strapped to a missile and now crawling through this fetid tunnel.

However, all of Lazuli's hopes and plans were about to be crushed and thwarted by nature with a little help from a dwarf named Vigor. He was the Horteknut Third and often referred to by his tunnel-mates as Booby Horteknut. This was not because he was forever making mistakes, but because he was the world's foremost expert on laying booby traps for any non-Horteknut who might try to utilize one of their tunnels. Laying traps for humans was child's play, as men did not have a single clue about tunnels or tunnel etiquette. They put their big feet down any old place, and they dug into the clay like they were looking for treasure. Humans didn't realize that the hole was already there in the ground, so to speak, waiting to be hollowed out, and all a talented tunneler had to do was find the path. So, crushing men was easy—but Vigor Horteknut was famous for squashing other dwarves who might be on the Horteknut band's trail. His favorite trick was to wrap a trigger string around a worm so when a hungry dwarf sucked down the morsel, he would unwittingly activate the trap and collapse the tunnel on himself. For any members of the Seven, these triggers were signposted with markers, but to anyone else, one stone in the soil was pretty much the same as another, even if one end was spiked and could conceivably be pointing at something.

Vigor had left one of these trigger worms in the Dalkey Island tunnel. He wasn't actually expecting interlopers, but interlopers were sneaky by nature, so one of Vigor's mottos was: *Caution at all times.* Another motto was: *Never bet against a gnome in a crunchball game*, but that was hardly relevant now.

And as it happened, someone did follow the Horteknut abduction band through their subaquatic passage, but when animal lover Beckett Fowl spotted the worm trigger, he did not slurp it down as a dwarf might. Instead, he gently moved the little fellow aside, wiggling his fingers in imitation of the worm's natural body language.

Calm, the finger wiggle said. *Friends.*

The worm wiggled in reply, saying, *Go away, pale monster.*

Which was fair enough, although what the worm should have wiggled was *Before you go away, pale monster, could you oh-so-carefully untie the string from around my tail?*

But that was a lot of information to squeeze into a wiggle.

And since the worm wasn't violently yanked, the tunnel did not immediately collapse in a chain reaction of cave-ins. However, Beckett had disturbed the string, which activated a slow release at that particular point in the passage.

The noise of the ocean was so terrifyingly awesome that

Lazuli did not notice the sound of a slow fill back toward the island until an icy sheet of Irish sea slid between her body and the tunnel floor like the specter of death.

"Beckett," she said, keeping her voice steady, "we need to hustle. We really—"

Which was as far as she got before the slow fill became an ultrafast fill and a tube of compressed ocean picked them both up like the insignificant beings they were in the face of nature and bore them along at speed toward the tunnel mouth. The same tunnel mouth they had been planning to approach like sneaky interlopers.

Perhaps it might have comforted Beckett sometime in the near future to learn that the worm was completely fine, but at that moment he was mostly concerned with trying not to drown.

It is recommended dwarf procedure that when excavating below sea level, the lower end of the tunnel should be stoppered in case of a breach. Many dwarves do not bother with this safeguard, especially for a short-term tunnel, but the Horteknut Number Three, Vigor, was a stickler for procedure and he knew he would have to answer to Gundred if their basement HQ flooded. Thus he demanded that each male Horteknut cough up a few gallons of spit so he could roll a giant luminous plug, which was then wedged into the tunnel mouth. This spitball was designed with a self-sealing seam that would trap any ocean leakage, or indeed unwary follower, before closing back up.

A proper plug could resist any amount of water pressure to maintain its seal on a tunnel mouth, but this one had been imperfectly placed, as what the dwarves had taken for a shiny rock was actually the corpse of a goat, which not only virtually disintegrated once the plug rested on it but also lubricated the rim.

Beckett could definitely be classified as an unwary follower, and he emerged from the tunnel only to find himself immediately trapped in the heart of a giant spitball, which ingeniously self-sealed behind him. Then, thanks to the goat paste, the ball popped out of its hole like a periwinkle from a whale's blowhole and engaged in a lumbering roll across the basement, leaving Beckett revolving slowly inside. Lazuli was the next one flushed out of the tunnel. The pixel slid across the floor of slick mud, still wearing her stolen suit of vines and losing her helmet in the process. Perhaps a thousand gallons of seawater washed her reasonably clean before the entire tunnel collapsed and self-stoppered.

The three Horteknut diggers in the basement took a moment to absorb this before reacting, and when they did react their reaction was unexpected, given the tension in the room. They burst out laughing, one even going so far as to slap his knees. This guy had one of those names that made him sound very tough, which indeed he was. The cool name was Axborn. He was famous in dwarf circles for a very unique relationship, which we shall learn about at a later time.

"Look at these idiots," Axborn said, "swimming into their own prison."

While Lazuli coughed, she thought that perhaps this dwarf was underestimating the Regrettables somewhat. After all, for them to get even this far, three things must have happened:

1. They had figured out the clone ruse.
2. They had disabled the Horteknut rear guard.

And . . .

3. They had navigated a Reclaimer tunnel.

All considerable achievements.

Admittedly, number two had been mostly due to Beckett, but the dwarves couldn't know that. But in spite of these achievements, the Horteknuts guffawed, chortled, and smirked.

Lazuli knew she should be afraid, probably even terrified, but the same indomitable spirit that had pushed her through the Academy drove her to her feet now. She spat a pint of salt water on the floor and said, "Specialist Heitz, LEP. You people are all under arrest. I don't even know how many laws you've broken, but if I had to prioritize, I'd say strapping me to a missile is at the top of the list. I traveled at the speed of sound outside that vehicle, people. And it was not a habit-forming experience."

Quite a cocky statement from a sopping-wet specialist fitted with a magic-suppressor and outnumbered three to one by a legendary band of fighters, but Lazuli was hoping that the Reclaimers might be cowed into submission. It was at best a million-to-one shot, and as is so often the way in these situations, those odds did not pay off.

"I see," said another dwarf, this one named Vigor. He was dressed in a simple shift that rippled with muscles as though his torso were composed of thickly coiled snakes. His vinesuit was resting in a bucket of water on a ledge behind him. Vigor took over the speaking from Axborn for two reasons:

1. He was the ranking Reclaimer

And . . .

2. Axborn was not the best at speaking.

"So, perhaps we should simply lay down our arms and surrender, eh, Specialist Heitz?"

Lazuli heard the sarcasm but chose to ignore it. "Yes, that's exactly what you should do, sir."

"Well, boys," said Vigor, not trying too hard to conceal his grin. "What do you think? Should we stitch up our bum flaps?"

Bum flaps being dwarf slang for the evacuation vents on the rear end of every tunneler's trousers. To stitch up one's bum flap meant a laying down of arms, so to speak.

Lazuli tried one more time. "You better stitch up that

flap, Reclaimer, before I come over there and do it for you."

Vigor's grin dropped right off his face. Enough was apparently enough.

"You don't even know what you're wearing, do you, officer?" he said.

Lazuli knew that dwarf vinesuits were made from a *kreperplont*, which was paired somehow with its wearer, but that was about the limit of her knowledge on the subject.

"I know all about vinesuits," she said, hoping to bluff it out.

"I see," said Vigor. "In that case, you know that Horteknut tunnelers are paired with their kreperplonts at birth and they share an almost telepathic bond."

Lazuli wondered if this guy might be doing a little bluffing himself. "Telepathic vines? Are you kidding?"

Vigor's grin returned. "I am, a little. It's mostly whistles, clicks, and gestures that control the kreperplont, to be honest. But it's amazing what vines can do. Axborn here may not be the brightest, but when it comes to kreperplonts, this fellow is a virtuoso."

Axborn stepped toward Lazuli, into the flickering light cast by the giant glob of gel that held Beckett immobile at its heart. This dwarf was a hulking specimen with a shaved scalp and long mustache tied in a bow under his chin, which was a grooming choice not many people could pull off, but Axborn managed it. His vinesuit was wrapped around his abdomen and limbs in thick coils that glistened as he moved.

"That's right, cop," he said. "This fellow is a virtuoso. And by *this fellow* I mean me."

"Most vinesuits are coded to their wearers," continued Vigor. "But there are general commands common to all suits."

Lazuli suddenly understood where this speech might be going.

I don't think anyone is surrendering here. These dwarves are toying with me.

And suddenly she wished that she had her magic, unpredictable as it was, to get her out of this hopeless situation.

"Now hold on a second . . ." she said, but there wasn't a second to be had.

"Commands like *squeeze,*" said Axborn, whistling a single note, and right on command the vinesuit tightened around Lazuli's body, forcing the breath from her lungs until she was only running on the oxygen in her bloodstream.

She wanted to cry out, but there was no air for that. All she could do was topple like a felled sapling and lie on the cold, wet floor.

Axborn squatted before her, and she could see the bow of his mustache in the corner of her eye.

"See?" he said. "Virtuoso."

Myles Fowl's hands were lacerated with cuts from the cardboard sheets he had bent to his will and design. On an ordinary day, he would have launched into a well-constructed rant at the discomfort and indeed inconvenience of a blood-slicked work surface, but this was no ordinary day, even by Fowl family standards, and so Myles labored on silently, slotting the pieces of his weapon into place, contenting himself with dark thoughts of rubber-band-centric revenge.

They will regret not Fowl-proofing this room, he thought. I cannot wait to see their faces.

The dwarves had left him alone in the storeroom for less than half an hour in total, but it was all the time Myles needed to assemble his contraption. It would have been most convenient to have NANNI on hand to plot the fold lines with her laser, but Myles had to make do with the blueprints in his head, which were very close to laser-accurate. The problem was the transfer of intent from his brain to his fingertips, as sometimes, it had to be admitted, Myles's fingertips were not as devastatingly effective as other parts of his body, such as his brains and sharp tongue.

"Nevertheless," he muttered to himself, "these Fowl fingers should work well enough to cope with bothersome dwarves."

Myles could not know this, but he was one of only half a dozen twelve-year-olds worldwide to use the word *bothersome* in a sentence that day, and the other five were reading aloud from a Victorian novel.

Myles had no sooner finished his construction than the dwarf Gveld Horteknut carelessly reentered his prison, making no attempt to protect her person in any way.

Such is her lack of respect for me, thought Myles. Well,

General Horteknut may come to regret underestimating Myles Fowl.

Myles felt so slighted by the general's general body language that he decided to voice this thought.

He jumped out from behind the stack of boxes, wielding his fully automatic rubber-band machine gun—which looked a little like the starship *Enterprise* festooned with multicolored stripes—and cried, "You may come to regret underestimating Myles Fowl, General Horteknut!"

For a moment, Gveld seemed genuinely happy. "What is that? A toy gun?"

"This is no toy," said Myles. "This weapon will see me clear of you and your gang of tunneling thugs."

And then he touched the battery to the trigger, activating the weapon and . . . shooting himself in the eye.

End of escape attempt.

Gveld escorted Myles out into the basement by the collar, her bemused expression hardening as she dragged.

"This Mud Boy tried to shoot me with rubber bands," she announced to Gundred, who had joined the Horteknut cluster around the giant spitball.

"I am so relieved that you survived, my general," said Gundred. "The other Fowl came through the tunnel and dragged the pixel along with him."

Gveld took in the scene, nodding once in seeming admiration that the two followers had made it this far, and a second time in satisfaction that the situation had been utterly contained. She transferred her grip from Myles's lapel to the hair on the back of his head.

"Do you see, Mud Boy?" she said. "We are Horteknuts. You cannot hunt us belowground, or you die."

Myles fought the panic rising in his gorge. Panic was of no use to Beckett. Panic was the enemy of rational thought. Artemis had once said to him, *Farm animals panic, brother. Are you a farm animal?*

And ten-month-old Myles had shaken his head, to which Artemis had said, *Well, then, change your own diaper.*

Little Myles had at that point decided that, rather than change his diaper, he would train himself not to need diapers anymore, which took him most of an afternoon.

He felt that panic again now, but something replaced this feeling: hope.

"But Beckett is not dead, General. I see his chest moving. He breathes."

"He does," said Gveld. "He does indeed breathe. Dwarf spit is a marvelous material. In an emergency, a dwarf can survive suspended in it for hours. Our saliva has everything a body needs, even nutrients, but your irritating twin won't breathe for much longer if you do not do what I need you to do, little human."

"I will do it," said Myles without hesitation. "My word on that."

Gveld grimaced. "The word of a human—any human, but especially a Fowl—means less than nothing to me, boy. You need an incentive."

Myles struggled to wiggle out of Gveld's steel grip. He was not successful.

"I am completely incentivized," insisted Myles. "My dear brother is suspended in your excretions."

"*Their* excretions," corrected Gveld. "Like most females, Gundred and I are non-excreters. In fact, Gundred is a surface dwarf."

Myles knew exactly what a surface dwarf was from Artemis's extensive files, though he did not let on. He did, however, subtly try to ingratiate himself.

"Though I suppose, technically, *excreter* is not a completely accurate term, as that material is certainly not waste."

Gveld shook Myles like a doll in Gundred's direction. "What do you think, my second? Is this brat trying psychological manipulation on us? Using sly compliments?"

"I suspect he is, General," said Gundred. "Do you find yourself warming to him?"

"That I do not," said Gveld. "In fact, I find myself disliking him more by the minute."

Myles felt the dwarf's thick fingers find the nerve clusters in his neck, and he had no trouble believing that she disliked him intensely.

"General," he said, "I will do what you ask. Just ask it."

Gveld forced Myles's face against the spitball, mushing it into the pliable surface so that Beckett's revolving image warped and stretched.

"You believe you will do what I ask at this critical

moment," she said into his ear. "But when the sunlight falls upon your face, you will ask yourself, *Is there another way? I am a Fowl, after all. Surely I can thwart this so-called general.*"

"That is not true," said Myles, even as he realized that it was. "I have a strong grasp of consequences and near total recall."

"Perhaps," said Gveld. "But in my experience humans need to be shown how dire their situation is. Most people have no context for these circumstances and believe them to be temporary. You need a demonstration that this is your new reality."

"A demonstration is not necessary, General," said Myles. "My brother's life is at stake and that is all the information I need. There is no reason to harm him."

Gveld pulled Myles from the blob and turned his face to a pile of vines on the floor. One of the other dwarves whistled and a gap opened up in the vines, revealing Lazuli's drawn face, blood leaking from the corner of her mouth.

"This is war, Fowl. People get harmed. Take your little police officer friend, trussed up in one of our vinesuits. Remarkable suits, those. They respond to our every little whistle and gesture."

Lazuli is hurt, thought Myles.

"So, you see, Mud Whelp, I do not intend to harm your *brother* . . ." said Gveld.

Myles suddenly knew what all this was leading to, and he set his mind fully to finding a solution. He had only seconds, but then, seconds to an ordinary person was a lifetime to Myles Fowl. The twin concentrated fully on recalling Artemis's files, which he had pored over for months, including as they did all the information from the LEP Core, which is what the fairy police called their Cloud. He also had time to mentally search the ACRONYM files, which he had helped himself to on a previous adventure (see LEP file: *The Fowl Twins*). These were woefully light on specifics, except for one interesting detail, which he put a pin in for later. Just when Myles felt he was circling a possible solution, Gveld finished her sentence, which was a sentence in more ways than one.

". . . but I do intend to crush the life from this pixel's bones to create an indelible impression."

To be perfectly honest, Lazuli seemed dead already, the only sign of life being a spasmodic jittering of two fingers on her left hand.

I must save her, as Beckett would be heartbroken if something happened to Lazuli, Myles thought. And then he realized: I myself would be heartbroken.

And so, before Gveld could issue a whistle or gesture, Myles was forced to interject with a plan that was considerably less than fully formed.

"General Horteknut," he said, "can I just say at this point that I would like to invoke an Irish Backstop?"

Gveld's cheeks were already puffed for a whistle, but she expelled the air harmlessly and fixed Myles with the most hate-infused stare he'd ever been subjected to, and he had been subjected to fourteen hate-infused stares so far in his life, the first being from a kindergarten bully whose weapon of choice was mean rhymes. On one occasion Benedict Keane and his friends had chanted at the brothers:

"The Fowl Twins, the Fowl Twins
Are making me sick.
The smart one is ugly,
And the other one's thick."

And four-year-old Myles had responded quick as a flash:

"Oh, what a disaster,
Is Benedict Keane.
He's dense as a neutron,
And bright as graphene."

Hence the stare.

And Ben Keane's stare had nothing on General Horteknut's.

"How dare you say those words?" said Gveld. "That term is for fairies alone. You may neither say it nor invoke it."

Myles was ready for that.

"My brother and I were declared to be of sufficient fairy heritage to avoid mind-wiping last year [see LEP file: *The Fowl Twins*], so I restate my desire to invoke the Irish Backstop. No true dwarf may refuse this request."

"I may refuse it," said Gveld Horteknut. "And I do refuse it!"

Vigor took a step forward. "Begging your pardon, General, but are you refusing a backstop that's been formally invoked?"

Gveld waved him away. "Don't listen to the Mud Boy's jabber, Number Three. He's no fairy. Humans cannot invoke anything."

"It's true what he claims," protested Vigor mildly. "Both twins were declared to be one-quarter fairy. They were possessed by one of Opal Koboi's ghosts. I have a source in the LEP, so I read the report." The Horteknut Number Three took another step forward, and there was a feverish light in his eyes. "An Irish Backstop, General. It's an omen."

This gave Gveld pause.

If this was indeed true about the twins' DNA, then she would have to accept the Irish Backstop. Indeed, she would be privileged to accept it. The Irish Backstop had been initiated during the Willows Wars and led to glorious victory for the dwarf army. It could indeed be an omen, and if there was one thing dwarves loved almost as much as gold, it was a vendetta—but omens were a close third.

Gveld took her time considering. Her initial impulse had been to kill the boy before the echo of his blasphemy faded, but . . .

But . . .

A glorious victory for the Reclaimers could only mean a full recovery of the Horteknut hoard. It was possible she could accomplish that with her band, the finest band of

Reclaimers to ever dig a hole, but omens had their own kind of alchemy. They gave the troops a feeling of destiny and right. So . . .

"Very well, Fowl. I shall allow your invocation, but I warn you, the terms must be met."

"I know what an Irish Backstop is, General," said Myles, unable to temper his haughty nature.

"Then you know that should you fail in your task, both of your coconspirators will die slowly and painfully."

"Unless I myself strike the fatal blows," said Myles, feeling the weight of those words in his stomach.

These were the terms: The contract invoker—in this case, Myles—was given a task appropriate for one with his gifts. Should he fail or abscond, then the nominated prisoners, Beckett and Lazuli, would suffer a slow execution and he himself would be hunted down to suffer the same fate. This slow execution could be avoided if Myles returned and surrendered himself to Gveld, in which case all three of the Fowl party would be dispatched quickly and relatively painlessly. This was also the case should Myles actually succeed. Succeed or fail, everyone would be dead.

It was an ancient and brutal contract, and Myles had just signed up to it using the lives of his teammates as collateral.

CHAPTER 9

THE IRISH BACKSTOP BACKSTORY

THERE may be some among you who are not familiar with the ins and outs of an Irish Backstop, even though the details are required reading in almost every fairy high school program besides the dwarves' own, as their code of secrecy forbids the keeping of accurate records. Dwarf texts are littered with deliberate lies and exaggerations seeded specifically to frustrate researchers. For example, dwarf bard Drollbag the Profound's history states that *A dwarf male's belly is so stretchy that it may comfortably accommodate the entirety of a bull troll within.* Which has proved false at least once a year, when some gullible dwarf has tried it. Drollbag's book also claims that if a dwarf *be rightly trunneled,* which translates to *trapped in a tunnel,* then he may spontaneously transform into:

1. The most sparkly of rainbows
2. A squirrel of the nimblest variety

Or . . .

3. A cloud of fetid gas

None of which are accurate, except the last one does at least have an element of truth to it.

In spite of all this blarney, any dwarf who's ever chewed sod knows the story of the first Irish Backstop, as this tale has been passed down through the generations and is considered the holiest and most inspirational of histories.

There are inevitably almost as many renderings of this story as there are dwarves to tell it, but the following condensed version has been woven together from common threads.

It began in wartime, as these things often do. Back in the days before humans took up the reins as the planet's main organized force of evil, the dwarves were having a tiff with the elves. Their issue was as follows: The dwarves felt that the invasive root systems of weeping willow trees were collapsing their tunnels and in certain places needed to be culled. The elves felt that willow trees were sacred and must not under any circumstances be touched by fairy hands. One thing led to another: a branch chopped here, and a limb sliced there, and within a century the dwarves and the elves were at each other's throats, and both camps had more or less forgotten the trees along the way. It all came to a head in Ireland, when an elf troop charged into a dwarf pit and was trapped utterly. The dwarf general, a lover of cruel games, offered to walk back from the traditional extended torture of the elfin captain's staff if the captain himself would report to the elf king's tent and strike him dead. In exchange for this traitorous action, she would execute him and his troops without the usual torture. If he failed or reneged on his agreement, then there would be the usual torture, unless he himself returned to strike the killing blows. This was the Irish Backstop, and it was indeed a diabolical arrangement. The twice-cursed captain left the battlefield but arrived back within the day, unable to complete his sworn mission. He had resigned himself to ending his own soldiers' lives with blasts from his magical lance rather than let them suffer. He aimed his lance, but the elf king, having heard of his captain's loyalty, showed up at the last second and surrendered to the dwarf general. The general's icy heart was melted by this gesture and she let the elves off the hook. There were hugs all around and the fairies never fought again, or so the story goes.

The only part of that legend which Gveld Horteknut did not buy was the merciful ending. "Take my word for it, human," she told Myles before prodding him from the basement room. "Dwarf generals do not show mercy. I personally would have killed them all, including the elf king when he showed up. Cut off the head of the snake, then slice up the snake's body. And then burn the snake segments. That's my philosophy."

Myles felt for that snake, even if it was just metaphorical.

Gundred was given the thankless task of delivering an expositional catch-up to Myles Fowl on their short journey to the surface. They were squashed side-by-side in a vehicle that was disguised to look like a discarded supermarket cart. It jerked forward in fits and starts while the nose rig pummeled and chewed the earth in front of it. The vehicle operated on a complicated hub of sealed gears and cogs ingeniously powered by Gundred's steady pedaling, a system that reminded Myles of Lazuli's backup flight mechanism (see LEP file: *The Fowl Twins*).

"I imagine this is a short-range vehicle," he said.

Gundred grunted as she powered the craft through a rock shelf. "That depends on the stamina of the pilot. A PIGLET can run forever with a robust operator at the pedals."

"A PIGLET," said Myles. "Let me guess: **P**ropulsion through **I**nternal **G**ears and **L**ocking **E**picyclic **T**ransmission?"

"It's *local*, not *locking*," said Gundred a touch grumpily.

"Locking is better," said Myles. "You should take a note."

Gundred pedaled a little more aggressively, but Myles either did not notice that he was needling the dwarf, or he did not care. Probably option B.

"Also, may I say, Gundred, this PIGLET of yours is not so very aerodynamic?"

Gundred had an answer for that. "We're not traveling through the air, human. I'm surprised you hadn't noticed."

"The principle is the same," said Myles. "In fact, a subterranean craft should be *more* aerodynamic, if anything."

Gundred was not taking notes on subterranean travel from a human. "Forgive me if I don't pay too much attention to a Mud Boy on his first ride in a PIGLET."

"Oh, I do forgive *that*," said Myles, not sounding especially forgiving. "What I shall not forgive is the incarceration, intimidation, and attempted murder. There will be a reckoning for those, you can count on it."

Gundred stopped pedaling, and the PIGLET shuddered to a halt in a layer of granite-speckled clay. Myles noted the buried skeleton of a horse frozen in mid-gallop and wondered what calamity had befallen the animal.

"Listen, boy. The general's plan may seem wantonly cruel to you, but we have been hunting this treasure for decades. Once the hoard is reclaimed, the Horteknut Seven may retire. My general will have restored the honor of her family."

"I know all about family honor," said Myles, "and the price that family members must pay for it."

Gundred resumed her labors, sending the PIGLET lurching forward. "You wouldn't understand. You were born into a loving family. I had no one until the general discovered me in the ruins of an ACRONYM facility I had demolished. I was half-buried, half-dead, and mute from shock and asphyxiation. Gveld might have left me to rot, but she risked her life to drag me out and nurse me back to health. The first words I ever heard her say were *I could use a hero like you*. And now, twenty years later, I am the Horteknut Number Two."

Myles lowered himself to a Beckettian joke. "Yes, you are certainly Number Two. Murdering pixels and children."

"That is perhaps not as I would wish it, but Gveld is my general. Now and always."

Myles disagreed. "Not always, Gundred. Very soon she will be a leader no more. In fact, if you would allow me to make a prediction based on both my knowledge of your plans and my faith in my own abilities, I would say that Gveld Horteknut's days as a general will be over before the sun comes out tomorrow *afternoon*." And as he said this, Myles watched Gundred's face closely. The dwarf flinched, and the twin knew he was on the right track when her tone became suddenly aggressive.

"If I were you, I would be more concerned with what my comrade Axborn will do to your parents if this does not go how we wish it to go. For although you did not nominate them for your Irish Backstop, your brother involved them by following you to our lair. My general has tasked Axborn to chew his way back to Dalkey Island and contain the situation."

Myles was concerned but not panicked. Panicking was only of use when all intellectual routes had been exhausted. He would panic if the time came that there was nothing else to do.

Gundred put all her energy into cycling for a long minute until the PIGLET broke through to open water. She cranked the digging rig around to the stern, where it operated as a propeller system, and for once Myles was impressed.

"That explains the angle of the blades," he said. "This is the first clever thing I've seen from you people."

The PIGLET made lighter work of the new liquid element, and their speed picked up by a rate of knots. Myles watched as the clear tidal water was infiltrated by murky harbor slicks and noted with some scientific interest a luminous weed he could not identify that seemed to be responding to the movement of fish rather than currents.

Gundred stayed silent for several minutes, channeling her anger into the PIGLET controls that she operated with violent gusto, but eventually she had to speak. "You think you're so clever? By tomorrow afternoon's sunrise, indeed."

Myles raised a finger. "Not sunrise. The sun will already be up relative to our position, that is. I meant after the eclipse. The solar eclipse tomorrow. That's when you Horteknuts plan to make your big move."

"You're guessing, Fowl," snarled Gundred, pedaling as though she were repeatedly stomping on a certain human's head.

"I am *deducing*," corrected Myles. "And if I may say so, it's an educated deduction. Hardly a deduction at all, really, considering the facts I have in my possession."

Gundred steered around a tower of partially sunken

shopping carts. "My job was to bring you up to speed, then give you your orders."

"Why don't you let me bring myself up to speed and you drive the PIGLET?" said Myles. "That way both of us are playing to our strengths."

Gundred was oh-so-tempted to jettison Myles there and then, but her general's orders specified *no killing humans* until the part of the plan that required the killing of humans, so she did not seal off the passenger compartment and flood it. Instead, she imagined the steering wheel was Myles's throat and squeezed it till the wood cracked.

"Why don't you do that, Fowl? I'll just sit here and marvel at your genius."

"Finally, you are speaking sense, Mademoiselle Gundred," said Myles, sitting up to deliver his speech. "I believe this entire misadventure was initiated last year, when I hacked the ACRONYM servers. The Horteknut band had probably insinuated a malware worm into their files, and so when I downloaded them, I unwittingly took the worm, too. Correct so far?"

Gundred decided to split hairs. "We don't call it a worm. We call it a *spyder*. I created it."

"A spider?" said Myles. "Oh, I see, you mean *spy*der, with a *Y*. How fun. To continue, I downloaded your spyder, and so now it's in my systems, keeping a close eye on my every keyboard stroke."

"You had no idea. We've been reading your secret journal for nearly a year."

"And during that year I was mostly concentrating on the ACRONYM sites. Watching as the LEP shut them down one by one."

"Until . . ."

"Until they set their sights on the penultimate facility, in Florida."

"Which was special because . . . ?" Gundred prompted.

"Because that is the most secure building in the world. It's inside an army base that is surrounded by a swamp and on an island, for heaven's sake."

"Impenetrable," said Gundred, who thought she was agreeing.

Myles corrected her yet again, which he enjoyed. "No. It's penetrable, but the penetrators would never escape. A one-way trip as it were."

"The entire facility was rigged to sink rather than expose ACRONYM's secrets. Which was not a bad idea."

"Not a bad idea indeed if you are an ACRONYM director," agreed Myles. "But General Horteknut did not wish this particular site to sink, because then it would be difficult to control the scene. And she needed to control the scene in order to extract ACRONYM's treasure."

"*Our* treasure," snapped Gundred. "The remaining ingots of the Horteknut hoard. ACRONYM has been using it for hundreds of years to fund their operations against the People. It is sacrilege that our own gold is used against us. Soon it will be returned to its rightful home."

Myles tapped his teeth. "In Gveld's mouth?"

Gundred bristled. "Her grill was made from recovered ACRONYM gold. My general wears it as a reminder of her mission."

"She really shouldn't," noted Myles. "ACRONYM tags its gold with radiation. It's in the files."

Gundred released a water-cam from the PIGLET's roof panel; it floated to the surface and broadcast a live feed to the craft's left porthole. Myles immediately recognized the industrial end of Dublin's docklands with its unusual mixture of cruisers and cargo ships tied up on the far shore.

"The general's mouth is the general's business," said Gundred as they passed below the East Link Bridge. "Tell me what you know of our plan if you wish to see your brother ever again."

"The general's plan was both elementary and ingenious, which the best plans often are," said Myles. "Gveld used her missile over Florida to trigger ACRONYM's contingency plan, which was to move the treasure to their backup facility in Dublin if Florida ever came under attack. I imagine you already tried to raid this facility and failed, so now you need me to try again."

"We tried from underground but were thwarted," said Gundred. "Now we must try from the surface."

Myles nodded. "And I have no doubt you will use your previous position to fake a small earthquake."

Gundred grunted an affirmative. There was no harm in confirming the boy's theories. In fact, he needed all available information if he was to succeed in his mission.

"We evacuated after the last attempt," she said. "But we left ourselves a way back in. Vigor and the two warriors your brother somehow incapacitated will take their positions in the sub-basement. Those two are most eager to make up for their shortcomings."

"The ideal time to mount the assault would be tomorrow during the solar eclipse," noted Myles. "When most of the city will be distracted and extremely photosensitive dwarves will not be in danger from the sun's rays. Before the sun comes out tomorrow afternoon." Myles tapped his chin. "But the big question is, why do you need me?"

"That's what I keep asking myself," said Gundred, steering the PIGLET starboard toward the Samuel Beckett Bridge.

"I understand why you tried to kill us," said Myles without emotion. "You realized that I was studying the Florida site and planning a reconnaissance flyover. It was perfect. All you had to do was strap Lazuli to a missile you had already planned to fire, and the wreckage would reveal both Fowl and fairy corpses. ACRONYM would lose their minds, thinking the facility was both compromised and under international scrutiny. And the LEP would quite reasonably believe that we Fowl boys had turned Specialist Heitz to our side and all this was some kind of botched Fowl scheme. In the end, the Horteknut band would get rid of their competition. But your plan to murder us failed, so you had to snatch me from the island instead."

"And replace you with a clone to fool your parents," said Gundred, eager to provide the Fowl boy with information he might be unaware of.

"I imagine it is a copy rather than a clone," said Myles. "Clones take a long time to grow. A copy can be printed up in a day."

As Myles casually displayed his brainpower, Gundred began to realize why they did in fact need the boy.

"And the only possible reason for the switch would be that there is an unforeseen problem that only I can help you with."

Gundred nudged the PIGLET into a cavity in the quay wall under the bridge and turned yet another crank, ratcheting out two stability clamps to hold the craft in place.

"I don't suppose you want to tell me what our problem is, Myles Fowl?"

"If you like," said Myles. "It's urgent, of course, if you are to stick to your new eclipse timetable. Since you apparently need a human to solve this problem, it must involve interaction with humans. If you need me in particular, then it is by nature a problem of the intellect, as Beckett would be the better choice for physical or dexterous work of any kind. And since we find ourselves moored here beside the Convention Centre Dublin, which is indeed a convention center, but also the top two floors are the ACRONYM field office that now houses the famous Horteknut hoard, I deduce that the problem is here and it is most likely an issue of access. How am I doing, Number Two?"

"Not bad," admitted Gundred.

"In conclusion, I would say that the only mystery here is why you have made me wait until now to reveal the specifics of your access issue, as my not-inconsiderable brain could have been working on the problem since we left the lair. It is almost as if you don't want me to succeed."

"Almost," agreed Gundred, and she mirrored a video from her communicator on the porthole screen. "But I'd prefer that you do."

"Ah," said Myles when the video was over. "I see. That *is* a problem."

The Convention Centre Dublin

Gveld and her band had been surveilling Dublin's convention center for months, ever since ACRONYM had realized, as had Myles, that their facilities were being shut down by mysterious raids or natural-looking disasters. The shadowy intergovernmental organization had also realized that it was only a matter of time before Florida came under attack, too, and when that happened, they would need a fallback base of operations. Florida had been the last stand, secure as it was, but whoever was infiltrating the isolated and fortified facilities seemed to relish the isolation and somehow glide through fortifications like they weren't even there. It made sense to the powers-that-be at ACRONYM that the *whoever* in question was probably the magical group they had been hunting for centuries, i.e., fairies.

Of course fairies would prefer to operate in isolated spots, and naturally their superior technology rendered any human defenses useless, so some months previously ACRONYM had gone a different route and relocated the hoard to the Convention Centre Dublin. They hung on to their defenses but chose a site in the middle of the city where people were encouraged to congregate on the lower floors so there would be no sneaking in for fairies.

This was not the problem, because:

1. The Reclaimers were used to blending in with humans.

And . . .

2. They didn't need to go any farther than the elevators anyway.

The problem was that someone at the fairy-hunting agency must have recognized that the fairy folk knew every play in the ACRONYM book. So this person had gone off book and old-school.

Up until the previous week the open-plan lower floors had been leased to a thriving 24/7 e-storage solution company by the name of Flash, which guaranteed constant activity in the center. Now, though, the company had completely vanished, leaving nothing behind but their oversized red FLASH signage. So instead of weaving their way through a crowded shop floor, any disguised dwarves would have to cross an open atrium under the watchful eyes of a highly visible security detail on the middle balcony and possibly a highly invisible detail somewhere else.

"When did this happen?" Myles asked.

"We're not certain," said Gundred. "Recently. They just kicked them out, which messes with our Plan B. They know we're coming and maybe the boss here decided to ignore the main office and get rid of distractions."

"And your original plan cannot be salvaged?"

"No," said Gundred. "ACRONYM didn't send in the gold by truck as we'd thought they would. They helicoptered it in from the airport. Our guys were sitting downstairs like dummies while the humans tucked the gold away in the safe."

"I see, but surely you have another strategy."

"Of course we do. In the event of a seismic occurrence, the treasure is shunted automatically into the executive elevator. That elevator is built to withstand the entire building collapsing."

"So what do you need from me?"

"I need you to get Gveld and me into that central elevator."

"And then what?"

"And then we fake a small earthquake and the gold is transferred to the elevator. You wanted an Irish Backstop? This is your Irish Backstop. Get us into that elevator during the eclipse. You have one hour to come up with a plan.

After that, the torturing begins, and just to be clear, *you die last*."

Myles spoke without thinking, which was unlike him. "If I were you, I'd kill me first, because, in all modesty, I am the most dangerous of your opponents."

Gundred nodded slowly, taking this advice to heart at least. "Do you know something, human? I just might see what I can do about that."

Truth be told, Myles had already put together a plan for what he would do should ACRONYM decide to switch up their procedures. Myles prided himself on plotting for *all* eventualities, not just Plan A and Plan B, and in this situation, he had calculated that there were six probable variations in procedure and thirty improbable ones. Most clandestine agencies remained in the shadows by being unpredictable, and ACRONYM was more shadowy than most, but what had happened here was straight out of the middle-management-mutiny handbook. The regional boss must have completely freaked out when major responsibility came his way and decided to ignore orders from Florida—he was the ranking officer on the ground in Dublin, and he was going to run security the way he saw fit. And he saw fit to double the guard and land the gold on the roof. Middle-management mutiny was number five on Myles's list and landing the gold on the roof was number six. So, the situation here was a combination of five and six with added improbable variation fourteen, which was *boot out the tenants.*

The solution to this was highly unusual but also already in place, and it only took Myles a couple of minutes to set it in motion on the PIGLET's smart screen.

He pointed a finger at the screen. "Look, Mademoiselle Gundred," he said. "All done."

Gundred took her time reading. "So, this will happen before the eclipse?"

"An hour before," confirmed Myles. "It's all right there."

"It's 'all right there' in theory. Are you sure these people will answer the call?"

Myles was sure. "I am aware that *human reaction* seems like a variable in this equation, but trust me, it's a constant. It happens every day. More and more, in fact."

Myles resisted the urge to lecture his captor, as he had no desire to antagonize her any further, especially with Beck and Lazuli in mortal danger, but it seemed to him that Gundred was taking an age to read through a plan that was already in motion.

We could be on the way back to that basement in Dalkey, he thought. We didn't need to waste time coming out here in the first place.

Myles tried to distract himself by looking around. He had never seen Dublin's port from this vantage and was surprised by how many access steps there were from the seawall to the dockside above.

From the age of barges, he supposed.

He also noticed how few of the pedestrians who hurried past, seemingly conversing with thin air, actually looked down at the water.

Too busy on their ear pods, he realized. And even if people had glanced downward, all they would have seen was yet another discarded shopping cart that had been tossed into the river.

And there is very little danger of anyone actually fishing it out.

After several minutes of Gundred checking through his plan, Myles let out a mildly irritated groan, which prompted her to ask, "Am I keeping you, Mud Boy? Do you have somewhere to be?"

Before Myles could answer, Gundred thrust her communicator into his hand. "Here, take this. There's a call for you."

Myles instinctively knew where this call was coming from, and he steeled himself for what he was about to see.

Stay in control, Dr. Fowl, he told himself. *Emotion is the enemy of intellect.*

Myles looked at the screen and saw his parents in Villa Éco's safe room. They were not holding a communicator, which meant that someone was pointing a camera at them. That someone was Axborn, Myles guessed. The dwarf with the funny bow beard.

"Myles," said his mother, "are you all right? Is Beckett safe?"

"We are both fine, Mother," said Myles. "Have you been hurt?"

It was his father who answered, in a brusque tone. "No, son. Just our pride. This is really intolerable, Myles. What happened to the fairy ban? You didn't even make it back to the villa before you broke your promise. And we had to watch that copy of you dissolve before our eyes."

"That is correct, father mine," said Myles. "It was a copy."

"Of course it was a copy," said Artemis Senior. "The organs were made of paper, mostly."

"I do apologize for all this palaver," said Myles. "Believe me when I say that it's not my doing and I will extricate the family from this predicament."

"And lovely Lazuli, too?" said his mother.

"Yes, of course. Lazuli, too." Myles thought of the pixel wrapped in a vinesuit and determined he should get back to the pressing issue of saving lives. He had just enough time to deliver one vital message.

"All you need to do is *stay cool*," he told his parents.

Artemis Senior was surprised to hear these words coming out of his son's mouth. "I'm sorry, Myles, my boy. Did my son Myles just tell his parents to *stay cool*?"

"I did," said Myles. "Just stay cool until I come to let you out of the safe room. *Stay cool*. It's an informal phrase, meaning to relax or avoid becoming agitated."

"We know what it means, Myles," said Artemis Senior. "It just seems strange coming from you."

Gundred had apparently finished reading the plan, because she snatched the communicator out of Myles's hand. "And that's enough of that, human. I just wanted you to see just how thoroughly you are outmaneuvered. Whatever you try, somebody close to you will die."

Myles thought this was probably true, but he had to try anyway, or else, he was reasonably certain, *everybody* would die.

Half an hour later, Myles was being bundled out of the PIGLET back into the Dalkey basement where Beckett and Lazuli were being held captive. General Gveld Horteknut was sitting on a crate in the light of Beckett's spitball, delivering a mini pre-battle pep talk to Vigor and two slightly shamefaced dwarves.

"They can take our land," she told her audience of three, "but they'll never take our gold!"

Myles, who was transfixed by the sight of his twin revolving in the glowing ball, ran his mouth automatically. "Technically, they *did* take your gold. You are merely taking it back."

Gveld froze, her fist raised, and swiveled her eyes in order to subject Myles to her familiar glare.

"Not that such a distinction is important," Myles added hurriedly. "Don't mind me, I'm just a stickler for details. Most irritating, I realize."

Gveld continued her speech. "They say that, on that fateful first night ten thousand years ago when the humans collapsed our warrens and stole our hard-mined gold, there was a Fowl among the humans. You heard that right. A mighty Fowl warrior was among the first to claim his share of our treasure."

"This one is no warrior," said one listener, who had a rune shaved into his scalp and an obviously dyed orange beard tied at the back of his neck and running over his shoulders like a cloak. "Nor his brother, neither."

Gveld did not point out that Myles's brother certainly had behaved like a warrior.

"Yes, Dyggar," she said. "These mud spawn are not warriors. But they have talents, nonetheless. And they will try to destroy us, as their kind have done for thousands of years. But let me promise you something: not this time. This time the Horteknut Reclaimers shall be victorious. This time the humans lose."

"This time the humans lose," echoed Dyggar, brandishing what Myles recognized from his schematic files as a lance version of an LEP buzz baton.

"About that," said Myles. "I have delivered on your Irish Backstop. You can walk into that elevator and claim the Horteknut gold."

Gveld nodded slowly. "Gundred sent me the file and I read it carefully. I have to say, boy, that, technically, you did not deliver anything. Not the way I interpret it."

Myles returned her slow nod. "I see. Because my plan hasn't yet borne fruit, you are choosing to categorize it as a failure."

"That I am," said Gveld. "And that is why Dyggar

volunteered to stay behind and make sure the terms of failure are met. You don't have a problem with that, do you, Dyggar?"

"No, my general. I can be relied upon. Dwarf law says the terms must be met."

Myles appealed to Gundred. "And you, mademoiselle? Does this seem like it is in accordance with dwarf law to you?"

Gundred could not meet his eyes. "Gveld, my general, the human delivered. His plan is sound."

"Yes, Number Two," said Gveld, resting a hand on Gundred's soldier. "His *plan*. But I don't trust human plans that seem solid but will melt like ice in the sun. A possible future result is of no use to me. I do not wish my last thought under this earth to be *The human betrayed us, and I let him live.*"

"But they are children . . ." said Gundred with an edge of protest in her voice.

"No," said Gveld. "They are *Fowls*. Believing the Fowls to be harmless children has historically been a deadly mistake for our kind. Fowl spawn are born dangerous."

Even Myles couldn't argue with that, and neither did Gundred.

"Of course, my general. As always, you show us the way."

Gveld smiled her dazzling golden smile. "I try, my friend," she said. "Now, is everything unfolding as planned?"

"Yes, General," said Gundred. "Vigor and the shamed will make their way to the basement with their charges. And I have chosen some appropriate disguises for the two of us."

"Very good, Number Two," said Gveld. "Fetch the outfits, and I shall meet you at the PIGLET."

Gundred bowed slightly. "Yes, General."

And she left, keeping her gaze glued to the floor, making zero eye contact with Myles.

Gveld nodded at Dyggar. "Is your lance charged?"

Dyggar pressed a button on the shaft and electricity fizzled at the tip. "Of course, General. I will not fail you."

"I never doubted you, soldier," said Gveld, clapping him on the shoulder. "Remember, once the clever one kills the stupid one, he must shoot the pixel before earning his own quick death. Those are the terms."

This was said as though the general were reading from an everyday to-do list of chores.

Dyggar counted off on his fingers. "Stupid one. Pixel. Clever one. Got it."

"Good soldier," said Gveld, and then once she had checked to make sure Gundred had indeed left the Dalkey basement, the general whispered into Myles's ear. "Sometimes Gundred wavers. She is not a born Horteknut, after all. But she's an invaluable sounding board for me and my dearest friend under the earth. But this mission is different. It's the last mission, and what Gundred doesn't need to know is—"

"You're going to kill every ACRONYM agent in that building," finished Myles. "Shut them down for good." Myles could not believe he had not seen this before. Perhaps it was simply too horrible an option for his mind even to consider. "You're not going to simply fake a seismic event. You're going to blow up that building and destroy any evidence that you were ever there."

Gveld smiled. "Maybe you are more like me than you thought."

Myles did not respond. He was thinking how he himself had ensured that thousands of extra humans would be caught up in Gveld's explosion.

Feel guilty later, he ordered himself. *Solve the current problem first.*

The current problem was Dyggar.

Dyggar, who was so eager to kill some humans.

Gveld curled the fingers of her right hand into a cylinder and peered through them at her soldier.

"Tunnel safely, my soldier. And do not talk to that human lest he worm his way into your head."

Dyggar returned the gesture. "Tunnel safely, my general."

And then the general was gone, and Dyggar took a human handgun from his belt.

CHAPTER 10
THE PIPSQUEAK

SO NOW Myles Fowl found himself in the unenviable position of having to shoot his brother and also execute that same brother's best friend.

This is a nice mess I've gotten myself into, he thought, adapting a phrase made famous by Laurel and Hardy, who were the stars of many Fowl family movie nights. Myles remembered that whenever Oliver Hardy used a version of this phrase, Beckett would exclaim in exasperation, *You're all laughing now, but anytime I make a mess, no one says "That's a nice mess, Beckett."*

Myles was finding it difficult to believe that Gveld had reneged on an Irish Backstop, which was supposed to be sacred.

I routinely mistrust humans, Myles thought. But somehow I had believed fairies to be a tad more reliable.

Apparently, he'd thought wrong. It was as Artemis had often said: *There are snakes in every species.*

To which Beckett had added, *Especially the snake species.*
Which was true.

Of course, Myles was not totally naive, and he had pre-
prepared a backup plan in case of this exact eventuality. But
he was a little less confident in this plan now that it seemed
he would actually have to whip it out. Especially since this
plan relied on motor skills and timing.

So now Myles was faced with a metaphorical snake of
his own, in the form of Dyggar with his strange back beard,
which probably drew impressed *ooh*s from the patrons of
a dwarf bar. To make matters even stranger, Dyggar wore a
tunic that was composed entirely of shaved aloe vera leaves.

Myles tried to make conversation in the glow of the
spitball that kept his twin suspended in slow revolution. "I
suppose those leaves keep you moisturized in the tunnels,"
he said in Gnommish, which was the fairy common tongue.

"Yeah. So what?" Dyggar seemed a little defensive. "Skin-
care regimens are not just for elves anymore. Being wet all
the time makes a guy dry, which is weird. I get these little
pustules in the crook of my arm. Do you want to see?"

"No, thank you so much," said Myles. "I think I'll just get
on with shooting my brother, if you don't mind."

"Suit yourself," said Dyggar. "Doesn't make any difference to me. I'm in no hurry."

"You're not going to the convention center?"

Dyggar pouted. "No, thanks to you. I gotta make sure
you kill these two, then finish you off. And after that I have
to wait here for Axborn."

"I do apologize for delaying you," said Myles. "Perhaps there will still be time for you to join the others?"

"Nah," said Dyggar. "We're on clean-up duty. Me and Axborn. The others get to find the treasure. Meanwhile, I'm stuck here with a twerp like you."

Myles filed this information, as he did all information. "Look on the bright side," he said. "At least you get to kill me."

"Yeah," said Dyggar, mollified a little. "There is that." He held out the gun to Myles. "There's one bullet in the pipe. You aim it anywhere but at that spitball and I'll blast you with so many volts your eyeballs will dry up. Also, you will be dead."

"You have thought of everything, my good fellow," said Myles, accepting the weapon.

Dyggar stamped a foot, annoyed with himself. "I just remembered. I'm not supposed to talk to you."

"Quite right," said Myles. "Don't say another word. Just rest your power lance on Lazuli's left arm—on a dead man's switch—in case I try something."

Dyggar beamed him a look that said *I was going to do that,* but he did not speak as he moved into position behind the spitball so Myles could not shoot him without also shooting through his brother.

Myles studied the handgun. It was a small .22, known as a pipsqueak pistol by those familiar with such things, but in spite of the nickname, Myles knew that at this range the small gun would have no problem killing his twin, even through a glob of gel.

Dyggar cleared his throat for attention and then pointed at his own body. The message was clear: *Go for the heart.*

Myles answered with a shake of his head and pointed to his own forehead. "Headshot, to be certain," he said. "I don't want to have to borrow a bullet and shoot my brother again."

Dyggar winked. *Wise choice.*

Myles squared up to the giant spitball. Inside the translucent sphere, Beckett was revolving slowly head over heels. A complete revolution, Myles calculated, would take fifty-eight seconds, which meant that Beck's head would move five degrees from the apex, or indeed any point, in slightly less than a second. The bullet would dip far less, as it would have considerably more momentum than Beckett, and even though the medium was at least a thousand times denser than air, the tiny missile should find Myles's actual target with barely any velocity left.

No matter, thought Myles. *All I need it to do is tickle him.*

Myles knew how to shoot a gun and had practiced simulations, but he had never shot one in reality. And he vowed there and then that he never would again. But, at this particular point in time, Myles couldn't see any other way to save Beck and Lazuli both.

What if I injure my twin?

You cannot. It's physics.

Myles closed one eye, sighted along the barrel (aiming directly at Beckett's head), counted to one, and pulled the trigger.

The recoil was negligible from such a small weapon, but the flash and smoke clouded Myles's view so he did not see what happened next, and the *bang* echoed around the room, so the twin did not hear the sound he was hoping for.

What happened next was that Myles's plan worked perfectly: the small bullet bored into the gel, destroying the sphere's integrity as it lost momentum. While it seemed initially that the projectile could not miss Beckett's head, the blond boy dipped a fraction more than the bullet, and the shot passed through one of his curls and onward through the sphere, holding on to barely enough energy to pop out the other side and dink Dyggar on the forehead.

The dwarf squealed, thinking he had been shot dead, and reflexively released his grip on his lance's dead man's switch, sending a lethal current coursing through Lazuli's tissue. This current shorted out Foaly's magic-suppressor, waking Lazuli's power, which responded like any antibody would when under attack by destroying its attacker. A corona of magical power bloomed around Lazuli, incinerating the vinesuit that contained her and slamming Dyggar into the sheetrock, where he made a vaguely dwarf-shaped hole.

"I shouldn't have talked to you," he said, before passing out.

"No, my good man," agreed Myles, though the dwarf was not a man. "You shouldn't have."

It was an understandable misclassification to make in the stressful circumstances, as mythological dwarves are virtually indistinguishable from human little people, and yet his error seemed to bother Myles perhaps more than it reasonably should. In fact, he sent the gun clattering across the floor and sat with his back to the wall.

"Stupid. Stupid," he said, knocking his own forehead with the heel of one hand. "Dyggar is a dwarf, not a man. And you have the temerity to call yourself a genius? A person may as well refer to an ionic bond as a covalent bond. Stupid."

And he continued in this vein until Beckett sat beside him and draped a sopping arm over his shoulder, at which point Myles stopped beating himself up and sniffled a little. When Lazuli crawled over to join the pair, Myles wept quietly for somewhere in the region of thirty-seven seconds.

"It's okay, brother," said Beckett quietly. "You saved us. You're the only one who could have done it. Artemis would have managed one, but you got two."

Lazuli tried to speak, but when she opened her mouth, nothing but smoke came out. She exhaled a long plume, then coughed a half a dozen times.

"Your magic's back," Beckett noted.

"Yep," said Lazuli when she had recovered her voice. "Luckily, the electricity shorted out Foaly's suppressor."

This comment brought Myles out of his funk.

"Luckily?" he said, somewhat insulted. "*Luckily?* I will have you know, Specialist, that your magical revival had little to do with luck, less to do with fortune, and nothing whatsoever to do with karma, kismet, or happenstance. I knew exactly how to activate your powers. My methods were a little crude, I grant you, but as we learned during our adventure on the island of Saint George, your trigger appears to be imminent death, which is morbidly humorous. So I thought a lethal shock would kill two birds with one stone. Obviously, you were not one of the birds."

Lazuli felt relieved but also angry, not to mention sore all over.

"So, you shocked me on purpose, Myles Fowl?"

Myles raised a finger. "I *saved* you on purpose, Specialist. There is quite a big difference."

Lazuli huffed. "Yes, about fifty thousand volts."

"I think you know, as a weapons expert," said Myles, "that it's the current that will kill you, not the voltage."

Then something occurred to him. "Specialist, are you trying to distract me from my feelings of guilt by using accusations and insults?"

Lazuli straightened her Gloop tie, which the magic had not incinerated, in an obvious imitation of Myles himself. "I am," she confirmed. "Is it working?"

Myles took his own pulse with two fingers. "I would say that it is. Thank you, Specialist."

"Good," said Lazuli. "Then I suggest that maybe we Regrettables pick ourselves up and go stop the dwarves."

"Finally!" said Beckett, punching the air. "I was in that rubber ball for even longer than forever. And I've been stuck here for nearly a minute. Any more of this waiting around and I'll turn into Myles."

I suppose I can examine my bruised psyche later, thought Myles, climbing to his feet.

He opened a second door in the basement, which led to a stairway that presumably ran up to Dalkey High Street.

"What say we use the stairs this time, my fellow Regrettables?" he said, grasping the wooden banister. "They are so much better suited for non-tunneling bipeds."

And then he promptly tripped up the first step.

Which was not easy to do.

CHAPTER 11
FLASHCON

OUR universe is so vast and varied that it is reasonably accurate to say that there is nothing new under our, or indeed any, sun. Everything that is currently happening has more or less happened before at some point. Any combination of character types and circumstances that you can possibly imagine has been combined somewhere along the timeline. Simply put, history inevitably repeats itself.

There are, of course, exceptions to this rule. In fact, there is a scroll in Haven City's Hey Hey Temple on which the pixie monks attempt to catalogue those exceptions as far as this planet is concerned, and they have concluded that there have been, to this point, forty-one events involving such outlandish and unlikely conditions that they could be considered truly unique. These events are known as *singularities*, and it is a testament to the Fowl family that they were involved in four singularities so far. The event that would become known as the ACRONYM Convergence increased the number of singularities to forty-two and the Fowl family's personal tally to five, which is a staggering statistic considering the hundred-billion-plus sentient beings who have so far existed on or beneath the surface of the earth. Having said that, those familiar with the Fowls' outlandish exploits consider the percentage a little on the low side.

It is indisputable that the ACRONYM Convergence deserves its place on the list, for the combination of players and events is bordering on incredible, but we must believe the monks that the convergence occurred as recorded. After all, to quote the famous elfin F-pop star Merry Sparx, *Hey, if you can't trust the Hey Hey, then hey hey?* Followed by several more elongated *heys.* This lyric does not really make any sense unless one is an F-pop devotee.

Perhaps the most damning indictment of the ACRONYM Convergence is the reaction of LEP Commander Trouble Kelp when he read the bare-bones report the following day. His exact words were:

"What?"

"Really?"

"Ha-ha, very funny."

"Is that even possible?"

"I am not buying this for a second."

"Are we sure Artemis Fowl is in space?"

"I'm going to lie down on the sofa in my office for an hour. Bring me two kilos of raw chocolate, then no interruptions."

"Oh, and ignore any sobbing noises you might hear."

It is tricky to establish the exact starting point of the Convergence. Perhaps it was when humans stole dwarf gold over ten thousand years ago. Or perhaps it was when the first team of Horteknut Reclaimers was formed to initiate their vendetta against humanity. Or perhaps it was when Gveld Horteknut took over the helm at Reclaimer Central. This, however, is a debate for historians. We will concentrate on the Convergence's events, leading up to and including the climactic showdown that takes place in and around the convention center on Dublin's Spencer Docks, which had recently been completely remodeled following a mysterious major subsidence some years earlier.

Let us observe actions as they unfold from the Convergence's event horizon, that being the point when the protagonists are committed to their goals and there is no chance the mission can be abandoned. For Gveld and her Reclaimers, this moment arrived when they took up their positions in the convention center environs. Gveld Horteknut and Gundred, her second, were across the street in the upper gantry of a hulking gray traffic bridge outside the center, both disguised from head to toe in manga cosplay as Sharkgirl and Yumi Dragonella, which made them look a lot less homicidal than they were. Vigor and an additional two Reclaimers waited in the bowels of the convention center, ready to blow shaped charges to bring down the building when the Horteknut hoard was secure.

Gundred was not privy to that last *bringing down the*

building bit but was shortly to find out. The original plan had been to trip the building's seismic sensors with a small explosion in the parking basement, which would automatically shunt the gold into the one section of the building that was indestructible, that being the executive elevator. Even if the entire building collapsed, anything and anyone inside would be protected. Gveld and Gundred would be waiting in the elevator to secure the gold, and once they had, they would override the elevator controls and ride into the sub-basement, where the Reclaimers would spirit away their treasure.

But . . .

Gveld had decided that, as this was the final ACRONYM facility, she had the perfect opportunity to shut down the despicable organization once and for all. And so she had instructed her demolitions expert, Vigor, to plant six charges instead of one.

"Turn this place into rubble," she'd ordered. "Then dig us out."

This was the final piece of the puzzle, which Gveld had kept from Gundred.

I can claim the collapse was unexpected, she told herself. Shoddy construction, simple as that. Gundred will be distressed for a day, but then she will be herself once more.

Gveld did feel a little guilty.

Not for killing the humans—she would not lose a wink of sleep over that—but for deceiving her Number Two, who was also her only real friend.

I also will be distressed for a day, she realized, which will make my story all the more believable.

But that was in the future. A future that would never come to pass unless Myles Fowl's plan actually worked.

Had killing him been a rash decision? Gveld wondered.

"Perhaps we shouldn't have killed the Fowl boy so quickly," Gundred said now, as though plucking the thought from her general's mind.

Gveld smiled. *She knows me so well.*

Aloud she said, "What have I taught you, my friend?"

Gveld had taught her friend innumerable lessons, but Gundred knew which one was most appropriate here.

"You told me, my general, that I should never regret the killing of a human. There are always more left alive."

"Exactly," said Gveld. "There are always more. Mischiefs."

A *mischief*, Gundred knew, was the collective noun for rats, which Gveld often applied to humans.

"And anyway, Number Two," continued the general, "we have time."

They did have some time, but certainly not an abundance of it. Perhaps half an hour before the eclipse began, and then seven minutes while it lasted to get into the elevator before it was called to the penthouse by the seismic alarm.

Thirty minutes to go, thought Gundred, and she knew in her heart that Gveld would go in whether they had cover or not.

My general will not miss this opportunity.

And then they would die together.

* * *

And what was Myles Fowl's wonderful scheme that would somehow provide cover for the costumed dwarves to penetrate the center's glass atrium? Myles would be the first to admit that it was a little on the fanciful side for his own liking, but in his defense, when he had put the plan together it had been hypothetical, as he had intended to steal the gold on its way across the Atlantic using one of his father's underwater lairs as a base of operations.

The problem was this: how to bring an unregulated crowd of unruly people to a specific point in Dublin within the hour. A crowd in which everyone wore a disguise and no one was identifiable. Myles knew that if that crowd were to be composed mainly of teenagers, the answer was simple: *the internet.*

So, Myles hacked the social media accounts of actor Dylan Dee (real name: Sean Barnes), who played starship captain Voopster Mab on the science fiction show *Supermassive.*

Dee was notorious for dropping online hints that led fans on treasure hunts to book signings, poetry readings, interpretive-dance flash mobs, special-effects-makeup tutorials, and even walk-on parts on *Supermassive.* The actor had sixty million followers on social media, and over a million of those were in Ireland, which amounted to more than a fifth of the country's population, and it had occurred to Myles that it might be very useful to harness the enthusiasm of the actor's ardent fans. And so, to this end, he had locked Dylan Dee out of his own accounts and posted the following:

FLASHcon, my little star warriors. Follow me one last time for MAJOR brownie points and rewards. Only for the faithful, CUZ you know who you are. Let's Con the World where the sun don't shine. #supermassive #walk-on #voopstermab

What did all that shorthand jargon mean? To anyone over the age of forty, probably nothing, but if a person was a Dylan Dee fan, and a million Irish people were, it meant that Dee himself was calling a flash convention during the eclipse at the site where Worldcon had just been, and whoever wore the best *Supermassive* costume would win a walk-on part as a major in the hit show.

Gveld considered this plan now. It seemed a long shot at best.

No matter, she thought. Cover or not, we are going in.

It seemed most unlikely that a swath of humanity could be mobilized in such a short time, but just then a mob descended on Convention Centre Dublin, flowing from the side streets and the harbor. Buses pulled over, disgorging legions of eager cosplayers. Cars triple-parked so that adults could eject kids from their back seats as fast as possible. Within minutes the entire area was shut down with human traffic. What had been a quiet dockside only moments before had transformed into a hive of raucous activity. There was quite of lot of squealing, shouting in alien tongues, toy lasers blasting, and dogs (also in costume) barking, and someone had brought a large hissing snake that had been painted gold, which was all kinds of illegal. Obviously, the sci-fi series featured a giant, as there were several pairs of teenagers on each other's shoulders, dressed in oversized furry onesies. Two of the giants had a fight. One of the dog/aliens joined in. A couple of dads got involved. The security men made a valiant effort to assure everyone that there was no flashcon here today, but nobody bought it, because the FLASH signage was right there!

Who are you kidding? they cried.

Get out of my way, humans, shouted some others, who were clearly human themselves.

And . . .

We want Dylan! was the chant that quickly spread through the crowd until it seemed the entire quayside rocked like boats on the river.

In the traffic bridge gantry, General Gveld Horteknut smiled. "It looks like the Fowl child did deliver," she said to her Number Two. "Do you see, Gundred? I was right to kill him."

It occurred to Gveld that all these children present would die, too.

But they were very annoying, and the world would be a better place without them.

A shadow fell across the river, and Gveld Horteknut checked the skies through her Sharkgirl visor. The eclipse had begun. Now it was safe for them both to stride across the plaza to the convention center without fear of direct sunlight should they be jostled and a gap open in their clothing, because there *was* no direct sunlight. This might seem like a minor worry, but most dwarves are catastrophically photosensitive and can be burned to a crisp by even milky rays. An elf TV pundit once quipped that *Even vampires love the sun more than the average dwarf.* Not that fairies believe in vampires, but that's okay, because vampires by and large don't believe in fairies. The point being that if a dwarf's sunblock flaked and a patch of skin got strobed by sunlight, the burn shock could kill them outright. Gundred had built up a resistance because she was a surface dwarf, but Gveld was especially vulnerable and had to be careful that her clothing was not porous. Gveld was not scared of dying as much as dying before her mission was completed. Now, at least solar burn would not be a problem for the next seven minutes or so.

The dwarves climbed down from the steel bridge gantry and cautiously crossed the road. Both had been out in public before—after all, they were human in appearance—but the security in this facility would be on the lookout for all kinds of fairies, including dwarves, so it was best not to reveal themselves as possible suspects. Also, the rune tattoos on Gveld's cheeks often shone when she was excited, and even through her Sharkgirl visor the glow was visible.

Gundred was nervous as they threaded their way through the towering humans, but she drew courage from her general, who strode to the lobby door as though she owned this building and was in command of everyone here.

My general, thought Gundred. My life.

A mere hour beforehand there would have been absolutely zero chance that the Reclaimers could have penetrated lobby security, but now the entire floor was a heaving zoo of irritated teens and their beyond-exasperated parents, who had given up their afternoon to drive into the city only to find these security guys denying that there even was a flash convention in spite of the dozen or so banners and signs displaying the word FLASH in bright red letters.

One dad was offering the receptionist a fat wad of euros to open the turnstiles. "Just let my son Ned, I mean Threepio, and his friends through. That's all I'm asking. We know the Star Wars guy is here."

"*Supermassive!*" squealed Threepio. "The *Supermassive* guy. It's Captain Voopster Mab. Why are you so stupid, Dad?"

Why indeed? thought Gveld as the Reclaimers ducked under the turnstile.

Of course they were spotted by half a dozen security men on the ring of the upper balcony, but Gveld bought them some time by switching on the speaker in her helmet and calling out:

"By the Ruby of Moonstar Twelve, there he is: Dylan Dee!"

A shrill howl rose from the teenagers. A howl of this magnitude once signified that a great tragedy had befallen the community, such as a Viking raid, or perhaps the eruption of a nearby volcano, but in modern times it could only mean one thing: Someone had laid eyes on a celebrity.

Gveld added fuel to the fire by pointing at a man guarding the elevator shaft and shouting:

"There he is! By the elevator door."

If Gundred had had the time or the inclination, she might have felt sorry for the elevator guy, who was swept away on a wriggling wave of superfans who literally tore the hair from his scalp looking for souvenirs, but the Horteknut Number Two had neither commodity. Her goal now was keeping her general in sight and getting into the right-hand elevator in the central column. The left one was useless to them as only the right would take delivery of their precious cargo.

The Reclaimers caught a break when they found the elevator at ground level. Usually the car would wait outside the penthouse in case it was needed by the station chief, but perhaps the station chief was already checking out the ground floor ruckus or perhaps he was being court-martialed for booting out the tenants. Whatever the reason, the elevator was where it was, which meant the dwarves wouldn't need to wait for it. Providing the NOK-NOK was up to the job of cracking its seal.

If there is one thing dwarves are experts on, it is breaking into places. And the NOK-NOK, or Network Override Key, was an ever-evolving piece of burglar's kit. It had been developed by the LEP as an electronic replacement for the battering ram and then adapted by dwarves to get around increasingly elaborate human security systems. It was the size of a hockey puck, and Gveld had it strapped to the palm of her hand. She held it close to the elevator's thumb scanner and let it do its thing. It was already finely tuned to ACRONYM's basic settings, but every site had its own quirks, and even the gauge of the various wirings could slow down the tool.

The NOK-NOK did indeed *do its thing,* but the ACRONYM elevator was no pushover and made the Reclaimers wait a full ten seconds before the door slid open, and in that time several people attempted to get close to Gveld. Gundred protected her general with gusto and expertise, incapacitating three security men with well-placed blows and turning back several teens who hoped that perhaps the elevator would ferry them into Dylan Dee's presence.

The Reclaimers lurched into the elevator and Gveld passed the NOK-NOK device to her Number Two.

"Can you feel it?" the general asked dreamily, her eyes locked on to the ceiling panel. "The gold calls. Destiny is almost in our reach."

Gundred stripped back the elevator panel and plugged in the electronic key.

"Time to bring down the house," she said.

More than you know, Gveld thought but did not say.

Ten Minutes Earlier

The Regrettables utilized a somewhat unusual mode of transport for their short trip to the convention center. It was certainly not the most unusual mode of transport the Fowl Twins would ever avail themselves of—that honor going to the time Myles had transmitted the brothers' consciousnesses along a length of an irradiated shoestring into a vat of swamp algae—but it was a memorable trip nonetheless, as it was undertaken on the backs of two dolphins that were none too pleased about being commandeered to ferry bipeds. The cetaceans were additionally put out by the fact that the water in these parts was teeming with bacteria, and furthermore, one of the dolphins, whose name was Ah-ah-eh-eh-eh, had planned to spend the afternoon working on his rom-com screenplay and not pumping out the toxic bilge lining his blowhole. But, as his pal Eh-eh-eh-blooeee had reminded him, *Neither of us relish being here, but that gangly human cut you out of those nets a few moon cycles ago, Ah-ah. We owe him a favor.*

To which Ah-ah-eh-ch-ch had replied, *Whatever, Blooeee. But if someone catches this little jaunt on film and we end up in a TV show, I'm holding you responsible. And let me tell you something for nothing: I am never going back in a cage.*

To which Eh-eh-eh-blooeee rolled his double split pupils and said, *Like you were ever in a cage. And at least you didn't have to puke up a package.*

To explain the package-puking comment: Myles had always been paranoid about losing his precious graphene eyeglasses, even though his need for them was more psychosomatic than anything else. Myles reasoned that it only made sense to hide several pairs on and off the island in case of emergency, and considering the Fowl lifestyle, an emergency was pretty much inevitable. To this end Myles had tucked away pairs of spectacles in several easy-to-find hiding places and a few less obvious ones. The least obvious one being inside a seaweed egg in the tummy of one of Beckett's dolphin pals, namely Eh-eh-eh-blooeee.

The poor aquatic mammal had been asked to hawk up Myles's graphene spectacles before they set out on their journey. These older glasses did not house a superintelligent NANNI, but the NANNI they did house was still more powerful than any other human techno-glasses in development.

Myles had been somewhat pleased though not delighted to be reunited with his less-than-ideal glasses, but even that was short-lived, as now, mere minutes later, he was irritated that his trouser legs and 3-D–printed loafers were soaked from repeated dunkings in the salt water. The twin had never enjoyed entering into possibly fatal confrontations wearing sopping shoes. The *squelch* could be quite distracting. But at least these spectacles had heated hydrophobic lenses to ensure they would not mist even in these saturated conditions.

"I imagine these dolphin chaps are doing their best, and I don't wish to appear ungrateful," he said more to himself than to Beckett, who appeared to be balancing on the starboard dolphin. "But a slightly higher waterline would have been appreciated."

Beckett pivoted one hundred and eighty degrees, commenting, "Moles. I think we have moles." Which would appear to be quite the non sequitur, though Myles did not so much as raise an eyebrow in surprise.

Lazuli seemed perfectly comfortable behind Beckett, even though this was, in fact, the first time she had straddled a common dolphin. She had once ridden a larger killer whale, but that mammal had been an even-tempered LEP agent wearing a translator. This dolphin was skittish and not affiliated with the fairy police force. Nevertheless, Lazuli resisted the urge to clamp her knees together and instead leaned forward into the spray.

"Myles," she called, "remember, this is an action situation, so I'm going to take point."

"Watch out for that rock," said Beckett, executing a backflip.

"I am aware, Specialist," said Myles, ignoring the rock warning. "You tackle the physical and I shall concern myself with the climactic supervillain showdown."

Lazuli spoke in short sentences between bounces. "Are you for real, Myles? A supervillain showdown? Those only happen in books."

Myles smiled tightly, thinking, Oh, Specialist Heitz, how little you know about supervillains.

Aloud he said, "There will most certainly be a showdown. Have no doubt about that. The moment General Horteknut lays eyes upon me, the verbal sparring shall begin. Our debate should buy you time to defuse the explosives. You should be fine, unless the Reclaimers catch you. Will that be a problem, if they catch you, do you think?"

"No problem," said Lazuli, then spat out a mouthful of salt spray. "There won't be more than three."

Three Reclaimers, she thought. No single individual has ever dispatched three Reclaimers.

But she would find a way. She had to, or thousands would perish, and she could not stand by and watch that happen.

In front of her on the dolphin, Beckett turned a cartwheel, which surely defied the laws of physics.

"I can see Mum in the window," he said, pointing across the River Liffey.

Another irrelevant comment.

Beckett will not be able to help me this time, Lazuli knew. Not in person, at least.

As previously instructed, Ah-ah-eh-eh-eh and Eh-eh-eh-blooeee pulled in beneath the iconic Samuel Beckett Bridge. Both dolphins reared up so that their passengers would slide backward, and then, with coordinated flicks of their powerful tails, they launched the bipeds toward the docks.

Lazuli stumbled a few steps forward before catching her balance on the concrete, thinking, Myles will never manage to stay upright. That Mud Boy would trip over his own shadow.

In fact, she had once thrown this accusation at Myles, who had replied, *That is a ridiculous assertion, Specialist. You embarrass yourself. A shadow is simply the lack of light on a surface upon which a light source projects. It is barely more than a photon in depth and cannot be held responsible for trips or stumbles.*

Which was probably the most Myles-y thing Lazuli had ever heard the twin say.

However, she was amazed to see that Myles had so catastrophically misjudged his landing on the service jetty that he had come back around to coordinated, if that made any sense, and actually landed walking as though the ground had come up to meet him.

"Beckett believes that this bridge was named after him," he said conversationally, as if he had not just stuck one of the greatest dismounts in history. "But between us two, it is the other way around. He is named for the person this bridge is named after."

Beckett ignored this comment and contented himself with squatting low, as though hiding behind an invisible ditch, and squeaking like a rat.

And so Lazuli and Myles faced each other beneath the spar and cables of the harp-shaped Samuel Beckett Bridge, both clad in matching black suits complete with golden ties, both a little the worse for wear due to the various exertions of the past few days but still reasonably functional.

"Do you think Beckett is all right?" Lazuli wondered aloud.

Myles focused on his scar. "He's fine. Communing with one rodent or another, I imagine."

"Maybe so," said Lazuli. "But I can't help thinking—"

Myles held up a hand, palm out. "Stop, Specialist Heitz. There is no percentage in second-guessing ourselves. Our odds are poor, but they are the best available to us. We shall, each of us, play to our strengths and hopefully prevail."

Lazuli was not so sure. If this situation were a virtual mission scenario, she would bet against the Regrettables every time. Could it be that Myles Fowl had just made an illogical statement?

The entire tableau reeked of ominous portent. The port should've been quiet on a Sunday, but instead the area was thronged by costumed teenagers and their attendant parent taxis, and an eerie half-light had settled over the city like a shroud.

Myles held out his hand for a formal shake. "Good luck to you, Specialist Heitz. Should we not meet again, it has been a privilege."

Lazuli took the boy's hand. "For me, too, Myles. A confusing privilege and a frantic honor."

Myles was not finished. "And should we beat the odds and meet again, I would expect the LEP to delete Beckett and me from the LEP *humans of interest* list. And of course, I shall be submitting my expenses."

"I would expect no less," said Lazuli, surprised to find that she could muster a smile.

We are probably going to die, she thought while smiling. And I never even got to take the captain's exam. But all she said was "Myles, your tie is crooked."

Myles's response to this was to stalk up the service steps,

muttering to himself. "How on earth is a chap supposed to maintain a reasonable level of decorum when he arrives astride a dolphin?"

Beckett crept on all fours beside his twin, whispering over and over again, "Something smells badly. Something smells badly."

Myles noted that his twin had used an adverb when he should have used an adjective, but even though he took issue with his brother's grammar, he agreed with the intended sentiment.

They split into teams. Fowl and fairy. The twins elbowed their way through the crowd at the convention center's front door, while Lazuli ran around the side of the building, hugging the wall until she reached the underground parking deck's pedestrian exit, which swung open easily. She encountered some humans on the short journey, but most did not spare her, a "child," a second glance. White-blond hair was no more than slightly unusual in this cosmopolitan city, and even blue face paint was occasionally seen slathered on the features of Dublin's cosplaying youths, who often turned up at movie theaters dressed as their favorite characters. And even if there had not been thousands of costumed children milling about the area, if a human's frontal lobe is forced to decide whether a small blue humanoid is a costumed human or a relatively diminutive unknown species, the brain's confirmation bias would opt for costumed human nine times out of ten.

One gangly teen even held out his fist for a bump, commenting, "Go, Neytiri."

Lazuli accepted the bump, wondering what or who a Neytiri was.

I'll Bugle that later, she thought. Bugle being her preferred fairy search engine, named for the instrument of Euphonius, the legendary centaur bugler who woke the gnome army during the great exodus.

But back to business. The stairway was wide and seemed like it had been built to accommodate serious foot traffic, but Lazuli didn't pass anyone on the way down, which annoyed her a little bit, because Myles had predicted that she wouldn't.

There shouldn't be anyone in the stairwell, but the Reclaimers might have tapped into the security feed, so watch for cameras, he'd told her earlier. *The parking deck is closed for renovation, but they'll leave the exit unlocked in case a fire marshal checks. When you reach level minus four, that's when you might meet resistance. The Reclaimers will wait there until the last minute to guard the charges, then take cover when it is almost too late. That's your window.*

Great, thought Lazuli. My window stretches from *almost too late* to *too late*. I wonder how long that is, exactly.

Seconds, maybe. A moment, probably.

Lazuli pitter-pattered down each step, farther and farther below sea level, and felt a little comforted by the slight change in air pressure. Like it or not, fairies belonged underground. They were generally safe there.

But not today, thought Lazuli. This fairy is not going to enjoy being underground today.

This prophecy fulfilled itself fourteen steps later, when Lazuli more or less bumped into Vigor, the first of the Reclaimers, who, conveniently enough for him, had already drawn his blade.

CHAPTER 12

NO INNOCENT HUMANS

WE HAVE arrived at that point in our narrative where, traditionally, the protagonists engage in an ultimate show-down. Our account breaks from this tradition, as we have not one but three—and arguably, four—showdowns. In order to keep these narratives straight in our heads, let us remind ourselves how our main combatants are arranged:

Gveld Horteknut and Gundred, her second, are in a central transparent elevator on the first floor, both disguised from head to toe as human little people in manga cosplay that makes them look less homicidal than they are. Gundred has interfaced with the elevator's control panel and from there with all the non-central elevators, of which there are eighteen cable-free, multidirectional, magnet-based drive units running through a network of vertical and horizontal shafts. Gveld's intrusion into the security systems has triggered an alarm, prompting the building's workforce of over three hundred ACRONYM agents to flash burn their computer drives and stride in rehearsed formation into sixteen of the aforementioned eighteen elevators, which promptly lock behind them. The lucky ones take the stairs, which proves to have more health benefits than simply getting their steps in, for they avoid getting stuck in the shortly-to-collapse building. And, of course, the building is bathed in the unnatural glow of its own lighting system, as the sun has tucked itself behind the moon and will be out of commission for a little more than seven minutes, ensuring that, even should the plan go awry, the Horteknut Reclaimers will have some leeway for their escape. It is a dastardly scheme that even Artemis Fowl would have to admire, if not approve of, and that was without even mentioning the cosplaying horde that seemed to be setting up camp in the basement.

Picture if you will twin central elevators constructed of silicon nitride, which is the hardest and toughest transparent spinel ceramic ever made. The right-hand elevator serves a dual purpose, both as a private escape pod for the ACRONYM station chief and as an unbreakable safe for the group's greatest treasure should the building's integrity be breached by missile attack or seismic activity. Currently, Gveld and Gundred are calmly riding in this right-hand elevator toward the top floor while all around them armed ACRONYM agents are wondering why the heck those two kids are traveling up while they themselves appear to be locked down inside their respective flimsier elevators. These agents are not trying to shoot their way out just yet, but it won't be long now.

This does seem like a lot to take in. So many plans and counter plans. Fortunately, our lead protagonists are fond of both monologuing and dialoguing, so the situation will shortly become abundantly clear.

Gveld shall begin:

"At last," she said, as the NOK-NOK burrowed deep into the ACRONYM network. "I am on the verge of taking back the lost Horteknut treasure. Our world shall be made whole. I am tempted to actually laugh, Gundred, honestly I am."

Gundred was not in the least tempted to laugh. "Gveld, I am not comfortable with this. We are exposed here, with all these witnesses."

"Oh, dear Gundred," said Gveld, deciding that it was time to come clean(ish). "We are not in the least exposed. The sun is safely behind the moon and we are in an indestructible box. And I have decided to not simply steal the gold but also wipe out the last remaining agents from this most despicable of organizations with a sequence of explosions."

This second strand of the plan was news to Gundred. "But aren't those humans in reinforced elevators, like ours? They are safe."

Now Gveld did laugh, though it segued into a consumptive cough. "I am afraid, my kindhearted friend, that the two central elevators are the building's only silicon nitride capsules. The other elevators are mere toughened Plexiglas. Those humans will be squashed by the very earth they poison. ACRONYM will be finished."

Gundred stood between her leader and the elevator interface. "This is not our way, Gveld. We do not create martyrs for others to follow."

Gveld shrugged. "What martyrs? The earth swallows a building. Will the humans punish the earth? Indeed, *can* they punish it any more than they already have? Trust me, no one except agents of ACRONYM would suspect mythological creatures. And the ACRONYM agents . . ."

Gundred inferred the missing clause: *will all be dead.*

A horrifying thought occurred to her. "But, my general, what of the innocent children?"

Gveld waved this question away. "There are no innocent humans."

From the atrium beyond came the muted sound of gunfire as a few quick-witted agents realized that they were, in fact, under attack. This gunfire had the effect of galvanizing the *Supermassive* fans, who decided en masse that perhaps a walk-on part in a TV show was not worth getting caught in whatever cross fire was going on here. Pandemonium erupted and ensued.

Meanwhile, Gundred chewed on Gveld's argument and could find no fault with it aside from the massive body count, which was only a human body count after all, which she shouldn't have cared about. But she did, because . . .

Gundred had a secret.

"We could simply take the treasure," she offered weakly, "and be gone before the sun shows her face."

This argument was so pathetic that Gveld returned to her work while she dismissed it. "In that scenario we become fugitives, and I will not set humans on our trail. These Mud People die, and that is the end of it. Our work can finally be done, and I can rest contented."

A bullet pinged against the casing of their elevator and cut short the conversation. The agents were growing restless.

"The eclipse won't last forever," continued Gveld gruffly. "The time has come to destroy this den of fairy killers."

The Fowl Twins went without hesitation into the building that was about to collapse around them. Myles had something of a spring in his step now that he had a pair of graphene eyeglasses cupping his ears, and he lapsed into his habit of lecturing while he walked.

"The convention center was more or less demolished some years ago, and the mortgage was picked up for a song, supposedly by an American vulture company," he explained to a disinterested Beckett.

"Worms are useless for conversation," said Beckett, determinedly off-topic. "It's all romantic poetry with them."

Myles rolled his eyes. "I don't know why I bother."

But he did know. The more Myles lectured, the less he worried, and so he continued to talk as they strode through the giant glass barrel of the open atrium against the tide of costumed teenagers whose flight seemed almost comical, made awkward by platform space boots and vision-obscuring masks.

Myles put a pin in his lecture when they reached the central double elevator shaft.

"Hack the building's systems, NANNI," Myles told his glasses. "Give me access to all security. I want to control everything from the sprinklers to the elevators. And, for heaven's sake, shut off that emergency siren."

"Yes, Myles," said NANNI.

And to Beckett, for appearances' sake, Myles said, "Keep up, brother mine. We have a city to save."

And a treasure to win, he thought, but kept that morsel of info to himself for the moment. A person could never tell who was listening. Myles knew this to be true, as he was usually the one listening.

The deafening siren mercifully sputtered out with a Morse code of final shrieks, and Myles estimated that his concentration levels increased 15 percent as a direct consequence.

Very well, he thought. Time to share a few painful truths with the Horteknuts.

The central elevator shaft had two cars. The right-hand car was elevated and peopled by two small figures.

Gveld and Gundred, Myles surmised.

The left-hand car was at ground level and waiting for someone with an authorized thumbprint to access it.

And guess who now has an authorized thumbprint? thought Myles, pressing his thumb against the sensor.

"Access granted," said the elevator in a voice that was, in Myles's opinion, a little smug. It seemed to say, *I am not just a common elevator; I am a private* executive *elevator.*

Elevators in general are smug, thought Myles, who was somewhat of an expert on the subject of smugness. But not as smarmy as sat navs, which are completely insufferable.

Nevertheless, Myles stepped inside when the doors *whoosh*ed open, with Beckett close to his side, still muttering his complaints about worms and their lack of conversational skills. "Worms are all me-me-me," he said. "They never think outside the tunnel."

The elevator took off remarkably smoothly.

Very low friction, thought Myles. But not as low as the cable-less multidirectional units, I imagine.

Which a person might think was a poor use of brain space at such a critical time, but it was all part of one of his many contingency plans.

A handful of seconds later, the Fowl Twins drew level with the second elevator in the shaft—the one housing two hostile dwarves who would be considered villains from a human perspective but possibly heroes from the fairy point of view.

Myles wasted no time, as there was patently no time to waste, and initiated the supervillain showdown with a suitably dramatic line:

"Ah, General Horteknut, we meet again."

Neither Gveld nor Gundred reacted. They kept beavering over a control panel with their backs turned to the Fowl Twins.

Myles tried again, aiming his mouth at the speaker in the wall. "I said, we meet again, General Horteknut. I imagine you weren't expecting to see me here."

Still nothing.

"NANNI," said Myles to his smart glasses, "did you get into all the building systems as I ordered?"

"Not exactly," said NANNI.

"Are you telling me you failed?"

"I half succeeded, Master," hedged NANNI.

"Half succeeded? Does that mean I control half of the systems?"

"Approximately. These systems are the latest tech, Master, and I have been in a dolphin's innards for the past year."

"No excuses," snapped Myles. "How am I supposed to communicate with the adjacent elevator?"

"There is a handset on the wall," said NANNI, vibrating the words into Myles's jawbone. "I can patch you through to the speaker."

Myles shuddered. "A handset? I am expected to use a handset now? The other supposedly identical elevator doesn't have a handset."

Nevertheless, Myles gingerly unhooked the handset as though there might be a deadly bacteria smeared on the handle.

"Half succeeded indeed," he muttered, and then spoke into the mouthpiece. "We meet again, General Horteknut."

"You have to press the call button," said NANNI.

"Oh, for heaven's sake," said Myles. "Why don't I simply write on the glass with my bodily fluids?"

"That is not actually glass," noted NANNI.

Myles missed fully operational NANNI. Oh, how he missed her.

He pressed the CALL button. "General Horteknut. I imagine you were not expecting to see me."

Gveld removed her Sharkgirl helmet but did not turn from her work. "I could hardly miss you, Mud Boy. You have been banging around in there for an eternity."

Myles stayed on script. "I believe it is time for our showdown."

Now Gveld did turn. "Showdown? Are you a child? Oh yes, that is exactly what you are."

Two burns for Myles, but perhaps he could claw back some ground by summarizing Gveld's plan. "I imagine your Reclaimers are going to blow the rods holding up this building, and when the seismic activity registers, the ACRONYM treasure will be shunted to the elevator to keep it safe. When the dust clears you will burrow out of here with the last of the Horteknut gold."

"Well done," said Gveld. "Although I believe I already told you most of my plan."

"You did," said Myles. "But some of it I worked out all by my lonesome. For example, how you trapped those ACRONYM agents in the elevators in order to kill them."

Gveld shrugged. "A bonus. We'll put an end to ACRONYM and restore the Horteknut name."

"And Gundred has no objection to this mass murder?"

"I do not, boy," said Gundred. "My general leads and I follow willingly."

Gveld was satisfied. "I hope that answers your question."

The remaining free ACRONYM agents were now firing at will toward both elevators. Not that their bullets had any effect on silicon nitride other than to make an odd musical tinkling on the surface. Myles could have sworn that he heard Rimsky-Korsakov's "Flight of the Bumblebee" hidden inside the pings, which was amusing.

"It seems the ACRONYM agents might have something to say about that," he said.

"They can say what they like," retorted Gveld. "No one can hear them. And soon no one will hear from them ever again."

Myles took a breath before playing his trump card. It was a volatile one, so to speak. "Of course, you won't be killing *all* the ACRONYM agents in the building."

Gveld sighed. "I was hoping to enjoy this moment, Fowl. It has been millennia in the making. Many of my own family died so that I may stand here today on the brink of ultimate triumph, so I would appreciate it if you didn't remind me of all the humans I won't be killing. The agency will be obliterated, and that will be enough for me."

Myles waited a moment to absorb this impressive rant,

staring at Gundred while he did so. "You're missing the point, Gveld. There's an ACRONYM agent closer than you know. She's been there for quite some time. Twenty years, I would think."

Gveld huffed. "Games, boy. Schoolyard games. People think we call you *Mud People* because that's where you lived when we ruled the surface: in the mud. But I think it's because of all the mud you sling."

Myles gripped the handset tightly. He knew how dangerous these waters were. "This is no game, is it, Gundred?"

Gundred did not answer, but Myles knew from the brimstone in her eyes that if she could strangle him at that moment, she would. Nevertheless, Myles forged ahead.

"I read the ACRONYM files, as you know, and they have tried many times to embed an agent with the Fairy People. But how could a human pretend to be a fairy? It just wouldn't work, unless that human looked like a fairy. In the way that perhaps a human little person might resemble a fairy dwarf. Even then it would have to be a female, because the males have tunneling abilities. But females—some could tunnel, yes, but most could not. And there is a recognized dwarf affliction called Boldart's syndrome, named after the dwarf who discovered it, in which dissolved nitrogen comes out of the bloodstream, forming gas bubbles in circulation. Those who suffer from this syndrome are called *surface dwarves*. It's rare, to be sure, but it means a dwarf cannot endure the same pressure as her fellows. So maybe a very clever female little person might persuade a band of dwarves that she had

Boldart's syndrome. Can you see where this is going, Ms. Horteknut?"

Myles was speaking to Gveld, but he was looking straight at Gundred, who was not enjoying this conversation one bit.

As for Gveld, she was staring at her communicator but not sending any commands.

I have their attention, thought Myles. I shall continue.

"My suspicions were first aroused when Gundred recognized an old ACRONYM call sign during my interrogation. And then you told me that Gundred was a surface dwarf. That would be very convenient for an ACRONYM spy. To never have to put herself in high-pressure situations of any sort."

Now Gveld spoke, without looking up. "Stop, Fowl. Stop this. Gundred is as a sister to me. More. She is my fellow warrior. She has done things to humans that no human would ever do."

Myles laughed, because Gveld's comment was either incredibly naive or just plain stupid. "You of all people should not be surprised by what humans will do to each other, especially when they're under orders."

"Don't listen to this toxic human, Gveld," said Gundred. "He is trying to distract you."

"I know that, sister," said Gveld, placing a hand on her comrade's forearm. "He is running down the clock in the vain hope that the pixel specialist will be able to stop our Reclaimers."

"That is exactly what I am doing," agreed Myles. "But that doesn't mean I am not also speaking the truth. So, since there is nothing you can do about it, I shall continue with my hypothetical, if that's what it is, and surely you can spare an ear to listen while I talk."

Gveld snarled. "I don't appear to have a choice."

It was true. They were all stuck in their respective elevators until the ACRONYM agents ceased firing.

Gundred had an idea. "We can destroy the speaker, Gveld."

But Gveld shook her head no, and Myles knew he had found the chink in their armor.

"So, article one for the prosecution was Gundred's supposed Boldart's syndrome. Then I found out that she was not a born Horteknut, which isn't damning evidence in itself, until you cross-reference it with the disappearance of an ACRONYM agent code-named Zelda a few months before Gundred's appearance in the rubble. And even that isn't conclusive, until you realize that Zelda Rubinstein was a famous little person actress in Hollywood movies. I think somebody was being a little obvious with their code name."

Something changed in Gveld. Perhaps she slumped a little, or perhaps her fist closed a notch tighter, so Myles forged ahead.

"But still I wasn't sure. Yes, there's a lot of circumstantial evidence, but no proof. *Give it up, Myles,* I told myself. You are making massive leaps to unlikely conclusions. But then I heard how Gundred was only half-buried by the rubble yet even so lost her ability to speak due to temporary asphyxiation."

"So, what, Mud Boy?" snapped Gundred. "It was worth it. I brought down an ACRONYM facility on my own."

"The thing is," said Myles, "if ACRONYM knew as much about dwarves as I do, they would know about something called *cloacal respiration*."

Gundred made what attorneys would call a rookie mistake, in that she asked a question she should have known the answer to: "Oh, really? And what is *cloacal respiration* supposed to be?"

Gveld knew then. Myles could see it in the sag of her features as the truth hit her square in the heart.

"The cloaca is an orifice that humans do not have but amphibians and dwarves do. In a pinch, a real dwarf can diffuse oxygen through the cloaca. Or, as my brother here might say, and please excuse the scatological language: a real dwarf can breathe through their butt. So, if Ms. Gundred's lower half was sticking out of the rubble, as you say, then she could not have been asphyxiated. I suspect that ACRONYM sacrificed a facility and carefully buried Agent Zelda in the ruins. The trauma was a cover so she would have time to learn the language."

This was quite a speech, especially in dire circumstances, and in his memoirs some fifty years hence, Myles would include it in his top ten monologues.

"My advice, General," continued the Fowl twin, "would be to finish up here and then ask your dear friend to subject herself to a simple scan. You will have your answer in five seconds. In fact, I could do it for you now with my fancy spectacles."

Gveld took several deep breaths, each one catching painfully in her chest. "Is this true?" she asked, then: "Gundred, my sweet sister. Tell me this human speaks false."

"Gveld," said Gundred, and there were tears in her eyes. "Gveld, it's been so long."

"Are you human?" asked Gveld, and there was a pain in her voice that went far beyond her own illness.

Gundred pleaded. "Sister. Let me prove myself. . . ."

"Is it true?" Gveld growled. "Does this despicable boy tell me the truth?"

"It was so long ago. I am something else now. Something in-between. This is my family. You are my sister, and I would die for you."

"Say it," said the Horteknut First. "Tell me."

Gundred found courage from somewhere deep inside and said, "My body may be human, but my heart belongs to you and the dwarves."

Gveld held out her communicator. "Prove it," she said.

And without hesitation Gundred pressed her thumb to the red button flashing on the screen.

Red button, thought Myles. That is probably not good.

He was right. It wasn't.

I do hope that I bought Lazuli enough time to disable the basement charges, but I doubt it.

Once again Myles was right.

He hadn't.

CHAPTER 13
IMMINENT DEATH

The Subbasement
Five Minutes Earlier

If we rewind some minutes before Gundred pressed the DETONATE button, we find Lazuli Heitz was missing her LEP equipment. Not all of it. The standard-issue sunblock was not at the top of her wish list, nor was the pee-straw, which, mercifully, she'd never had to put to the test. But, ideally, she would have faced this Reclaimer with her Oxalis pistol primed to wrap him in genetically modified micro vines, instead of going into battle dressed like a mini version of Myles Fowl without a single armored plate to protect her blue flesh and without any implement that could be considered a weapon.

Unless my mysterious magic shows up again.

Mysterious magic was, she supposed, better than nothing.

The Reclaimer, Vigor, was certainly no class of criminal mastermind, as he did not bother with the melodramatic and pun-laden witticisms typical of that ilk when faced with an opponent.

For example, upon spying Specialist Heitz, Sir Teddy Bleedham-Drye might have quipped, *Ah, Lazuli, it's about time we took our duel to new Heitz.*

Or the pixie Opal Koboi, who was quite the one for shrieking, may have shrieked, *You think you're blue now, Heitz? I'll show you just how blue you can be.*

Which is quite a lengthy shriek, but Opal was a practiced shrieker.

This particular Reclaimer simply body-checked Lazuli through a plastic tarp and into the excavation area without uttering a single word. The air huffed from Lazuli's lungs and she lay in the dust, her eyes rolling back just far enough so that she could see the network of steel rods holding up the building. She should not have been able to see the rods, for a couple of reasons: 1) because they were usually encased in concrete pillars, and 2) because it was generally pitch-black down there when the crews were not working. There was no human crew currently on the job, but a group of Reclaimers had fired up the arc lights so that the underground site was awash in a white glare, and the concrete had been chipped away from the rods so that the aforementioned Reclaimers could smoosh their spitballs around them.

Come on, magic! thought Lazuli. Didn't Myles wake you up?

What was it he'd said? *Your trigger appears to be imminent death, which is morbidly humorous.*

Lazuli heard something between a slash and a rip and knew the Reclaimer had cut through the plastic sheeting.

She wondered, How soon is imminent? This seems pretty imminent.

But it was *nothing doing* on the magic front, it seemed, and Lazuli could not even rise to meet her fate as the dwarf's boot suddenly stamped on her chest, and whatever air she'd had in her lungs left in a blurt.

Blurt, the pixel thought. I'm going out with a *blurt?*

She was tempted to laugh but didn't, because maybe then the magic wouldn't feel that death was imminent.

My mind is melting, she thought. That's what happens when you hang around with the Fowl Twins.

While Lazuli's mind was melting, Vigor set about doing the job he'd been doing for centuries, that being the dispatching of enemies as efficiently as possible. To this end he spun his crystal blade so that the pointy end was aimed at Lazuli's heart, and then covered the pommel with his palm for an extra push.

Imminent, thought Lazuli and managed to raise a hand. Imminent.

Evidently the Reclaimer decided that a little blue hand couldn't stop his thrust, because he plunged straight down. Lazuli felt the cold crystal touch her skin, but it did not pierce it, because the magic finally showed up and did its job—though it took a moment for that fact to register with

Lazuli, as she was too busy watching her life flash before her eyes.

It was only when the crystal blade melted down to the hilt and a concussive force blasted Vigor clear across the basement—and rather unfortunately into one of the rod clusters, playing them like a xylophone—that Lazuli realized she was still alive.

"Ha!" she said, when her breath had returned. "Myles was right. The boy was right."

Of course he was.

But there were still two Reclaimers left to tackle. When her magic had finally shown up it had flitted across her mind that she could use her power to inflict magical damage on the other dwarves, but it seemed that her particular brand of magic was more defensive than offensive, so . . . *If you wouldn't mind, brain, I need a new plan, please.*

No plan arrived, perhaps because Lazuli was distracted by the sight of her own hands glowing orange, with steam rising from the pores.

Concentrate, Specialist, she told herself. *There's a building about to come down on your head.*

The underground chamber was vast by fairy real estate standards, possibly the dimensions of three crunchball fields. The space was so big that the human earthmovers strewn around the excavation site seemed like discarded toys. It was difficult to gauge the size for certain, as it stretched off into darkness beyond the supports. Gathered around the giant central column were the last two Reclaimers, their vinesuits coated with mud and dust. They had noticed Lazuli but seemed perfectly content to let her observe the proceedings, making no move to halt any progress the specialist might make or, for that matter, to help their comrade. The dwarves simply packed themselves inside a transparent blue hemispherical structure and waited.

Lazuli guessed this was a tunnel pod—a superstrong structure used to survive cave-ins.

The pixel was seized by the urge to flee. Who would blame her for removing herself from this basement? She doubted there was a place for her in the pod.

But if I leave here without stopping the detonation, Myles will die for certain.

Because there were some situations that even a Fowl could not talk his way out of.

And also, Lazuli knew that the only reason the Reclaimers were ignoring her was that she was too late. They figured there was nothing to be done.

I need to prove them wrong and do something unexpected, Lazuli realized. I need a plan that's so far out of the box it can't even *see* the box.

And so Specialist Heitz posed a question to herself that no one should ever pose, unless circumstances are so positively dire that good sense no longer applies.

What would Beckett do?

The answer came easily. *Beckett would marshal an army of*

rats to hold up the columns with their furry bodies before declaring himself emperor of all rodents.

The question needed to be modified.

What would Beckett do if marshaling rats were not an option?

Beckett would use whatever was on hand to cobble together an outrageous save-the-day solution.

So, what is at hand?

Earthmovers, dwarves safe in their indestructible blue tunnel pod, not to mention glowing hands. And perhaps less than a minute to combine these elements.

Lazuli got to her feet.

Think big, she told herself. *Think Beckett. Be Beckett.*

Just as a really bad idea was forming in Lazuli's head, her five minutes ran out. Some floors overhead, Gundred pressed the red button, sending the detonation signal to the first spit bomb in the chain. The first column blew, and Lazuli knew that a bad idea would have to suffice. So, like a runner from the blocks, she was off sprinting across the chamber, leaving scorch marks wherever her magic-infused knuckles made contact with the earth.

Dwarves pride themselves on the discretion of their demolition skills. The point being, if no one knew a dwarf had demolished a building, then they would never guess a dwarf had ever even been in the vicinity. In the case of the convention center, they had planted spit bombs deep in the heart of each cable cluster, all linked by a wireless signal networked to organic chips. Myles had guessed that the Reclaimers would remain on sentry duty until the last minute, but for once Myles had been wrong—the dwarves intended to stay on-site until *after* the job was done, safe inside their blue pod, and then pack up and chew their way out.

Lazuli ran, dust rasping in her throat, the explosion shock wave knocking her a few degrees off course, but she tucked her chin and persevered, ignoring the ringing in her ears and the swirling clouds of debris that were obscuring her vision. She could make out the bulk of the massive excavator maybe twenty feet away.

The dwarf. Don't think about the dwarf.

The dwarf entangled in the pilings of the pillar who had been squashed by the chomp of a concrete mouth.

The dwarf you put in that position.

Don't think about it.

On she ran while the pillars were truncated neatly by shaped and focused charges. It was almost surgical. The entire structure would not collapse until the central support came down.

That support cannot come down.

Lazuli reached the giant yellow excavator, hauled herself onto the top of its caterpillar tracks, and from there leaped into the cab, which, of course, had been built for a full-sized human and not a small blue pixel.

Though the color of her skin was not important right now. What was slightly more pertinent was the fact she was without an ignition key.

"But I have magic hands!" Lazuli shouted at the machine. "Magic hands, do you hear me?"

And she wrapped the fingers of those magic hands around the wire cluster below the dash and sent whatever residue lingered in there scurrying into the belly of the engine. She could not contain a hysterical laugh as she thought, Are magic and electricity even compatible?

The excavator roared into enthusiastic life, confirming that combustion engines could indeed run on magic.

All I have to do now is find the drive gear.

Outside the cab, two more columns collapsed, one with a little less finesse than its comrades, spraying steel spears across the space, one *thunk*ing into the seat over Lazuli's head. The basement's ceiling of rock and concrete sagged dangerously with an operatic shriek. The section of the floor that had already been slabbed with concrete cracked as though struck by the hammer of Thor, and a jagged wave spread across it.

"D'Arvit!" Lazuli shouted and immediately regretted the expletive, as dust coated her throat.

After a brief spell of hawking up dust and blood, Lazuli saw through a miraculously clear square inch of windscreen that both Reclaimers were enjoying the spectacle.

Lazuli got very angry very fast.

Those worms are cheering!

Perhaps she could change their tune.

Lazuli dragged a gear lever the size of her torso into

drive, checked that the excavator was pointing roughly the right way, and then climbed under the seat and jammed both feet on the accelerator.

One in a million chance of this working, she thought. One in a billion.

The excavator jolted forward, made a little jumpy by magic, its gigantic shovel gouging troughs in the mud.

Lazuli realized what was happening.

I should have raised the shovel, she thought.

But she needn't have worried. Magic trumped friction, and the vehicle lurched forward. The Reclaimers stopped high-fiving each other pretty quick when they saw what was bearing down on them.

It would have been nice if Lazuli could have seen their faces, but she was wedged in the excavator's footwell, keeping her boots pressed down on the accelerator.

One of the Reclaimers turned to his comrade, his hands held up in a pacifying manner, and he may have said something along the lines of *It's fine, buddy. This pod is indestructible. A mountain could fall on us, and we'd be okay.*

But this guy didn't know Specialist Heitz. She wasn't trying to destroy anything—she was trying to *preserve* something. In this case, the building and everyone in it.

The excavator's shovel scooped up the indestructible tunnel pod at the exact time the last charge blew. A wedge of concrete and steel vaporized, leaving a grinning hole. Heitz promptly—and conveniently—filled that void by tossing in the pod, leaving the two dwarves inside to wonder what exactly had just happened. The immediate result of all this unlikely activity was that, though the building sagged quite alarmingly, it did not collapse.

And there we have the bones of the ACRONYM Convergence. But there was even more to come. . . .

CHAPTER 14

TIC-TAC-TOE

The Convention Center's Central Elevator Shafts

The occupants of the Convention Centre Dublin were experiencing quite drastic mood swings. The ACRONYM agents trapped in the locked multidirectional elevators had gone from irritated to terrified. The agents who had until recently been determined to save their comrades had abandoned that effort entirely and fled the building. And the Horteknut leader was wondering why the entire structure had not collapsed into the dust.

Beckett Fowl was atypically still, crouching in the corner of the elevator, teeth chattering as though the boy were stuck in a loop. And as for Myles Fowl, he was alive when he'd fully expected to be deceased, which made him happy, but he was also puzzled as to how exactly the building remained relatively intact when detonation had obviously taken place. So, on the whole, and given Myles's nature, it would be safe to assume that he was slightly more annoyed to be puzzled than happy to be alive.

"NANNI," he said to his smart glasses, "scan the basement area for humanoid life-forms."

"Umm," said NANNI, "I see three."

Three? thought Myles, letting the *umm* go for now. There should be four.

There were many explanations for the missing heartbeat, including spontaneous molecular relocation, but the most likely reason was that someone was dead.

Someone like his pixel friend Specialist Heitz, perhaps. He had a thought. "NANNI, what are the groupings?"

"Two and one," replied the eyeglasses promptly.

"Good," said Myles. And then to the chattering Beckett: "Best-case scenario, Specialist Heitz is alive."

He took a quick look down at the floor, which had sagged and cracked drastically around the sides but not in the middle, leading him to conclude that the central column was the sole intact support. "That is, until the building collapses," he added, for it was obvious to Myles, a student of architecture and anarchitecture (the architecture of anarchy), that the convention center was destined to crumple in the very near future. Myles was put in mind of a beleaguered circus tent with only its central pole to hold the canvas aloft.

"How are we on the building's systems, NANNI?"

"We still have half the elevators and thirty percent of the shafts, including the top two floors and some communications," said the smart glasses. "And the main power is out, so the center is running on backup systems. Should I open as many elevators as I can?"

Myles considered this. Opening the elevators would certainly be the humane thing to do in the short term, but if Gveld had one more trick up the sleeve of her Sharkgirl suit, then that humaneness would be short-lived, as would the humans who embodied it.

"Not just yet, NANNI," he said. "Let's keep those horrid ACRONYM agents where they might be able to do some good for a change."

Myles thought he might as well try to intimidate the Horteknuts one car over. Perhaps they would simply surrender now, though he doubted it.

"Do you see what happens when you go against the Fowl Twins?" he shouted into the handset, which, amazingly, was still operational. "When will people learn?"

Gveld and Gundred had been tossed about somewhat by the shuddering foundations, but they were sturdy warriors and soon in command of their rattled marbles. Gveld climbed Gundred's frame to get to a standing position, glowering all the way up.

"Human!" Gveld said accusingly to her, as though being involuntarily born into that particular species was in itself a crime.

"I pressed your button!" said Gundred. "I proved myself."

Gveld added another accusation to the mix: "Liar!"

Gundred pinned Gveld to the side of the elevator with

her forearm. "Once, perhaps. But I am a dwarf in my heart."

"Words," said Gveld. "You infiltrated my group to spy on us. You are a liar."

"As are you!" said Gundred. "There is something you are not telling me!"

Myles grew weary of both the bickering and the fact that he was not the center of attention. "If I may interject," he said, "you are both, in point of fact, liars. And if I might elaborate on that: Gundred is in reality a human little person who grew to identify with her undercover role—her legend, if you will. And Gveld is lying through omission. That omission being that she intends to kill many more humans than are in this building."

"What's the Fowl boy talking about?" Gundred asked, pressing Gveld harder into the wall.

Gveld barked a laugh. "Why do you need to know? So you can report back to ACRONYM?"

In Myles's opinion, Gveld was dodging the question, so he felt he had no choice but to answer it himself.

"If this building collapses into the river, it will bring half the docklands with it, including the toll bridge, and the theater, which I believe is hosting an eclipse viewing on their IMAX screen. Thousands will die, including the teens I mobilized, and I cannot allow that to happen."

Gundred was visibly shocked. "Is the Mud Boy right?"

"Mud Boy?" said Gveld. "*You* are a Mud Person. The one I trusted. The one I loved most dearly is everything I despise."

These words lashed Gundred and she relaxed her hold.

"I don't know what happened. I don't remember who I am, but I would never harm you or the band. Believe me, I've had my chances."

"And perhaps you took them," retorted Gveld. "Perhaps you are the reason we lost so many soldiers."

"No!" said Gundred. "*You* are the reason. You lost your way. You are cruel, and this plan was reckless. You involved humans in it."

"Apparently that is a weakness of mine."

Myles had a theory about Gveld's recklessness, but he thought he might resist sharing for once so the dwarves could talk themselves out of time. Already a scintilla of sun was poking itself around the full moon's curve, the light creeping across the river like a slow bleed of yellow watercolor.

Keep talking, thought Myles. Your time is almost up.

But then, somewhat belatedly, due perhaps to the drastic nature of the subsidence, the ACRONYM treasure was shunted into a compartment above the dwarf section of the elevator, announcing its arrival with a loud *thunk* and the illumination of a green roof light.

Gveld moaned, reaching toward the treasure. "It is so close. So very close."

Gundred grasped her leader's shoulders tightly. "Gveld. This day is not lost. There is a way."

Gveld opened her gold teeth just wide enough to spit out an insult, then reconsidered. What if there *was* still a way? After all, she had nothing to lose and immortality to gain.

Gveld nodded once. *Tell me,* the nod said.

Very well, thought Myles, who had, of course, already considered how the building might be utterly collapsed if a person had control of the elevators. We're about to play a game and I am excellent at games. Just ask the Komodo 13 chess computer.

While the Horteknuts huddled, whispering their plans, Myles had NANNI bring up the elevator schematics on his lenses and also set up some shortcuts so he could move things with finger gestures.

To onlookers it will seem as though I am using psychokinesis, thought the Fowl twin. And I most probably will have mastered that skill by the time I'm fifteen.

In this, Myles was being optimistic. He would, in fact, be seventeen before he managed to move an object with his mind. (That object being a large rock, about which he would comment with uncharacteristic levity: *It was not as heavy as Artemis's ego.*)

But back to the present.

Myles glanced over at Beckett, who remained huddled in the corner. "You would enjoy the game that I am reasonably certain is about to take place," he said to his catatonic brother. "There promises to be plenty of action and perhaps an explosion or two should I lose, which is, frankly, unlikely."

Beckett did not react. But then again, Myles had not expected him to.

Traditionally with games of this type—chess, checkers, tic-tac-toe, and so on—players offer each other a courteous handshake or, at the very least, some verbal salutation before the game begins. But in this case a handshake was neither likely nor possible. Gveld simply turned to face her opponent and hissed the following sentence:

"You humans will all die!"

Which impressed Myles, because it is difficult to hiss a sentence containing so few sibilants. It was not, in any form, a salutation, but Myles took it to mean the game was afoot.

"After you, General Horteknut," he said gallantly.

If Gveld was surprised that Myles had perhaps anticipated her new plan, she did not show it; she simply swiped the surface of her communicator. This might not seem like the first move in a deadly game where the consequences were multiple deaths, boxes of broken bone, the echoes of screams, and mingling of the worst body odors, but it was. Deep in the innards of the convention center, one of the elevators under Gveld's control sped laterally to the extremity of its rails. The center's magnetic elevators were smaller than the traditional models, but still the weight shift was considerable, since the car was carrying a burden of two thousand pounds of humanity. The elevator *thunk*ed into its new position and the building, already on tenterhooks stability-wise, actually shuddered, plaster falling from the walls and a door fluttering down from on high like an autumn leaf.

"Ha!" said Gveld.

"Oh, please," said Myles, and he flicked his index finger,

sending one of the elevator cars he controlled careening southward to restore balance to the center.

"He knows!" said Gundred. "The Fowl boy knows what you're doing."

Gveld was not speaking to Gundred unless she had to; she simply repositioned herself so that Myles could not possibly peek at her screen. Then she made her second move, which was to send two elevator cars to the northern wall, piling over four thousand pounds of weight onto that face of the building and causing an alarming yaw. Girders sang like fiddles, and three seagulls flapped through one of the myriad wall cracks like low-rent movie doves. Gas flooding through a broken main in the basement level caught fire, transforming the fractured floor into something resembling the gaping mouth of an active volcano.

Myles was a little disappointed. "In most games of this nature," he commented, "a double move would be counted as illegal and you, Ms. Horteknut, would forfeit a turn. But I suppose this is not most games."

Myles's counter was to swivel one finger, which put a single fully loaded elevator car through an L-shaped ride to the top floor overlooking the river, nicely offsetting Gveld's illegal play and causing the building to right itself.

"I could do this all day," he said. "But your window of opportunity has already closed. The sun has returned, and the authorities are on their way."

Myles knew it was rash to taunt Gveld Horteknut, a homicidal criminal at the end of her rope, but there was a chance that enraging the dwarf would break her concentration. He also knew that he could not, in fact, *do this all day* as he had boasted. Half a dozen more moves in this oversized checkers/tic-tac-toe hybrid game and the convention center would shake itself to smithereens. And the people in the elevator cars, whom Myles himself had opted to leave inside, would not survive the devastation.

I need to end this, Myles thought. Perhaps the oldest trick on the chessboard is in order.

Now, as all chess players know, the oldest trick on the chessboard would be the sacrifice of a pawn, but what pawn could Myles Fowl have in mind? Surely not his own twin.

In spite of Myles's warning regarding windows and their closing, Gveld unsurprisingly opted to play on, confirming this choice by spitting a challenge over her shoulder: "To the death, Mud Boy!"

To which Myles retorted, "Quite the opposite, General Horteknut. To the life, as it were."

"We shall see," said Gveld, and then she spoke to her Number Two, because there was no other choice. "The Mud Boy broke into the building's systems. You break into his. Show me you are a dwarf in your heart. Take control of his elevators."

So, I fight on two fronts, thought Myles. I'm surprised they didn't think of this sooner.

There followed a frankly mindboggling series of maneuvers, all caught on camera by both bystanders and broadcast media, where it almost seemed as though the convention center itself was coming alive and seeking to throw off the bonds of its foundations. The edifice shook and shuddered, reared up and listed, all accompanied by a deafening cacophony of howls and roars as the concrete and steel were stressed and compacted into shapes they were never meant to assume. Fourteen hundred panes of glass—which the manufacturers had claimed to be unbreakable—shattered, and the shards fell in tinkling showers. Water tanks ruptured, sending mini waterfalls cascading off the various balconies that fought a losing battle with the raging gas flames, and solar panels shimmered to earth, then exploded in sparkling blossoms. It was, as a Radio Nova radio host put it during his live broadcast, like the end of days.

Armageddon is here, folks. So sacrifice a goat and dig yourself a hole.

Inside the animated building, Myles Fowl was under pressure, or rather, NANNI was. With every thrust and parry, the graphene-housed computer seemed to be losing the battle with the more powerful Horteknut devices that overflowed her buffers with malicious commands.

"'Screw your courage to the sticking place,'" quoted Myles. "A few more moves and we will end this, NANNI."

But, alas, a few more moves were not to be, as Gundred had apparently found a pinhole in NANNI's firewalls.

"I have him," she said. "We can take back all the elevators, but it will cost us air-conditioning and some shafts."

"Do it!" snapped Gveld. "Do it *now!*"

Gundred obeyed the order, and Myles could do nothing but watch the progress of Gveld's elevators on his lenses. Gveld was all in, plotting the only available route through the shafts to send all of her elevators to the top of the building for a coordinated pile-driver action. Myles imagined that she would release the dampers and send the cars plummeting to earth, where they would pulverize the floor entirely and leave the building no choice but to collapse in a heap of rubble.

"You left me a way through," she gloated. "I expected more from you."

"You were right to expect more," said Myles. "I left you a way through and you took it. You control the elevators, but you relinquished some shafts to me. And you have placed your cars in my shafts. Delivered the mice to the traps, as it were."

"More human doublespeak," said Gveld. "What do I care for shafts? Prepare to be buried alive, Fowl. I doubt you have enough oxygen in that box to last you both. My dearest wish is that one of you kills the other for five minutes of air."

Gveld released her stacked elevators, which should have plummeted earthward, smashed into the foundations, and made an unappealing meat stew of the humans inside. But, ironically for a dwarf, the Horteknut general had underestimated the importance of shafts. It is true that, with traditional elevators, shafts are merely glorified holes for cars to pass through. However, with multidirectional magnetic rail elevators, the shafts are as important as the cars, as the rails are on wall-mounted turntables that rotate automatically to send a car in the direction it wishes to go. So, consequently and crucially, if a person controlled the shafts, then that person could also control the turntables. And if that person were Myles Fowl, then those elevators were going where he wanted them to go, or rather, staying where he wanted them to stay. With a click of his fingers, Myles locked his shaft turntables in the horizontal attitude, and Gveld's cars not only remained stacked on the top floor but also balanced out the entire building somewhat.

"The elevators are stuck!" said Gundred, pounding the screen of her device, which of course had no effect on the situation.

"Oh, don't sulk so," said Myles. "You have been outmaneuvered by Myles Fowl. You are not even the first one today, and you will certainly not be the last."

Gveld beat her fists on the transparent wall. "Fowl!" she said. "Fowl."

"They all say that," Myles noted, absently straightening his tie. "And then they try to kill me."

Gveld stopped her pounding and fixed Myles with a murderous gaze. Myles could have sworn that the rune tattoos on her cheek were glowing, which was probably impossible but improbably possible. And, as Myles was learning, the border between those two countries was shrinking by the day.

"Kill you," she said. "Good. Absolutely. I shall kill you both. But first I want you to know that your parents are dead." Gveld raised her phone and traced a pattern on the surface. "There. I have sent the kill command. Axborn—remember him?—will gut your dear family like fish with his beloved homemade blade, the *skovl*. Your precious mother and father will watch their own innards slide onto the floor."

Myles winced. "That is quite an image. But do not fret on my parents' account, as someone will be there to stop your burly assassin."

Gveld might have laughed some minutes earlier, before she had been so comprehensively hoodwinked by Myles Fowl.

"And who might stop him?" she asked now with a serious visage affixed. "The buried pixel? You? Your twin brother? Perhaps you might try if the two of you were not stuck here in front of me plain as worms on a platter."

In response, Myles simply plucked the spectacles from his face. When he folded the frames, Beckett disappeared. For, of course, Beckett was a hologram. The same hologram that had been running around Dalkey Island for the past several months bamboozling the LEP surveillance, and that had, until more recently, been beamed from the arm of Myles's glasses.

"I am here, it's true," he said. "But Beckett has never been here. I must bring him to visit when they rebuild this place. Now, as you can see, your warriors are defeated. Your plan has failed utterly."

As if on cue, the convention center's emergency power decided to shut off, which automatically opened all the multidirectional elevators but not the traditional cable ones. So now the ACRONYM agents were free, but Fowl and fairy were locked in their own respective elevators.

"Ah," said Myles. "And there is the final nail in your coffin. There is nothing you can do but accept that you are beaten and wait for the LEP to take you into the custody you so richly deserve."

Myles had thought Gveld Horteknut could not get any angrier.

He was wrong.

The Fowl twin's general manner did that to a person.

That and his face.

CHAPTER 15

BLOOD ON THE ROCKS

Dalkey Island

On the Fowl island, two people were trying very hard to stick to their respective orders. Axborn of the Horteknut Seven's instructions were undoubtedly the more straight-forward in that they only had two steps. He mentally reviewed them as he lay in a shallow ambush trench on the beach below the Fowl residence, a building which, in Axborn's unimpressed opinion, looked like a higgledy-piggledy assembly of children's building blocks.

Step one: Keep an eye on the LEP surveillance feed in case the Fowl Twins somehow returned to the island. And if they did, then kill all the humans on the island. And all meant *all*.

Axborn had asked whether seals counted as humans and was told, *No, they do not.*

And step the second: If the order came through to kill all

humans on the island, then kill all the humans on the island even if the twins had not returned.

Axborn would have preferred to skip step one altogether and simply proceed directly to step two, as step one was, in his opinion, long-winded and confusing. Also, step one had the extra element of surveilling the surveillance, which was not as straightforward as it sounded. The LEP, in spite of their promises to desist from spying, were still keeping an eye on the island from one of their satellites. This surveillance, which Axborn had open on his phone, consisted of a bird's-eye view of Dalkey Island with live icons representing the Fowls.

Axborn had pointed to the trails left by Myles and Beckett and said to Vigor, "Look, the Fowl boys are already on the island."

And he was told by Vigor, "No, Axborn, you total dunce. I explained this. Those trails are avatars set up by Myles Fowl to outfox the surveillance. We can't switch them off or the LEP will know we hacked into their feed."

Axborn did not understand any of this aside from the fact he was being called a dunce.

"So, can the LEP see me?"

"Not as long as you're wearing your vinesuit. It will show up as vegetation and not raise any flags. Just to be safe, you shall burrow into the earth for an extra layer of camouflage."

"So, do I kill the yellow trails?" Axborn had asked.

"No," Vigor had told him. "The avatars are on a loop, which I was able to flag as yellow. The real twins will deviate from this loop, and when they do, their avatars will turn red."

"So, I kill the red things?"

"Yes. Anything red shows up, you kill it. And then get out of there before the LEP arrive."

"What about that brown thing?"

"That's a house."

"Do I . . . ?"

"No, you don't kill the house."

"Just the red things? What about those gray things?"

Vigor had sighed for a little longer than necessary, and perhaps Axborn would not have been too unhappy if he knew that his superior looked decidedly pasty now, having been mashed into the innards of a building support.

"Those are the parents. Look, here's what I'll do: I can make it so that if either of the twins shows up, all the human icons turn red. So here's a little memory trick: *gray is okay, but red is dead*. Got it?"

Axborn repeated the rhyme, which he considered a little patronizing. "Gray is okay, but red is dead."

"Good. So, kill only red, unless the kill order comes through. Then kill everything."

"Do I . . . ?"

"No, dummy. Not the house. You can't kill a house."

Axborn checked his phone now. Nothing red and no kill order.

You can too kill a house, he thought. I could burn that place to the ground—did you ever think of that, Vigor? Who's the dummy now?

* * *

Beckett Fowl was also trying his very best to stick to his instructions, which were more complicated than the Reclaimer's. "You must follow a very specific path back to the villa," Myles had told him after they'd escaped their captivity in the dwarves' HQ. "A route that is cobbled together from seven stages of your avatar's various routes. If you go the exact way I tell you, the dwarf guard should not see you until it's too late."

And then Myles laid out the route in terms Beckett would remember.

"Any necessary combat maneuvers I will leave to your discretion," Myles had added. He was tempted to tell Beckett how to fight, but that would have been akin to telling a monkey how to peel a banana, so he simply said, "Farewell, brother mine. I trust you to save our parents should they need saving."

"I will save them, Myles. And you'd better stop that building from collapsing."

"Have no fear, Beck. You may consider that building un-collapsed."

The boys wrist-bumped and went their separate ways, which was unusual in itself, because the Fowl Twins generally went the same way.

Beckett had a third dolphin drop him off at a shingled beach on the slope behind Villa Éco. Actually, *drop him off* is a misleading term, as the dolphin, whose name was Eeeeoooo-eh-eh-eh-flaaarb was famous in the dolphin community on account of her tail strength, and she more than justified her reputation by flipping Beckett directly onto the grassy ledge that was the starting point of his journey to the Fowl homestead.

Beckett enjoyed being flipped off a dolphin's tail immensely and vowed that he would beg Myles to submit tail-flipping as an Olympic sport when this whole Horteknut thing was over. Beckett had already badgered Myles into filling out the complicated Olympic Programme Commission's inclusion form for several other potential sports, including troll wrestling and the long fart. Beckett was confident that he could bring home the gold in these sports, having certainly put in the hours of training.

Beckett had written his travel instructions on his forearm, and he consulted them now. Number one was *Get off at the ledge where I fought the dwarves.*

Check.

Next was *Walk directly to the monks' well*, which was where all the trouble with the troll venom got started (see LEP file: *The Fowl Twins*). Beckett remembered now, as he walked along a path worn in the grass, that Myles had designed and 3-D–printed a most excellent cross-section model of the island. It illustrated, among other things, how it was possible to have a fresh-water well on a small salt-water–bordered island as long as a person didn't draw the fresh water too quickly, as this would result in a rise of salt-water levels. Beckett wished now that he had thanked his twin for the effort instead of pretending not to understand simply to infuriate Myles.

I give your model an A++, he broadcast into his scar, even though Myles did not believe that anyone was qualified to grade him on any subject, except perhaps physical education, which he didn't consider actual education anyway.

Step three in Beckett's route was a series of cartwheels toward Artemis Senior's office, where his father had scolded the twins earlier in the week. Beckett knew that his father and mother had planned to watch the eclipse from Villa Éco's observation roof deck just outside the office, but Myles had assured him that Mum and Dad wouldn't be able to spot him, for they would be locked in the safe room while Axborn awaited instructions. The ideal outcome for this mission would be for Beckett to get his parents off the island before Axborn even realized he was on it. But, obviously, if Axborn were guarding the safe room door, a showdown would be unavoidable.

Beckett was 180 degrees into his third cartwheel when it became suddenly obvious even from his upside-down vantage point that Myles's plan was a bust. The blond twin would have to rely on improvisation—which, fortunately, was the only type of plan in which Beckett Fowl had even the slightest interest.

What happened to foil Myles's plan was this: just as Beckett reached the monks' well, the overly aggressive and frankly distasteful dwarf with the testosterone-loaded name Axborn received the kill order from Gveld Horteknut some miles upriver.

"Hooray!" cried Axborn, or some word to that effect.

And without a moment's consideration for anything except his order, the dwarf sprang from the shallow ambush trench.

As Beckett cartwheeled, he noticed the spade-shaped digging tool that doubled as Axborn's weapon of choice. It was on the dwarf's right forearm, and Beckett hazarded a guess that perhaps the Reclaimer's intention was to fill in the trench he'd excavated.

But then he saw the dwarf stride with some purpose toward Villa Éco's front door, and he revised his guess to: I think that fellow intends to murder Mum and Dad.

As this was unthinkable, Beckett had no choice but to cartwheel away from the proscribed route and make himself a target.

The moment Beckett left the safety of his path, Axborn's phone sounded an alarm over and over until the dwarf stopped what he was doing, removed the sharpened skovl from his forearm, and checked the screen of his communicator.

"Yes!" he crowed. "Finally."

For his killing orders had suddenly been streamlined:

Do Kill: All the humans on the island.

Do Not Kill: Seals or the house. *Unless seals interfere with killing the humans.*

Axborn had added that last piece himself.

And bonus good news: he didn't even have to search for the Fowl who had set off the alarm, as the Mud Boy's avatar was pulsing.

He's right behind me, Axborn realized. I bet he tries a surprise attack. Typical human. This will be so funny.

* * *

As it turned out, Axborn was correct in his assumptions, both regarding the sneak attack taking place and the attack being somewhat funny—initially at least, because while it was true that Beckett preferred honorable combat as a rule, on this occasion his parents were in danger, and that fact trumped sportsmanship. Therefore, Beckett threw himself into a floor routine that would make Olympian gymnasts cry into their protein shakes as he approached Axborn at high speed and varying altitudes.

Axborn didn't even bother to turn around, for, while he might have been slow in many ways, he was very quick when it came to combat. And so, just when Beckett believed this fight might end with a single blow, something unexpected happened: Axborn whistled, and the sleeve of his vinesuit unspooled from one of his arms and twirled into the air behind the dwarf.

Beckett couldn't help thinking, That vine looks like it's aimed right at me.

And indeed, it was, for even though Beckett was in the middle of a maneuver that he had dubbed an AFWEBS, or **A**rabian **F**ront **W**ith **E**xtra **B**eckett **S**auce, the vine tracked his movement perfectly. For those who might be interested, an Arabian front is an aerial movement where the gymnast does a half turn, then flips twice in the air before landing. Beckett liked to flap his elbows like a chicken while performing this advanced move, thus providing the extra Beckett sauce.

However, extra sauce or no, the vine plucked Beckett out of the sky and wound about him in slick coils, squeezing tight enough to make his ribs groan. It was all Beckett could do to keep one arm out of the package, for all the good that might do him, trussed as he was neater than a harpoon handle in the coils of a sailor's rope.

The vine delivered Beckett to Axborn's feet, and the hulking dwarf leered down at him. "Hello, Mud Boy," he said. "You've met my little kreperplont. His name is Bud, which is short for Budacious. These kreperplonts are one of our big secrets. The dwarves, I mean. We have many big secrets."

It was perhaps ironic that, although Beckett was a polyglot, he found it difficult to understand English spoken with Axborn's almost impenetrable accent.

"You're doing really well with English," Beckett said in the Horteknut dialect of Gnommish. "But we can speak your language if you prefer. It's got less words and is also a lot cooler."

"Yes!" exclaimed Axborn in his own tongue, as if he had scored a point. "It is a lot cooler, you idiot!"

"I like Budacious," said Beckett, trying to stay calm, though he was very close to panic due to the restriction of his movements.

"Me too," said Axborn. "Did you know that Horteknuts are often placed into their kreperplonts as babies?"

Why does everybody lecture me? Beckett wondered before answering, "No. I totally did not know that."

"It is true, vile human," said Axborn. "I was delivered

into Bud's embrace. We grew up together, in fact, and each vine, leaf, and tendril does what I tell it to do. Including holding you in their grip and forcing you to watch while I kill your vile parents."

"That's mean," said Beckett.

Axborn fitted the skovl to his bare forearm. "It would be mean. But you are a human, and you deserve what you get because of some things you did a long time ago that I don't care about."

Beckett attempted to bond. "That long-time-ago stuff is called *history*," he said. "And I don't care about it, either."

"Me, too, neither," said Axborn, essentially agreeing with himself using questionable grammar. "But Gveld told me your family did things with a tunnel and gold. I think there were some kittens in there, too. So you deserve to watch your parents die."

Beckett could believe that some of his sneakier ancestors might have been involved in tunnel-and-gold shenanigans, but no Fowl would ever harm a kitten (except maybe Artemis).

"There were no kittens!" he shouted in a tone that apparently the dwarf did not appreciate, because Axborn made a funnel from his tongue and whistled a couple of notes until the kreperplont tightened its grip on Beckett.

"Shout not, human," said the Reclaimer, "or there will be trouble for you."

Like I could be in more trouble, thought Beckett, taking tiny, rib-creaking breaths.

"Now, my loyal Budacious and I must be about our orders," the dwarf said, making a few practice thrusts with his blade. "My skovl has human blood to spill."

And then, in response to another note-specific whistle from Axborn, the vine hoisted Beckett aloft and trailed him behind the dwarf, who strode along the beach toward the villa whistling a merry tune.

Time to lose the rag, thought Beckett, and wriggle out of here.

Losing the rag was, as Myles had told him, a whimsical phrase meaning to become suddenly agitated and was arguably based on the older phrase *Loosing the rage*. There were, Myles had inevitably proceeded to expound, several other possible origins for the term, which he listed in some detail, until Beckett actually did lose the rag.

As he did again now.

Beckett was a slippery customer by nature, and had historically proved almost impossible to keep ahold of. In fact, during his toddlerhood, when Artemis was in Limbo (see LEP file: *The Lost Colony*), Beckett Fowl had retired four human nannies, and two of those had come with special-forces training. They simply could not be responsible for the boy's safety. One of the nannies, a Sergeant Dirge McDoon previously of the SAS, left his quite-shrill resignation message with the answering service. A message that included the passage: "I cannae take it, Missus Fowl. The lad is a security nightmare. He nivver sleeps. Wee Beckett learned to walk in an afternoon, and by the next day he was jumping over walls. I tried to catch hold of him, I did truly. But you may as well try to catch a greased seal. You might as well attempt to hold on to a wisp o' the wind. It's nae natural. The bairn is not . . ." (From this point on Sergeant McDoon's testimonial dissolves into sobs and sniffles.)

There were other messages and letters, but you get the gist: Beckett was difficult to contain. He learned early on that the most effective way to escape even the tightest grip was to move unpredictably. Never follow a full-body jerk with another full-body jerk, for example. Mix things up. And this was the philosophy he employed now during his tantrum. Beckett thrashed and roiled, contracted and expanded, vibrated and squirmed in his efforts to wear out the tendril. Even a kreperplont must get tired at some point, he reasoned. Then maybe it would lower him a little so that his free arm could grab on to something useful.

Axborn was amused by Beckett's antics.

"It is true what they say, Mud Boy," he called over his shoulder. "You are indeed the slow learner. Here is a lesson you would be wise to learn quickly."

He whistled again and a thin tendril reached out and slapped Beckett on the cheek, leaving a nasty welt. Beckett flinched, which is unavoidable when struck by foliage, and then continued in his diverse thrashings with only the briefest of pauses.

Another whistle, and another sharp strike on the cheek, this time drawing blood, and while it seemed as though Beckett might have avoided the second blow with a simple duck of his chin, which would have been well within his capabilities, it also seemed as though the twin had accepted the blow on purpose. People who did not know Beckett might possibly exclaim, *Good grief, I do believe the boy's had an idea*, or words to that effect, but in actual fact Beckett did not generally have ideas in the traditional sense, if ideas are defined as thoughts that suggest a course of action. Beckett acted on instincts, those being the inheritable tendencies of an organism to take complex action without involving reason. Myles had, during a relatively calmer moment when the twins' lives had not been in any immediate danger, tried to explain this to Beckett, who could not have cared less about inheritable tendencies, so Myles reduced the theory to a single interesting statement: *Simply put, brother mine, when you act on instinct, it is because our grandfather once had an idea.*

Which was just intriguing enough to penetrate Beckett's mental defenses.

So, although Beckett did not even know precisely why he wanted his own blood drawn, he knew exactly what to do with it when it pulsed onto his cheek. He smeared the viscous liquid across the palm of his free hand and made one final desperate lunge toward the pebbled beach.

Thanks, Granddad, he thought.

If Beckett had been hoping that his entire person would touch down, then he must have been dismayed, for the only part of him to make contact with the beach's pebbled surface was his bloodied hand, and even that barely grazed a single flat stone.

And following that final gargantuan thrust, Beckett seemed to accept defeat and hung limply in the kreperplont's gnarled embrace as Axborn took the shingled path from the beach to the main house.

To kill Mum and Dad, thought Beckett.

Unless . . .

Unless . . .

But he could not even complete the thought, for there is an inherently Irish belief that happy thoughts jinx happy endings. Usually the Fowl twin did not indulge in this kind of superstitious twaddle, but today, he was prepared to grasp at straws.

The path to Villa Éco was a short one, and on this Sunday afternoon, with the post-eclipse light creeping across the island, the surroundings were quite melodramatic. There was even an obliging mist rolling from the crags of Howth on the outer rim of Dublin Bay. Beckett, who was usually a major fan of spooky nature, had no time for this vista as his head was chock-full not of despair, as one might reasonably expect, but hope.

Axborn had set the screen on his wrist communicator to *reflect* and was using it as a rearview mirror to check on his captive.

"Hello, up there, Mud Boy!" he called cheerily to the elevated twin. "You didn't see this coming, I bet. No one ever does. My kreperplont is the best and coolest of all vines. He has won three rosettes from the secret dwarf games, which I shouldn't tell you about, because they are a secret. I never even mention them to humans unless they will shortly be dead, like you."

Usually Beckett would jump on a wacky conversation-starter like this, but he was concentrating on not completing his hopeful thought in case he would jinx it while still remaining hopeful, which he was finding was an incredibly difficult state of mind to maintain.

"Very well, don't talk," said Axborn, a little disappointed. "Save your breath for screaming."

The dwarf took the slight incline to the front door at a strange angle, as though leaning into a heavy wind, because, as strong as the kreperplont was, Beckett needed to be counterbalanced.

With every step Axborn took, Beckett felt his own strength ebb away, as restricted breathing diminished his energy, which Myles had once told him had something to do with oxygen in his bloodstream. And as of now, quite a lot of blood seemed to be streaming down his face.

At least when I'm dead I'll stop bleeding, he thought, and it was without a doubt the second-most negative thing ever to cross Beckett's mind, right after *Axborn is going to kill Mum and Dad*.

And just when Beckett was down to the last grain of sand in his egg timer of hope, Axborn was blindsided by what seemed like a furry cannonball, which sent him staggering to starboard.

CHAPTER 16
SILLY TROLL

IT QUICKLY became obvious, when the cannonball grew claws and teeth, that it was not in fact a cannonball, but a living thing.

"Whistle Blower!" called Beckett. "You got my signal."

If you ever have need of me, paint my feeding stone red.

The toy troll did not reply, as he was busy tearing at Axborn's vine helmet while growling his way through a rough approximation of . . .

"It's our theme song!" exclaimed Beckett. "The Regrettables' theme song."

The twin thought his heart might burst with pride, but the fact that a kreperplont was squeezing the organ's valves might also have had something to do with it.

It took Axborn a moment to realize that he was under attack, but once that fact hit home, the Reclaimer recovered quickly. It was not the first time the dwarf had been under attack, or even the first time he'd tangled with a troll—not that he was yet aware that his assailant was a troll, as Whistle Blower's breed was so rare that toy trolls were virtually nonexistent, and most fairies would never see one in their lifetimes.

But regardless of whether he could categorize his assailant or not, Axborn had several sequences of practiced moves he could employ in a surprise attack situation. The first priority was to regroup, and to this end Axborn knelt on the ground and drew in his extremities, shielding as much of himself as possible while he assessed how much danger he was actually in. He whistled a few instructions to his kreperplont, which sealed up any crevices in his body armor, leaving only his skovl arm partially exposed.

It became clear almost immediately that while his attacker was certainly enthusiastic, the troll's vigor was no match for the tough hide of a kreperplont, and although it was true that Axborn's beloved vine was being shorn of bark, it would take several hours at this rate for the injuries to be anything like fatal to Budacious.

Thus comforted, the Reclaimer launched his counterattack, which was swift and efficient. Whistle Blower may have been an instinctive young buck when it came to a frenetic bust-up, but Axborn was a trained special-forces operative clad in functional bio-armor.

All it took was a few whistles for Axborn to weaponize a vine and send it flashing Whistle Blower's way like a bolt of organic lightning. The vine curled its tip into a vegetative fist and clobbered the toy troll in the side of his mohawked skull. The stunned troll blinked in surprise, and that was all the time it took for the kreperplont to truss him up like a tiny hog ready for the barbeque spit. To add insult to injury, Axborn ordered the creeper to tie a bow at the end of the package.

The dwarf spat a stream of blood through his square teeth and grinned. "That was good with the trying, tiny troll," he admitted. "But we fight as one, my kreperplont and I. We are unique even among my people."

Whistle Blower struggled valiantly against his restraints, but it was patently obvious that the toy troll was wasting his energy.

Axborn stood and whistled so that both Beckett and Whistle Blower were elevated and separated.

I have summoned my friend to his death, thought Beckett, which was an unusual thought for the boy, firstly because it was quite negative, and secondly because it was succinct and comprehensible to a third party should a third party be able to read his mind. To explain, Beckett's inner monologues were usually both rambling and random, and they rarely dwelled on blame or guilt. For example, Myles had once hypnotized his twin in an attempt to understand his thought process, and Beckett had mumbled the following: *Never trust a donut, because donuts look all sparkly and stuff but are empty on the inside.*

Which was about the most intelligible thing he'd said for the entire session.

But back to the present:

Axborn swished his blade a few times to warm up his killing arm and called up to his prisoners, "I am truly enjoying your doomed attacks, but to you this entire campaign of war must seem regrettable."

Beckett frowned. *Regrettable?* It *was* regrettable, he thought morosely. Maybe the Regrettables *is* the right name for our team. We can't even beat a plant.

Below him on the path, Axborn tootled a whistle that resulted in Budacious crashing the captives together in the manner of orchestral cymbals.

"I am doing that just for the fun," said the dwarf, confirming just how wide his mean streak was.

Protected as they were by bio-armor, Beckett and Whistle Blower barely felt the impact, but their self-esteem was shattered.

Axborn ballooned his cheeks for a further whistle, and Beckett thought, Allow me. And he whistled the cymbal command, sending himself speeding toward Whistle Blower.

The troll had just enough time to brace himself before the two friends crashed into each other, but this time Whistle Blower held on for long enough to say, "You speak to plants now?"

Beckett was about to deny this when he realized: I *do*. I speak to plants. This one, anyway.

He tried the whistle again and once more the friends were bashed together.

Axborn chided his kreperplont. "Calm down, Budacious. There will be plenty of unnecessary violence later."

That was not Budacious, thought Beckett. That was me: Beckett Fowl, the Plant Master.

Beckett grabbed on to Whistle Blower's baby banana–sized tusks. "I knew you'd come back," he said. "My elbows told me."

Whistle Blower rolled his eyes. One of the few theories Beck had any faith in was his own about having psychic elbows.

"Of course, they did," said the troll, as clearly as he could with digits wrapped around his tusks.

"And I do talk to plants," whispered Beckett. "Are you ready?"

Whistle Blower's response to this was a look so menacing that Beckett was relieved the menace was not directed at him, but even so he promptly released his grip on the troll's elongated incisors.

"Sorry about that." he called as he swung away. "Friends?"

"Friends," confirmed the troll.

Then Beckett made a funnel with his tongue and blew a sharp whistle.

Budacious instantly relinquished his grip on the Regrettables, and they dropped to the earth the way cats might, that is to say landing on their feet ready for fight or flight.

In this case, it was most definitely *fight*.

Axborn immediately noticed the change in counterbalance and retracted Budacious's tendrils to cover his own arms.

"It seems my Bud has grown weary," said the Reclaimer. "A little dehydrated, perhaps. No matter. I will kill you right now. It messes with my timetable a little, but these things happen."

Axborn slashed the air with his skovl as if warming it up. "Very well, runts," he said. "Who goes first? Let's get this over with. I have places to go and parents to kill."

As a point of information, the Dalkey Island beach confrontation was submitted for consideration as a singularity as it was the only time such a battle took place, specifically between a human, a toy troll, and a dwarf. The confrontation was not ratified, however, due to two objections:

1. A human, a dwarf, and a troll were previously involved in the Fowl Manor siege (though not a toy troll; see LEP file: *Artemis Fowl*).

And . . .

2. The Dalkey Island beach confrontation could be seen as an extension of the ACRONYM Convergence.

But to return to the confrontation itself:

Whistle Blower decided that he would go first, even though the little troll had not understood the particulars of Axborn's challenge. The toy troll roared as best he could, considering his tiny vocal cords and lung capacity. His vocal efforts did not have the desired effect, unless the desired effect was the shudder of chuckles that momentarily overcame Axborn.

"Oh, look," said the dwarf. "The puppy wants to play. Come on, fella. Come and have a try."

It must have seemed funny to a trained killer that the diminutive fur ball would persist with his aggression in spite of the obvious mismatch. It was like a stinkworm taking on a python.

Axborn removed the skovl and balanced it on his head like a silly hat. "Look, little stinkworm. I am without any defense."

And then came the ultimate insult to the toy troll: Axborn closed both eyes.

Which turned out to be something of a tactical error, as Axborn really should have known that his kreperplont was not simply pooped. After all, the two had been through shallow and deep together. But, as often happened with the Regrettables, their opponent underestimated them, which was to cost Axborn dearly, both physically and emotionally, considering the demeaning trauma he was about to endure.

Whistle Blower did not have to be a trans-species polyglot to know that Axborn was taunting him, and so piqued was he by this rude display that he sprang from a low rock in a full-frontal rage attack that would have left him wide open for a fatal strike in other circumstances.

But these were not other circumstances, and Axborn's eyes were shut. In fact, the Reclaimer was considering chanting a dwarf nursery rhyme that was not very complimentary toward trolls:

> *Silly troll, silly troll,*
> *Fell into a deep dark hole.*
> *Humans beat him with a pole,*
> *Silly troll, silly troll.*

Silly troll, thought Axborn, and snickered just as Whistle Blower crashed ineffectively into his vinesuit.

Which was what Axborn had anticipated would happen, but it was not actually what *did* in fact happen. Axborn snickered, but Whistle Blower did not crash into his armor, because the vinesuit conveniently opened a toy-troll-sized hole just as he impacted. This meant that Whistle Blower's attack was not ineffective in the least. In fact, it proved to be very effective indeed, as toy trolls are pound-for-pound the third-strongest creatures on the planet, after dung and rhinoceros beetles, which still did not make the tiny troll anywhere near as strong as Axborn, but it certainly gave him enough force to rock the Reclaimer back on his heels, dislodging the skovl from its perch and cracking a couple of dwarf ribs.

"Silly troll," said Axborn, as the words had already been en route from his brain. And then: "Aaaaaarrrrrrpnnnnn!"

Which was a more appropriate response to broken ribs, but still should be dissected, as it gives us a glimpse into Axborn's psyche.

The *aaaaa* was a typical involuntary vocal reaction to sudden pain.

The *rrrrr* was stage two of the reaction, which demonstrated that the warrior was angry that he had been injured. And . . .

The *pnnnn* was the dwarf's attempt to internalize his reaction, so that he might:

1. Pretend that he was not, in fact, injured.

And . . .

2. Not draw attention to his own presence from other possible combatants.

But still the dwarf did not realize that his kreperplont had been hijacked. And why would he? The very idea was preposterous. Unfortunately for him, Beckett Fowl specialized in the preposterous, had a degree in the ridiculous, and was a doctor of the unbelievable.

Once Axborn had managed to subdue his own pain response, he set about reacting, and to this end whistled a command to his kreperplont.

Crush the troll was the essence of his command, and he released the section of vine on his right leg to carry out the order.

Beckett Fowl prevented the liquidation of his friend's organs by whistling an order of his own, which freed up

Axborn's left leg and set the two sections of vine tangling with each other.

Beckett could not help smiling, as it seemed for all the world as if the tendrils were performing one of those extremely complicated handshake routines that inevitably concluded with a high five. This time, however, no high five was forthcoming, as the tendrils became entangled with each other more comprehensively than two phone-charging cords tossed into a handbag.

Axborn cottoned to what was going on and, forgetting the point of the *pnnnnn* portion of his previous exclamation, opened his mouth to proclaim his disbelief. It was this parting of the lips that was to be his undoing on the kreperplont-control front, for the moment Whistle Blower noticed a flash of tooth, he decided to put the dwarf's whistling apparatus out of action. This was accomplished with a roundhouse swing of the left fist, which mashed Axborn's lip like raw steak. His lips split and swelled immediately, as though being pumped from the inside.

Whistle Blower drew back his fist before the dwarf's remaining teeth made short work of it. A little-known fact about dwarf teeth is that even though they are referred to casually in the normal classifications, they are, in fact, all molars. No incisors or canines—crushers each and every one—and to a dwarf, an entire toy troll would be little more than an hors d'oeuvre. And so Whistle Blower was perfectly correct to sharply withdraw his digits, for this Reclaimer was far from down and out.

Axborn spat blood, then attempted further whistling, which was corrupted by the air's passage through his pulped lips, and instead of ordering Budacious to attack the Fowl twin, he ordered it to *knit a sweater of ants*, which confused the creeper so much that it went into a spasm and fell away from Axborn completely, scurrying down the beach into the water, where it was picked up the following day by LEPretrieval.

And just like that, threat number one was neutralized. Axborn was left without armor or clothes, aside from a knee-length shift and the crumbling coating of clay-based sun protection that many dwarves paint on just in case.

Beckett had mixed feelings about the kreperplont's tumbling exit. He was glad they wouldn't have to tangle further with an innocent plant, but he would have dearly liked to keep it around as a new member of the Regrettables and maybe teach it to juggle chain saws.

Whistle Blower detached himself completely from the dwarf and lined up beside Beckett. The message was clear: two against one. Classic triangle brawl.

Axborn's lip quivered at the loss of his bio-armor, and it seemed like he might actually weep for the kreperplont, but then he shook his head like a wet dog and plastered on his game face.

"That was a neat trick, human," admitted the dwarf, hitching his shift and squatting to reclaim his skovl. "But one dwarf with his blade is still more than a match for two pups."

There was more Axborn wanted to say, about how tough he was and how much pain he intended to inflict on his opponents, and so on and so forth, but he was feeling a little insecure about the mumble factor in his voice, and he wanted to put this whole episode behind him so he could swallow a few anti-inflammatories and fish Budacious out of the water. So he decided to end this confrontation now, before his mouth got him into even more trouble.

In the movies, climactic hand-to-hand fights tend to be stretched out over several minutes so that viewers feel like they've gotten their money's worth, but in the real world, it's more often the case that whoever lands the first decent strike wins. The Reclaimer/Regrettables' tussle mostly followed that rule, except for the fact that it could be argued that there were two winners, but also two losers, which might seem confusing.

To explain:

Whistle Blower and Beckett launched a beautifully coordinated attack, which to an observer might have seemed as though the pair had been practicing it for years. The troll went high and the boy went low, both keeping an eye on the skovl, which could, theoretically, do both of them in with a single slash. Axborn decided in the moment to use the implement in shield mode to bat away the oncoming troll, who he reasoned (correctly) would attempt to further damage his lips and gums. His mistake was to underestimate the toy troll's ability to manipulate himself in the air. Whistle Blower wrapped his toes around the skovl's blade and used the metal as a springboard to propel himself toward Axborn's mashed mouth.

Meanwhile, Beckett was swinging in a low arc, which should have brought him nicely in line with the dwarf's kneecap so he could administer one of his trademark cluster punches. All that Beckett could hope for was that he wouldn't be in the line of fire, so to speak.

All very well and good, you might think, but you would be absolutely wrong, for the Regrettables had regrettably forgotten about the dwarf male's greatest talent, that being the spring-loaded unhinging of the lower jaw to accommodate buckets of clay and debris while tunneling. To many dwarves it seems as though their lower jaw has a mind of its own, as they reflexively unhinge when they sense danger coming. Axborn had one of these hair-trigger jaws, and so when Whistle Blower clenched his fists for a double strike, the Reclaimer popped his jaw and swallowed him whole.

And just like that, even quicker than Axborn had lost his armor, Beckett Fowl lost a friend.

Perhaps *lost* is a slight exaggeration. Whistle Blower was more misplaced than lost.

And even that was temporary.

But when the toy troll came back some moments later, a certain innocence had been left behind in the dwarf's digestive tract, and it would take quite a few weeks before the little fellow slept peacefully.

Readers of a more sensitive nature are advised to skip over the next paragraph, as it ranks among one of the most disturbing events to be chronicled in the Fowl files. Yet it must be included in the name of historical accuracy.

Whistle Blower disappeared into the cavern of Axborn's open mouth without even hitting the sides. His left big toe did clip one of the dwarf's tree-stump teeth, which curved his body to the exact angle necessary to descend through Axborn's esophagus into his stomach, where the dwarf's aggressive stomach acids would dissolve him down to the bones in seconds.

"Oh," said Beckett. And then once more for good measure: "Oh!"

The twin decided that he would go ahead and throw a cluster punch anyway, but the sight of his friend being swallowed whole stayed his hand momentarily, and this hesitation gave the special-ops dwarf plenty of time to stomp on the boy's punching arm.

The dwarf grinned a leery loose-jawed grin, and for a moment there seemed to be a measure of satisfaction on his bloodstained teeth. This satisfaction was diluted somewhat moments later when the dwarf's stomach distended and stretched as though there was something inside trying to get out.

In fact, it was exactly like that.

Yes, Whistle Blower, thought Beckett. Fight!

Axborn did not seem overly concerned by all this stomach upset, because dwarves can train themselves to regurgitate at will. Given the choice, dwarves would prefer to send recyclings south rather than north, so to speak, but in a pinch they can spit up blockages. And in this case Axborn decided that north was infinitely preferable to south. He hunched himself over, made a series of bullfrog croaking noises, and hawked Whistle Blower out of his gut just as quickly as the troll went in.

The little troll lay shivering on the grass, displaying none of his usual vim and vigor.

He's injured, thought Beckett, then he called to his friend. "Whistle Blower?"

The troll could not respond, as he was overcome by violent shivers.

He must be cold, thought Beckett. But alive, at least.

The Fowl twin laid a hand on Whistle Blower's skin. The troll was not cold to the touch. He was being eaten alive by the same liquid that was now burning Beckett's hand.

Beckett did not know what to do.

Myles would know what was wrong, and he would know what to do.

The boy was correct on both counts; Myles would certainly have diagnosed stomach acid as the problem and prescribed a dip in his seaweed silo as the cure. But of course Myles was not available for consultation. He was several miles away, endeavoring to stop a building from falling.

Maybe knowing things *is* important, thought Beckett now, for maybe the third time in his life. Then: *I have no friend to help save Whistle Blower's life.*

Beckett was wrong in this regard. He did have a friend to help.

More than a friend, in fact.

A Fowl.

CHAPTER 17

STAY COOL

TO EXPLAIN this, we must shift our focus several hours into the past and several yards northwest into Villa Éco's safe room, where the Fowl parents were incarcerated. In order to preserve the narrative flow, we shall summarize this episode as much as possible and omit several conversations, which, while admittedly amusing, do not, strictly speaking, contribute to the story. These conversations may be summarized as follows:

1. "I can't believe we have been locked in our own safe room by warrior dwarves." (This conversation was repeated in various guises several times.)
2. "Some genius you turned out to be."
3. "Trust me, I actually *am* a genius."
4. "Our boys, our wonderful boys!"
5. "We'll get through this together."
6. "But what if we *don't* get through this? I don't think I can survive losing one of my boys again."

Once the Fowl parents had exorcised these various issues from their systems, they set about finding a way out.

Artemis Senior left no stone unturned looking for something that could help him open the steel door. The stones that the twins' father turned were part of a pyramid that Beckett was building and considered important enough to store in a safe room. In fact, the twins used the basement chamber as something of an overflow room for whatever they deemed valuable. Artemis Senior could not find a single useful item in the various crates. Of course, there had been a manual release cord on the inside of the door, but the Horteknuts had literally snipped that off at the root, and the cable nub had retreated into the wall. The dwarves had also taken the precaution of removing anything from the room that could possibly assist the Fowls in their inevitable escape efforts but had left the twins' various crates upended on the floor, before quite smugly informing the Fowl parents that they had infected the entire security system with a fairy virus.

Artemis Senior was understandably frustrated. "Of all the things Myles could have left in here," he said, actually kicking a box, "he leaves beach gear. Why on earth would Myles consider ragged beach gear important?"

Angeline was suddenly thoughtful. "He wouldn't. Myles rarely swims. And he never sunbathes."

Artemis Senior frowned. Perhaps this beach stuff merited a closer look. He squatted and sorted through the various items: a towel—folded, of course—a pair of trunks sporting an anchor motif, goggles with tiny motorized wipers, and a sun visor bearing the legend STAY COOL.

Stay cool. Where have I heard that recently?

The twins' father examined the visor. "This is the most un-Mylesy thing ever," he said. "It is quite trendy, which Myles would hate, plus the letters on the plastic would obscure his view, which our son would find intolerable."

"Try it on," urged Angeline. "You never know."

Artemis Senior did so. "Nothing," he said. "Just a visor."

"*Nothing* is ever *nothing* with Myles," said Angeline with conviction. "And *just* is never simply *just*."

She thought for a moment and then read the legend aloud. "Stay cool," she murmured, and then Artemis Senior remembered hearing the phrase from Myles himself mere hours before.

All you need to do is stay cool.

He had thought it strange at the time, as Myles detested such colloquial turns of phrase.

"That must be it," he pronounced. "Stay cool!"

And this did the trick. The visor became a screen and flickered into life, and NANNI spoke through tiny speakers on the frames.

"Pass phrase accepted," she said. "Welcome to NANNI lite."

"It's NANNI!" said Artemis Senior, excitedly. "Our sneaky son snuck NANNI in here."

"Of course he did," said Angeline. "Now open the door."

Artemis Senior echoed the command. "Open the door, NANNI. Now."

"NANNI lite," corrected the program. "Someone shut NANNI down. I will do my best to open the door, but the house system has been corrupted, and the damage is considerable."

"Just do it," said Artemis Senior, who could not help thinking that it was he who had disabled NANNI and how he could never forgive himself if something happened to the boys as a result.

What had I been thinking? he chided himself. To leave us even partially undefended?

While the Fowl patriarch thought, NANNI lite poked the Horteknut virus, rebuilding bridges where she could, zapping malware as she went, running thousands of commands per second in an attempt to clear out the fairy software. Luckily, the Fowl systems had some foreknowledge of fairy code, and in less than half a breathless minute she managed to crack open the door a few inches.

"She's doing it!" said Angeline. "I can see daylight."

The twins' mother flattened herself against the door and stuck her arm through the gap. "I can almost fit."

"Wait, honey," said Artemis Senior. "It's not stable. Without a safety sensor, those doors could bite you in two."

"I can fit now," Angeline insisted as the door cranked open maybe another centimeter.

"Negative," said NANNI. "It is not physically possible for you to fit through yet. I have scanned the available space and the dimensions of the object."

Angeline wiggled farther into the crack. "Are you calling me *the object?*" she demanded, and then: "How much longer, NANNI?"

"I estimate a point somewhere between five seconds and eight months."

"Eight months?!" said Artemis Senior.

Angeline could not wait that long and so squeezed herself through the tiny space and was off running up the stairs, leaving her tennis jacket snagged on the door's teeth.

"Angeline has done the impossible," commented NANNI.

"She often does," said Artemis Senior.

There is an old saying that Irish people employ when they are subjected to a sudden fright. Upon hearing a banshee wail, for example, an old farmer might swear that *the heart was put crossways in me*. Being of Russian descent, Angeline had never quite come to grips with this particular phrase, until the moment she raced past the sea window and saw her son battling one of those horrid Reclaimers. The dwarf was hefting a weapon, and Angeline felt as though her heart had slid across to the right side of her chest.

Beck, she thought. My Beck.

Angeline's instinct was to press her nose against the window and pound the toughened glass for all she was worth, but those would be the actions of a defeated parent, and she was not prepared to accommodate the notion that she might be too late.

And so she ran toward Villa Éco's front door, and the hardest part was the single second when Beckett was out of her sight.

What should I do? she thought with some considerable desperation. How should I fight my enemy?

In times like these Angeline missed the Butler family, who had been bodyguards to the Fowls for centuries, but Artemis had swept one Butler off to Mars with him, and the other was in the United States pursuing a career as a professional wrestler. Perhaps if there'd been some time available to gather weapons or call for help, Angeline would have felt some measure of confidence in her own chances of success, but she couldn't halt her forward momentum for even a split second.

Grab whatever you can lay your hands on, she told herself.

Unfortunately, all that Angeline could lay her hands on was the fire extinguisher hanging by the front door. She adored this particular fire extinguisher, as it had been molded to look like a metal grouse and it spewed foam when its beak was opened. But right now, she was not appreciating its artistry, just its heft.

Angeline grabbed the Fowl fowl from its bracket, ripped open the door, and rushed without hesitation toward the confrontation unfolding on the lawn.

As she neared the conflict, things seemed dire for Beckett and his friend. Angeline had never met Whistle Blower, but she had heard about his prowess on the battlefield.

This prowess was not in evidence now as the little fellow writhed on grass that was blackening beneath him.

He's burning up, thought Angeline, still running directly toward the dwarf and that cavernous mouth of his, which could easily accommodate a whole family's Christmas dinner. Beckett was on the ground, too, his forearm trapped beneath the dwarf brute's foot.

Oh, no, sir, thought Angeline. Not my boy.

From an objective point of view, one might think that Axborn held the advantage here, for wasn't he a trained and veteran soldier imbued with all the gifts his species had to offer? And yet history has taught us that it is unwise to wager against a protective mother, as often the universe sides with this particular energy. And such proved to be the case in this situation.

Axborn's finely tuned senses detected Angeline's approach and he swiveled his head to face her, his unhinged jaw dragging into the turn after his skull, just in time to be whacked on the cheekbone by a metal grouse that was a lot sturdier than its living counterpart. Axborn stumbled backward a single step, unpinning the human boy's hand. The dwarf's jaw was fractured, but Axborn was still conscious and determined. He had fought through worse pain and against worthier adversaries, or so he thought. He was right about the pain but dead wrong about the standard of his adversaries.

Angeline took in the scene with a glance and pulled the pin on the fire extinguisher, dousing the toy troll liberally and incidentally cooling Beckett's burned hand in the process. She swung the extinguisher back toward Axborn so that she might be ready to strike again, only to find the dwarf a yard closer than she anticipated. So Angeline sprayed the foam directly into the dwarf's mouth, leaving him with no option but to chomp down on the extinguisher itself, which he did. Angeline reacted quickly to the scything teeth and escaped with nothing more than scraped knuckles. The extinguisher was not so fortunate. It went down the path Whistle Blower had recently taken, still hissing foam.

I'll just regurgitate that, Axborn might have thought, but he never got the chance to, because . . .

Beckett threw his cluster punch and Axborn was plunged into a world of trauma. Landing the blow in the first place was difficult enough, but pinpointing the exact spot necessary to cut off the artery that controlled the dwarf's supplementary intestine was a one-in-several-million shot. When Beckett had tussled with the previous two Reclaimers earlier in this adventure, the cluster punch had caused the constricting sphincter muscle to fail, allowing the release of up to a thousand pints of compressed gas and supercritical fluid, but now he was punching directly onto a skin unprotected by a vinesuit, which supercharged the blow's effect.

Dwarves have a physiological get-out-of-jail-free card, which gives their bio-jet some extra oomph in times of dire emergency. This card can only be played once a decade, as overdoing it can prove fatal. The act of using it is known by many names: Trimming the Weight, the Big One-Two, and Watch Out Below, among others, and it involves the high-speed expulsion of not only the contents of the dwarf's stomach but also a third of the body's store of runny fat.

Beckett's punch activated this process, and Axborn found himself overcome by sickening dread as his body prepared for liftoff.

"D'Arvit," he said. "Not this. Not now."

But it was this.

And it was now.

The dwarf might have held on. He was a wind virtuoso, after all, and had once retained over a thousand pints of assorted recyclings for over a week when he was being held prisoner by humans in South America. And so, under reasonable circumstances, he might have waited out the crisis. But these circumstances were far from reasonable in anyone's book, and the jostling and fizzing of a fire extinguisher in his abdomen pushed him over the edge.

Axborn's linen shift fluttered, then ballooned like a sail catching the wind. The Reclaimer made a sad whimpering noise and then his heels left the ground, followed by his ankles, and finally, his entire person. A trained dwarf can ride a jet wash, but not when there is an alien element such as extinguisher foam involved.

Beckett rolled aside before he was pounded by a back-wash of decompressing air and assorted detritus. Contained in the column were the contents of the Reclaimer's stomach, which included but were not limited to the eroded remains of:

The skull of a small horse . . .

. . . fourteen diamonds . . .

. . . a small medieval millstone . . .

. . . one BAFTA Best Cinematography award . . .

. . . three shark's teeth . . .

. . . a burger patty from a popular fast food chain (no damage) . . .

. . . assorted stones and clay . . .

. . . a dog collar, which read either FOODLESS or TOODLES (most likely the latter) . . .

. . . and two soda cans (diet).

All of which missed Beckett by a hairbreadth, except for one of the shark's teeth, which nicked his forehead.

Axborn sustained substantially more damage than the Fowl twin. He flew in an erratic line, flailing as he zoomed to a height of thirty feet, at which point his engine sputtered out and he plummeted to earth headfirst, plunging into an ancient well that used to serve the monastery some five hundred years previously. Unlike Whistle Blower on his descent into the dwarf's stomach, Axborn did hit the sides on his way down. Several times, in fact. Luckily for the dwarf, the well had been dry since April, so he would not drown in the dark shaft; unluckily for him, the well had been dry since April, so his impact was not softened by several feet of water.

Beckett took Whistle Blower in his arms and was mightily relieved to find that his friend was resting comfortably.

"We saved him!" he exclaimed, turning to his mother. "You were outstanding, Mum, attacking a dwarf with a duck. Not just a dwarf—a Reclaimer. And he took off like a rocket. I wish I could do that. Just the taking-off bit, though, not the landing, if you could even call that a landing." Beckett had a sudden idea. "Mum, after what you did, you could join the Regrettables! I was thinking of inventing an initiation ceremony. How would you feel about eating grass?"

Angeline was not in the mood for her son's excited chatter. She'd had experience with loss. She knew about consequences.

"Beckett," she said, "are you hurt? Are you in pain?"

Beckett focused on his own body for a second, then shook his head. "No, Mum. There's no need to worry about Beckett Fowl."

Angeline suddenly saw the world through a film of tears. "You don't understand, my precious boy. Of course there's a need. Don't you know what I would do to protect you? How you break my heart with every foolish stunt?"

"I do, Mum," said Beckett, but he didn't fully comprehend the depth of his mother's constant fear for her sons' well-being. And he would not understand it for almost three decades, when it would become his time to worry.

Angeline wiped her eyes. "Where is Myles? Is he safe?"

Beckett was glad to have an easy question to answer. "Oh

yes. Myles is safe inside the collapsing building in the city."

Artemis Senior joined them just in time to hear that statement. "Let's go," he said. "We'll take the *Fowl Star*."

Beckett stifled a squeal of excitement. The *Fowl Star,* which his father tinkered with in the boathouse in his spare time, was a foiling yacht that could theoretically exceed sixty knots at top speed. Artemis Senior was perfectly aware that his boys might *borrow* the yacht for test runs if they could, so it was coded to his own biometrics. Myles had overridden the biometric settings armed only with copper wire and his genius, but the twin had never taken out the boat, as he wanted to leave his father with a shred of dignity. Beckett rightly guessed that, given the gravity of the situation, and indeed the effects of gravity on unstable buildings, a squeal of excitement from him might not be appreciated.

CHAPTER 18

A TOXIC RELATIONSHIP

The Convention Centre Dublin

Let us return now to Dublin's iconic convention center, where thousands of lives hang quite literally in the balance. To recap: Myles has, in the past fifteen minutes, managed to:

1. Foil Gveld's plan to reclaim the famed Horteknut lost gold.
2. Keep the convention center upright on its foundations.

And . . .

3. Reveal that his twin brother is, in fact, a holographic decoy.

Imagine what I could do in an hour, Myles thought, and he spent a nanosecond considering this intriguing notion.

Off the top of his head, Myles conservatively estimated that, given sixty minutes, he could:

1. Come up with a viable alternative to Ireland's various border issues.
2. Devise a plan to make the entire island energy self-sufficient (actually, that would only take fifteen minutes).

And . . .

3. Design rocket thrusters that could move Dalkey Island to a warmer latitude for the winter months.

But at the moment, Myles certainly did not have a leisurely hour to scheme and plot, for there was a most irate dwarf general one elevator shaft over who seemed quite intent on killing him, and he was pretty much out of ammunition ideas-wise about how he should sidestep being killed. Myles's only hope was that the general's irrational behavior patterns would scuttle her own plans.

And Gveld's behavior was indeed undeniably irrational. It was undeniable, unless you were Gveld Horteknut, who was convinced that she was reasonably calm under the extreme circumstances.

"I am calm," she was telling her second-in-command. "I have never been calmer. And once I kill this human child and grind his bones into sand, which I will then use in my hourglass, all will be well. Of course, my closest friend is a human, and my lifelong ambition has been denied me, and I've had a headache for the past year, but one can't have everything, eh, Gundred dearest?"

"Ah," said Myles, as though he were part of the conversation. "I do have a theory about that. The headaches, at least. How long have you been wearing that golden grill on your teeth?"

"Shut your mouth, human filth," said Gveld in reply. "Do not draw my attention just yet."

Myles nodded as though the dwarf had given a reasonable response, such as, *Six months, or quite some time, thanks very much for asking.*

"I see," he said. "It strikes me that over time some natural gold compounds have broken down and released gold ions into your system. These ions can have toxic effects on living organisms. The effects could possibly present as extreme paranoia, atypical behavior, extreme anger, and a hatred of people smarter than you." Myles smiled. "Actually, I added that last one, to show I have a good bedside manner."

"I am a dwarf," said Gveld. "Perhaps Gundred is susceptible to gold toxicity, but real dwarves are not."

Gundred couldn't help but groan. It seemed that Gveld was somehow going to make every single conversation in the foreseeable future about Gundred's deception. Having said that, the foreseeable future could be quite brief.

"Unless," said Myles, "the gold has been radioactively

tagged, which the ACRONYM gold has been, according to their own records."

This was a very good point.

And well made.

Even Gveld would have to take notice of that, unless, of course, she was suffering from gold toxicity and therefore paranoid.

"Nice try, Fowl," she said, sneering. "If I have toxic poisoning, then my decision-making process is flawed. How convenient for you."

"Not at all," countered Myles. "Paranoia is almost justified when facing an opponent of my caliber. In fact, delusions of persecution are possibly the only things that would give you the necessary edge to beat me. They do, however, make life tricky for those in your command."

Gundred took up the thread. "Gveld, this explains everything: the dangerous missions, the fallen comrades. . . . And all for what? Gold that we don't need? Foolish pride that will likely kill us all? You need to take a step back, General."

Speaking of taking a step back, perhaps we too should step back from Gveld and Myles's repartee to remind ourselves of the precarious mastermind cocoon our protagonists find themselves bantering inside. It is unlikely that the entire *collapsing building* scenario would slip our minds, but perhaps we have been distracted from the attending circumstances. Circumstances such as the tiny fact that the entire city was in absolute uproar. One of Dublin's major landmarks seemed to have come alive of its own accord, complete with teetering and moaning, during a solar eclipse. People had no idea what was going on, but they were certainly prepared to hazard some guesses, which were broadcast to the world at the speed of byte on various social media platforms, the latest being an app called Humblebrag, which encouraged users to misrepresent their own lives by posting only the most extreme moments, and guaranteed that at no point would any facts be checked. Ever.

So, on Humblebrag, people saw various service cables being torn from the sidewalk and whipping around like skipping ropes.

One wrote: *Freaky Egyptian snake invasion. #ragnarokishere*

An embarrassing mangling of two mythologies.

From the nearby bridge, someone put up a video of sparkling glass showers with the tagline: *It's raining glass. Hallelujah.*

Even though the glass was obviously falling from the building and not the sky overhead.

Yet another account holder, @OpenYourEyesPeople, posted, *Dublin city center is on fire and shaking itself apart. I bet warrior dwarves are behind this.*

Of course, hardly anyone took any notice of this spookily accurate wager, even though, in fairness to @OpenYourEyesPeople, her assertions were correct. Dublin city center *was* indeed shaking itself apart, and warrior dwarves *were* the culprits, for the most part.

If one were to take a bird's-eye view of the situation— though, in fact, there was not one actual bird's-eye view available, as all the birds, not being stupid creatures, had fled the area as soon as the first explosion cracked the center's foundations—but if one *could* have taken a bird's-eye view, then that view would have been both awesome and terrible. It was as if a circle of hell had dropped neatly onto the convention center and its environs. At ground zero—that being the center's lobby area—the entire floor had dropped half a level, creating a rubble-filled crater that was spiked with steel rods and jagged glass and had jets of multicolored flame shooting through the cracks. This rubble was mostly a uniquely veined marble tile, fragments of which would become highly collectible over the following years. The atrium was clogged with a particulate dust that spread through the empty and twisted window frames and across downtown Dublin like a Victorian pea-soup fog. The walls bolstering the Liffey's banks had been toppled entirely in places, and four of the river's bridges had been compromised; two would eventually collapse completely. In fact, the safest place in the entire zone was inside the earthquake elevators, where our protagonists were trading insults and arguments.

Unfortunately for them, their safety bubbles were about to burst, for when Gundred made the statement *You need to take a step back, General,* Gveld Horteknut, who felt herself attacked on two fronts, countered with a classic confrontation tactic, that being to throw the attacker's comment back at her, opposite-style.

"No, Gundred," she said. "I need to take a step *forward.*"

Which didn't make much literal sense in such a tight

space, but when Gveld drew her crystal sword and began hacking at the silicon nitride plates separating them from Myles Fowl, her intentions became abundantly clear.

For his part, Myles was surprised it had taken her this long. And there we have it, he thought. The irrational homicidal impulse.

Gveld was, he knew, at the crossroads of a mental anguish born of paranoia, single-mindedness, betrayal, and the reality that her centuries-old ambition now lay in ruins at her feet.

Her own life is not as important to her now as the termination of mine, Myles realized.

The crystal sword was sharp enough to carve a diamond and soon made a jagged hole in the toughened silicon nitride, which mildly surprised Myles.

No matter, he thought. It is only a small hole, and at that rate it will take her fifteen minutes to reach me.

Gveld obviously came to the same realization, because she pulled a crystal dagger from her belt and began hacking with both hands.

Myles studied her technique silently for a moment before calculating. *Taking into the account the smaller blade and Gveld's increased rate of speed, I would estimate that, if circumstances do not change, I will be dead in ten minutes.*

Myles upped his internal warning system level to critical. He searched his mind for a solution, but he was trapped in an elevator with no power. There was no workaround. All he could hope for was a change in circumstances.

"I know it is highly unlikely," he said, putting on his glasses, "but I don't suppose you can suggest a way I might extricate myself from this predicament, NANNI?"

NANNI was a little punch-drunk after the various explosions and said, "Can you change your state from solid to liquid, Myles?"

Myles rolled his eyes, an expression that was wasted on the AI. "I am mostly liquid anyway, NANNI, but if you mean can I phase-change voluntarily, then the answer is *not at the moment*."

"Then you are toast," said NANNI, which was hardly scientific, but Myles got the message.

"Hmm," he said. "There must be *something* I can do."

"What did you think was going to happen when you confronted General Horteknut?" NANNI asked.

"I presumed Gveld would bow down before my superior intellect," said Myles. "Oh, and yes, I also expected a tantrum, but usually good sense prevails."

But not in this instance, Myles realized. In this particular case, death shall prevail.

And he really wished he had made the toxic-poisoning deduction earlier in this particular adventure.

Gveld seemed possessed by the desire to kill Myles and was drawing an almost supernatural strength from somewhere. Myles knew he was witnessing a very rare case of *hysterical strength*, in which an individual's system is flooded by proteins and enzymes to facilitate extraordinary feats of might and stamina, and he realized that he would have to revise his estimate as to his own time of death, as Gveld would not slow down until the job was done.

ETD four minutes, he thought. At most.

It appeared Gveld had abandoned her rational self completely, as she was devoting quite a lot of energy to an extended rant as she worked.

"You are—*grunt*—not walking away from this—*grunt*—Fowl," she said. "You are not walking—*grunt*—or crawling, or flying. You will be—*grunt*—carried out of here in—*grunt*—several containers. The last thing you see—*grunt*—will be my blade penetrating your—*grunt*—eyeball on its way to your brain. Now, what do you think of that?"

Myles was reluctantly impressed. "Good sentence structure. Clear statement of intent. I would have to say that, as unhinged rants go, yours was not too shabby, especially given the circumstances."

Which enraged Gveld even further. She attacked the elevator wall with renewed vigor.

"I really don't understand why compliments would make you angrier," said Myles, who lacked the good sense to be terrified.

Gundred took Gveld by the shoulders. "He doesn't understand, my general. He is a child."

"I am not your general," spat Gveld. "*Your* general is an ACRONYM agent who is either dead or escaping from one of the other elevators."

"You *are* my general," insisted Gundred. "My general and my life. I will die here with you to prove it."

"That is your choice," said Gveld, returning to her work. "The choice of a human who means less than nothing to me."

Myles was of two minds about this statement. "Can there be 'less than nothing'? I suppose, in mathematical terms, less than nothing would be a negative number, which is something. In the real world, it could be argued that dark matter, and indeed vacuums, are less than nothing. . . ." Then Gveld's blade poked through the cables between their elevators and cracked the silicon nitride pane in front of his nose and Myles thought that maybe this was not the time for a philosophical debate on nothingness.

Gveld's strike not only cracked the silicon nitride but also shaved a few strands from one of the elevator cables. These elevators were the only traditionally operated cars in the building and not held in place by shaft turntables— meaning they could plummet to the earth. The earthquake protocol would protect Gveld and Gundred, but Myles's car had no such dampeners.

"Ah," said Myles.

"Yes!" spat Gveld, expressing the exclamation point with another strike. "We all fall, but only you die."

Myles thought about this. It was true that he had thwarted Gveld's plan and saved thousands of lives, but imagine how devastated the world in general would be if he himself died in the process.

I imagine they will rebuild this center and change the name to the Myles Fowl Memorial Hall.

Perhaps they will even initiate a humanitarian award and call it the Myles.

While both of these eventualities were pleasant to think about, Myles decided that on the whole he would prefer to live, and so he put his mind to the problem.

"You could very well die, too, General," he pointed out to the hacking Gveld Horteknut. "You have breached your own elevator's skin. Its integrity is no longer assured."

Gveld did not respond verbally, but she did redouble her efforts in slicing strands from the cables and widening the hole in the silicon nitride panes.

Either Gveld will get me, thought Myles, or gravity will.

As if the universe could read his mind, one of the cables snapped entirely, and both cars dropped a sickening yard.

"Weep for a world without me!" blurted Myles. These had long been his last words of choice, and the fact that his subconscious threw them up now reconfirmed for him just how much danger he was in.

One car over, Gveld's eyes shone in triumph, if such a physical manifestation of an emotion is possible. She picked herself up to begin again, only to be confronted by Gundred.

"Are we murdering children now, my general? Even though all is lost?"

"We are avenging our family's shame," said Gveld, her gold teeth glittering. "Or perhaps I should say *my* family."

It seemed Gundred was not prepared to meekly swallow any more barbs, for she said, "You are not avenging anyone's family. You are poisoned, my general. I beg you to come away with me. We can escape this place and regroup. Then I can leave forever, or I will accept your blade. Either way, you need never see me again."

"I don't see you *now*," said Gveld. "You are invisible to me."

Myles was grateful for their argument, as it served to both run down the clock till the authorities arrived and give him time to think.

"NANNI," he said, "how much power do we have in the laser pointer?"

"Enough to point a laser," said NANNI. "Certainly not enough to do any damage to anything or anyone without two more lenses."

And not just any lenses, Myles knew. One concave and one convex, which he didn't happen to have on him.

Perhaps I might improvise.

"NANNI," he said, "scan the silicon nitride pane. It has warped in several places. Is there perhaps a section we could use as ad hoc lenses?"

NANNI ran a quick scan. "Oh, I see a bubble. That might work."

The AI marked the spot and Myles realized to his chagrin that he was not tall enough for his purposes. He turned to Beckett, for his twin always ran point on physical tasks, but of course Beckett was not present.

"Bother and damnation," Myles swore, and then shuddered. "It seems one will be forced to climb."

When it came to climbing, Myles was often undone by

stepladders, and so perching on the handrail of an elevator was a daunting prospect.

"I suppose it must be done," he muttered and set about the task of first clambering on top of and then balancing on the railing.

With Myles thus occupied, we return to the actual dwarf and the human little person, who are having their own crisis one car over.

"Stop your sulking," snapped Gundred, angry now. "You are planning an act of mass murder. Nowhere in the dwarf charter is this called for. We know where the gold is. We can return to claim it. But this day is lost, and if you do not see that, then you are not the general I have followed these past few decades. The general I love as a sister."

Gveld froze momentarily, as though she might allow some sense to filter through, but Gundred's betrayal was simply too great for her to accommodate.

"I am not your general, and you are not my second-in-command. And since that is the case, I shall kill the Fowl boy and then I shall kill the spy."

"Yes, I was once a spy, though I can barely remember it," said Gundred. "I was a different person. A poorer person. You gave me purpose and worth."

"I was wrong to give it," said Gveld. "I take it back. You are worthless once more."

"You cannot take it back, my general. I shall die with self-worth. The only person you cheapen here is yourself. Even the Horteknut hoard will remain in human hands. It is so close, almost within your grasp, but it seems you are more interested in murder."

"You talk and talk," said Gveld. "But it is only words in a language you have stolen. I see you for what you are. You are the worm in my ear. You are the slow knife between my ribs. You are the breaking of my heart."

This one hit home, and Gundred cried openly. "Gveld, please! We can still escape."

Gveld laughed bitterly. "How does one escape one's heart, Gundred? There is no escape."

By which point Myles had just about managed to perch on the corner of the railing and was feeling quite proud of himself. "Are you ready, NANNI?"

"Of course, Myles," said his spectacles. "Congratulations on your climb. You have now achieved a level of agility comparable to that of a three-year-old human child or two-week-old chimpanzee."

Better than expected, thought Myles, even though he was reasonably sure his own AI had just insulted him. "How many bursts do we have?"

"Five, or possibly four. I wouldn't be surprised by three, and there is a chance that two will be our limit."

This is not science, thought Myles. But they were attempting to shoot a laser through a bubble at a dwarf who was in toxic overload, so allowances had to be made.

At that moment Gveld renewed her attack on the panes and cables. Her blades were fans of light and impossible for

Myles to target manually, so, reluctantly, he had to relinquish control.

"Target the ulnar nerves in Gveld's forearms," he ordered NANNI. "They control the grip in humans, and that is most likely to cause her to——"

By which time NANNI had already refracted two bursts through the bubble, pinpointing exactly the correct points, and though Gveld felt little more than two pinpricks of pain, her nerves and reflexes gave her no choice but to release both weapons. The crystal sword and dagger plinked harmlessly through the shaft's mechanisms, disappearing into the dust cloud.

Gveld's power of speech momentarily devolved to an animalistic level, and she howled as the blades fell. The Horteknut general thrust her arm into the hole in the silicon nitride and stretched her fingers to the limit of their reach as though she could somehow reach her lost blades.

"I would say that our antagonist is not happy," said NANNI.

Myles nodded. Even he could read a social cue like howling. "I concur," he said.

Now, he thought, surely the general will surrender. Her howling will downgrade to sobbing, and then she will accept her fate. To continue with this struggle is not logical.

But it seemed as though Gveld Horteknut was not ready to give up her ghosts just yet. She charged the elevator's wall, ramming it with her shoulder, causing the entire capsule to shudder. This was dramatic, certainly, but hardly effective, unless the goal was to give herself motion sickness.

"Really, General," said Myles. "This is not becoming. Think of your legacy—one might even say, your legend."

Gveld's power of speech returned(ish). "Fowl," she grunted with each shoulder charge. "Fowl! Fowl!"

The Fowl name itself is an expletive, thought Myles. And probably not for the first time.

While Gveld persisted with her attack, it was clear to Gundred that all avenues were closed to them but one: retreat. To this end she drew a tiny vial from her Dragonella tunic and twisted off the top, which had a dropper attached. The Horteknut Number Two oh-so-carefully dripped a single drop onto the elevator door seal, which began to dissolve immediately and with startling rapidity. The toxic fumes would possibly cause severe lung damage over time and were impossible to ignore. Even Gveld was distracted from her murderous mission.

She sniffed the air. "What do I smell? Could that be rock polish?"

It was, and her second-in-command was applying it to the door seal in an attempt to get them both out of this predicament.

"Are you a deserter as well as a spy?" asked Gveld.

Gundred kept her hand steady and applied another drop. "No, my general. I am ever your soldier. A prudent retreat is simply a delayed attack. You taught me that. Do you even remember that word, *prudent*?"

Gveld was not interested in hearing her own maxims turned against her. "All this time you had rock polish?"

"Yes," said Gundred. "Which I was not in a mind to volunteer so you could murder a human and kill yourself."

"With rock polish we could finish this job and be gone."

Gundred was unrepentant. "Rock polish can spread if not handled carefully. The crystal bottle can barely contain it. This is not an environment in which to splash the most corrosive organic compound known to fairies."

"I'll be the judge of that!" said Gveld, lunging for the bottle.

From atop his perch, Myles flattened himself against the elevator wall, as he had read all about the destructive power of dwarf rock polish in Artemis's files. Only master dwarf polishers were licensed to wield it, as they could gauge how many milliliters were needed in any situation. It was not simply the amount that had to be considered but the direction of pour and method of application.

With her reckless lunge for the vial, Gveld Horteknut was disregarding one of the most basic rules of dwarf society, that being to always and without exception take the utmost care with dwarf rock polish. And she was to pay the price for her impulsive action, as this single move would put a different and tragic complexion on this entire affair, for, as Gundred had warned: *Rock polish can spread if not handled carefully.*

Certainly, no one could ever classify Gveld's current handling of the crystal vial as *careful*, but she was a desperate individual in the throes of heavy-metal poisoning, and a combination of *desperate* and *poisoned* do not careful fairies make.

Before Myles's horrified gaze the drama in the adjacent elevator car unfolded as follows:

Gveld made a lunge for the rock polish and managed to get two fingers wrapped around the vial, which was a decent grip considering that Gundred also had two digits in play, those being forefinger and thumb. But while Gundred's handling of the vial was considered, Gveld squeezed as though she might shatter the bottle as she prepared for a heave. Gundred's initial response was to tug the vial toward her own chest, a tug that was met with only token resistance.

So far so good. One might think that Gveld had come to her senses, but no. Gveld was not relinquishing her hold but rather allowing Gundred some leeway to facilitate a run-up for her own uncontrolled yank.

She's going to try and tear the bottle from my grasp! the dismayed Gundred realized. The polish will go everywhere.

The polish would not in fact *go everywhere*, as the aperture was barely wider than a pinhole, but should even a dribble escape, it would be enough to melt them both to the bone, and Gveld did not seem in the right frame of mind for careful application even if she had been licensed, which she was not.

Gundred now had a choice: Should she wrestle with her general for the vial, which would certainly lead to an uncontrolled spillage, or should she relinquish her hold and hope that if the vial traveled in a smooth arc and remained unshaken then the anti-spill nozzle would fulfil its purpose?

In any such situation there is a third and indeed a fourth choice.

The third choice is to do nothing.

The fourth is to hesitate before choosing.

Gundred could not decide, so she opted for a combination of all four choices, which made for the worst possible outcome. To explain:

First, Gundred did nothing while hesitating. Then she instinctively held on, before belatedly realizing she really should let go.

This meant that initially Gveld's big tug had no effect, leading her to pull harder at exactly the same moment that Gundred released the vial, resulting in Gveld suddenly staggering backward, the vial bobbing overhead erratically. And, as any container expert knows, an erratic bob is precisely how to override a drip nozzle.

Dwarf rock polish was sprayed on the ceiling, wall, and floor, and immediately began to hiss on contact.

"My general," said Gundred, "you have disastrously over-applied."

Gundred was momentarily snapped out of her paranoia by the ramifications of what she had done. "I have indeed over-applied," she whispered.

Around them the elevator car began to melt like ice in direct sunlight. The polish's contact points went first, followed by chomp-sized sections that widened across the silicon nitride. Soon Gveld and Gundred were forced to lift their feet in a macabre dance as they avoided the spread.

There was no time to do anything. The floor was disappearing too fast.

Gundred and Gveld looked into each other's faces and cried tears of anguish. Not only would they die today, but they would part on bad terms, which both now realized was unacceptable.

"I am sorry, my general," said Gundred. "Believe that now as we die."

Gveld's only reply was to hold out her arms for a final embrace. Gundred stepped into that embrace with all her heart, preferring a death with her commanding officer to a life without her respect.

"I never betrayed you," whispered Gundred.

"I know," said Gveld, clasping her colleague's shoulders. Then something glinted in the dwarf general's eyes, distracting her. For a moment it seemed as though sunlight was falling across Gveld's face, dappling her features, softening the anger that lived in the creases.

It was not sunlight. It was ambient light reflected by bars of gold. The gold that Gveld had hunted for so long was in a huge banded slab, right over her head.

Myles understood immediately what had happened. Gundred's polish had splashed on the overhead panel, burning through to the treasure above, which was now so very nearly within Gveld's reach. The ceiling shriveled and disappeared, and for a moment the gold formed a new ceiling that shone in the low light. Gveld smiled wistfully for what had so very nearly come to pass, then whispered in her comrade's ear:

"Tell the families what happened here."

"What?" said Gundred, puzzled.

Without another word, Gveld used the last stable plates of the floor beneath her feet to brace herself, and with a mighty push sent Gundred flying backward, crashing through the weakened door and onto a drooping girder beyond.

Gundred was initially stunned but quickly realized what was happening. "My general!" she said. "Gveld, jump. Please come to me."

But there was no jumping. Nothing to brace against, and no space to jump through, for the gold fell in a clanking mass, the slab holding its integrity for a twinkle then blossoming into a shower of ingots, each one the weight of a concrete block.

Gveld barely had time to make a cylinder from the fingers and thumb and look through the makeshift hole. . . .

The Horteknut salute, thought Myles. *Tunnel safely, friend.*

And then Gveld was gone, borne into the bowels of the building by a torrential downpour of irradiated dwarf gold. Myles followed her descent into the dust cloud and heard the earthshaking crash as the bullion drove the general's body through the dust and flames and deep into the foundations. The crash was so loud that for a moment Myles thought Gveld might take the entire building with her. But the Convention Centre Dublin held on through this one last trauma, although the whining from stressed supports was constant now.

Gveld is unequivocally dead, Myles realized once he picked himself up from the elevator floor. There was no surviving such a ferocious impact.

The Horteknut hoard claims another victim, thought the Fowl twin. And the dwarves lose their greatest hero.

Myles knew that he had contributed to Gveld's literal downfall, and the thought made him sick.

This was never my plan, he thought. Why did the general not simply surrender?

He would never understand people's insistence on acting irrationally, even unto death.

Myles brushed himself off and looked to Gundred to pose this question, but he found the ACRONYM double agent's gaze already burning into him.

She spoke before he could. "That was the greatest dwarf who ever lived. And you killed her, human."

This was somewhat inaccurate in Myles's view, and he felt he should disagree. "A couple of points, Agent Zelda. First, I did not kill the general. Your own polish facilitated that. And second, you too are a human and so, by referring to me as a *human* in such a pejorative tone, you are effectively insulting yourself."

Gundred scowled. "I am not a human and I am not a dwarf. You have cast me into a gray area."

Myles could not argue with that.

"What will you do now?" asked the Fowl twin.

Gundred picked herself up on the girder. "I will find my general's body and ensure that she is given a hero's recycling." She pointed a warning finger at Myles. "And you, Fowl, will stay out of my way."

Myles nodded. "I will not interfere. But remember, Gundred, you are not a true dwarf. You cannot survive a collapse, and I would estimate that this building will fall in less than five minutes. The gold was the final nail in its coffin."

Gundred spat. "Gold. All this for a shiny metal. Gold poisoned my general in every way." The ACRONYM double agent tugged the hood of her Dragonella costume over her forehead. "Do not look for me, Myles. For once in your life, rein in that famous Fowl curiosity."

Myles considered this. He was already curious to see how Gundred's journey would play out, but perhaps the little person deserved some space in which to grieve. He peered into the abyss and could see nothing but flickering dust and a deadly lattice of twisted metal.

"My curiosity is of little importance here, Agent. I fear there is no way through to your general. You will probably die trying to reach her body."

There was no reply from across the divide, and so Myles looked up to find that Gundred had already gone into the dust. The only sign of her was a vaguely dwarf-shaped hole in the cloud, which filled itself in as he watched.

"Bravo," said Myles in genuine admiration. "A most excellent tragic sidekick exit."

Then a stray drop of polish melted the last strand of supporting cable, and Myles's elevator dropped thirty feet to be skewered by no less than five steel rods, all of which missed Myles's person but gave him the fright he deserved for being so insensitive as to make the *tragic sidekick* comment so soon after actual tragedy. Myles squealed all the way down, and if Beckett had been on-site, he would have excitedly informed his brother that the squeal was not just a squeal but also the first six letters of the seagull alphabet. Not in the correct order, which would have been *beyond incredible*, but intelligible nonetheless to a person who spoke seagull.

Myles hung inside the elevator, looking for all the world like an art installation with a steel rod running between his jacket and shirt, and wondering if:

a) Someone would rescue him.

Or . . .

b) The building would finally and inevitably collapse.

He really hoped it was option A, as he would miss his family terribly, and anyway, he was not overly fond of dying, having tried it once before.

CHAPTER 19
DWELF ARRIVAL

AS IT happened, it did indeed turn out to be option A, which was accomplished in such a manner as to take care of both the *missing family* and the *dying* issues. For when the elevator door was finally cranked open, it was done so by a man in a rumpled beige velour leisure suit. That man was none other than Artemis Fowl Senior, whose arrival had coincided nicely with the gas fires burning themselves out.

Myles was so relieved, he actually said "Dad!"

Then immediately corrected himself. "I mean, of course, *Father*."

"I don't know where all this formality comes from," said Artemis Senior, popping Myles's jacket button to free the boy from the garment. "A little affection every now and then wouldn't kill you."

Myles slapped dust from his hair. "You are quite needy, Father, but I suppose a five-second hug couldn't hurt."

"I concur," said Artemis Senior, holding out his arms.

Myles stepped into the hug and found that he had been wrong—the hug actually *did* hurt just a little—but Myles held on, as he felt his father needed a boost.

Outside, it seemed as though the world was converging on the Convention Centre Dublin. Emergency services were advancing through the three states of matter, those being land, sea, and air. To the casual eye, the Fowls were no different from any other refugees from the convention center, coated as they were from head to toe with gray dust.

The eclipse had fully pased by now, and the extent of the devastation was becoming clear. Downriver, droves of people were being herded from the theater, away from ground zero.

"All those people would have died if it hadn't been for you, son," Artemis Senior told Myles.

"Indubitably," said Myles. "And you and Mother would have perished if it hadn't been for Beck."

"And the little troll fellow," said Artemis Senior.

Myles thought he might get a dig in. "It was fortunate Whistle Blower returned after you so rashly sent him away."

Artemis Senior was not in the mood for a guilt trip. "I have a feeling he never actually went away, my son. In fact, I do believe that the more I look into this bizarre affair, the more I might find out about your various side projects."

Myles was offended. "Father, I do not have 'side projects.' Everything Myles Fowl does he does one hundred percent."

"I am disappointed by that hyperbolic comment," his

father said sternly. "It is impossible to devote one hundred percent of your effort to several projects at once."

Myles was chastened. "You are correct, of course, Father. I was attempting to make a point."

They walked side by side to the river, ostensibly a couple of survivors fleeing the beleaguered building. A team of paramedics attempted to shepherd them into one of a fleet of ambulances, but Artemis Senior waved them away, saying, "The boy scanned himself already with his eyeglasses. He's fine."

While Myles automatically blurted, "The Fowl family deny all charges."

That statement drew some confused looks, but the Fowl patriarch ushered his son down the jetty steps before anyone could formulate an objection.

"But back to my initial point," said Myles as he carefully negotiated the steep stairs. "It was a mistake on your part to separate us from the fairies. Lazuli, most especially. She was invaluable in this affair and even now needs our help quite urgently. I think that if we commandeered two of those construction cranes across the Liffey, one river barge, and perhaps a dozen electric bicycles, I could cobble together quite an effective excavation mole."

"No need to worry on that front, son," said Artemis Senior. "Commodore Short has already been in touch. The LEP have a Retrieval team moving toward Lazuli as we speak. The pixel is in good hands. Holly will contact us the moment Specialist Heitz is safe."

"Excellent," said Myles, somewhat relieved, as he was in dire need of a nap.

The Fowl electric yacht bobbed in the churning waters, and on deck stood Angeline and her blond son. Beckett had a wriggling mass in his shirt that Myles took to be Whistle Blower.

"I found Myles safe and sound in the elevator," Artemis Senior announced when they stepped on board.

"I told you," said Beckett, holding up his wrist. "The scar never lies."

Angeline wept with relief when she saw her son alive and more or less well, though it was hard to tell what minor injuries were possibly hiding beneath his coating of dust.

Myles was upset by his mother's tears and thought he might comfort her by employing a childish endearment. "Mum," he said, "no need to go on so. I am perfectly fine."

Angeline did not seem comforted. "Oh my god, Artemis! He called me 'Mum.' Is this another clone?"

Beckett laughed. "No. It's Myles pretending to be normal."

Angeline was not convinced. "Are you sure, Beck?"

Beckett pointed to his scar. "Totally sure."

"Say something Myles-y," ordered Angeline.

"Oh, for heaven's sake," said Myles. "Is my very name an adjective now?"

"Myles, it *is* you!" said Angeline, and she took her son in a hug that raised quite the dust cloud.

Beckett stepped in close and joined the hug.

"I did a brain thing," he said to his brother. "Painted the rock with red blood."

Myles was impressed. That was clever.

"I did a physical thing," he said to his twin. "I climbed on a rail."

Beckett frowned, thinking that perhaps this Myles was a clone after all.

Some levels below, Lazuli was huddled inside the excavator's cab, as though it could save her from the crushing impact of a collapsing building.

I will be obliterated, she thought. I will be atomized. I will be paste.

Which was not a comforting trilogy of thoughts.

The building yawned above her like the maw of some ravenous kraken demanding food. A wind funneled down from above, tainted by the fetid gas from ruptured septic tanks. Sparks tumbled through the wreckage, creating horrific shadows from twisted steel and stone towers.

I need to move, thought Lazuli. I need to get out of here.

But there was nowhere to go. No way out. She was trapped in a jagged dome supported by a trembling central column.

I can't . . . she thought. This is not how . . .

This is not how I want to die was the thought Lazuli was too shell-shocked to complete. But the finality of this situation wasn't a surprise to her, not really. It had to come to this sooner or later. A person could not continuously present herself at the sharp edge of Fowl adventures and expect to come out the other end alive.

Just ask Commander Root.

But were the Fowl Twins at fault here?

Were they really?

The answer to that was probably a no. After all, it was not the Fowl Twins who had glued her to a rocket. It was not the twins who tried to collapse a building in the name of honor.

This was a fairy problem, and she was to be a fairy casualty.

But . . .

She did not regret anything.

Lazuli laughed bitterly. A Regrettable who did not regret.

And the remaining Horteknuts? Lazuli snuck a peek through the struts of the steering wheel and saw that the two Reclaimers in the blue pod had activated an air recycler and were passing around freeze-dried rations. This made her suddenly furious—that the instigators of her imminent death would be completely safe and comfortable as they waited for their comrades to come and dig them out, while she, on the other hand, waited to be pounded flatter than a pixie-wafer tart.

A phrase from that train of thought struck Lazuli: *Imminent death.*

Hadn't Myles said that imminent death was the trigger for her magic? Hope surged through the pixel . . .

Then died.

There was no magic powerful enough to lift a building. Not even the great and mysterious demon warlock known only as N°1 (see LEP file: *Artemis Fowl:The Lost Colony*) could perform such a feat.

Lazuli saw now that the Reclaimers were waving at her—waving and laughing—and a rage grew inside her that she did not think she was capable of.

I would destroy them all if I could, she thought. In a heartbeat.

Lazuli looked at her hands and saw that they still glowed orange, veins tracing black in the blue skin.

And I *could* do it, Lazuli realized. I could.

This savage notion was squashed by an image of Beckett, who, apparently, had become her conscience. How would Beck feel if the last act she committed was a murder? He would be so disappointed in her.

And just like that, her rage faded almost entirely. Five more seconds and the magic would have subsided utterly, but then, with woeful timing, a dwarf punched through from outside the dome, his tunneling momentum sending him skidding across the cavern floor. Two more dwarves followed in quick succession, like artillery shells, and Lazuli thought, No. I am not having this.

The dwarves had obviously come quite a distance to rescue their comrades, and they whipped up more air currents than a fleet of landing helicopters as they expelled their pent-up tunnel air and came to rest like spinning tops winding down.

These new dwarves wore heavy mining suits and were strapped with sidearms, shoulder cannons, and more blades than a person might reasonably expect to see in a superstore that exclusively sold blades.

The only question here is whether those dwarves kill me first, or they rescue their friends and then kill me, thought Lazuli, not liking either possible scenario. So she decided to take the initiative and incapacitate three more dwarves.

How many is that in a single day? Four? Five? An underworld record, surely.

Perhaps she could be remembered for more than being taken prisoner by Reclaimers.

Twice.

And then, determined to go out with at least one bang, Lazuli swallowed her fear of nearly every element of this bizarre situation and hopped down from the cab of the excavator, hoping that her mood-sensitive magic would believe her life to be in danger. It did, and Lazuli was relieved to see the orange glow spread to her elbows.

The dwarves did not notice her coming. They were flat on their backs, taking a breather, when Lazuli stepped out of the dust, her eyes glowing like hot coals, though she did not realize it.

"Looking for someone to outnumber?" she said. She blasted the first dwarf, and he spun away on the fulcrum of his behind, yodeling with shock as he went, his bum flap flapping like a flag of surrender.

"Anyone else?" asked Lazuli, and even though he didn't

actually present himself, she kicked the second dwarf in the chest. Her magically turbo-powered boot sent him head over heels, his unhinged jaw clacking in surprise.

"You're . . . so . . . tiny," he said, one word per revolution, which did not calm Lazuli one little bit. She was vaguely aware of the fact that more figures were coming through the tunnels, but there was no time to deal with them now. She would have to disable the third dwarf and then see what she was up against.

The dwarf in question managed to get on his feet, and in his panic, he decided to clamp his mouth over Lazuli's arm. This was not the brightest idea he would ever have, as it was such a blatantly aggressive move that the pixel's magic escalated to auto-defend mode. It sent a bolt of energy so concentrated it was almost liquid straight into the dwarf's recycling system. The dwarf, in turn, automatically opened every internal pathway he could except his mouth, and as a result, the poor fellow went up and over, making it seem for all the world as though Lazuli was swinging him like a fairground mallet. The dwarf hit the ground with such force that had there been a bell, he would have rung it.

All this expenditure of energy was not without side effects, such as dehydration, nausea, and extreme disorientation, and so when Lazuli turned to face the latest arrivals, she was not in tip-top form.

"Come on, then," she slurred, and wobbled, wishing there were a nearby wall to lean on. "I've got plenty more where that came from."

Lazuli half noticed from the corner of her mind that the lead new dwarf did not cut a very dwarfish figure. Indeed, they seemed too slender and moved all wrong and it was entirely possible that the dwarf was an elf, and probably a female.

"A hybrid girl like me!" said the groggy pixel. "A dwelf."

The figure pulled off their helmet and by amazing coincidence looked a lot like Lazuli's LEP superior, Commodore Holly Short. The resemblance was, frankly, uncanny.

It *is* Commodore Short, Lazuli realized, and she told Commodore Short that she was Commodore Short, which was probably something Commodore Short was already aware of.

The elf's little voice told Lazuli that the best thing she could do in the circumstances was pass out now and explain later.

And so she did.

The *Fowl Star*

The debriefing was held three days later aboard the *Fowl Star* yacht, which was actually the second craft to bear that name. The original *Fowl Star* was a cargo ship that Russian gangsters had sunk some years earlier in the Bay of Kola, where it remains to this day wedged into a crack in the Barents Sea floor, preventing further movement of the tectonic plates. Which just goes to show that even Fowl possessions can save the world.

Myles decided that, since everybody's security had been compromised (mostly by him), it would be safer to talk on a vessel in international waters. This way, even if something incriminating was recorded with echo-sounders or vibration microphones, it would be difficult to find a path to prosecution. And anyway, he was growing weary of denying charges thrown at him by adults he neither respected nor recognized as valid authorities.

NANNI steered the boat to the agreed-upon coordinates five miles off the Irish coast and then toggled the engines to resist the pull of shore-bound currents.

It was a fine summer morning with only the occasional wisp of cloud to provide cover, so Beckett cranked open a striped awning, which laid a patch of shade over the lower deck. Myles gently chastised his twin for hand-cranking when he could have simply swiped a sensor, to which Beckett responded bilingually that only a *scritch-scritch-arrrrr* would swipe when he could crank. It would seem to the casual or even professional observer that all was well in the Fowl Twins' intrapersonal bubble, which it was, because Beckett had no time for the effects of trauma, while Myles was seeing a counselor for an hour every day in order to come to terms with the events of the past week. The counselor was, predictably, his own reflection in the bedroom window, which, in the right light, gave him a view of himself and the world beyond, in keeping with counselor objectives.

As a concession to the weather, Myles was wearing a white linen suit with a matching fedora hat and of course his Gloop tie, while Beckett wore Bermuda shorts and of course his Gloop tie, and flippers, as he intended to swim back to shore after the meeting.

They waited for several minutes until Myles grew impatient, slamming his Fowltini glass on the table before crying out melodramatically, "For heaven's sake, Commodore. I am wearing glasses with fairy-based technology in the lenses. I can see you."

There followed a brief speckling in the air accompanied by a sound reminiscent of a baby owl's shriek, and Commodore Holly Short appeared in the wooden slatted chair facing Myles, the Opti-sequins of her green LEP uniform sparkling as they settled.

"Sorry about the shrieking noise, Master Fowl," she said. "My shield harmonics need tuning."

Lazuli's shield did not need tuning, and so she appeared noiselessly at her superior's shoulder, also dressed in LEP green.

"Myles," she said, and to Beckett, "Beck."

"Laz," said Beckett, and once again: "Laz."

He said this twice to emphasize his affection, but also because Myles had requested that he not bowl over his pixel friend with one of his trademark hugs until they assessed the state of fairy-human relations, and not embracing Lazuli was causing the boy some distress.

"I'm under no-hugging orders," he explained.

Me, too, mouthed Lazuli.

"Commodore Short," said Myles. "Specialist Heitz. How lovely to *see* you both."

Holly raised one eyebrow pointedly. She was very adept at eyebrow-raising, which could, in fact, cause problems when the smart visor of her flight helmet misinterpreted the motion as a head tilt and sent her off-course as a result.

"Lovely to see you, too, boys," she said. "I had hoped to see Whistle Blower, too."

"Whistle Blower is a free agent," said Myles innocently. "He does as he pleases. We have no idea where he is."

"Really?" said Holly, and she directed the next questions to Beckett. "Is that true? You have no idea where the toy troll is?"

Poor Beckett's stress levels skyrocketed. "I have no ideas about anything," he said vaguely. "That's my policy."

"I see," said Holly. "Nevertheless, it is nice to see you boys. Though I had hoped it would take a little longer for you to break our agreement."

Myles smiled thinly. "Not *our* agreement. Your agreement was with my parents. Believe me when I tell you, Commodore, that the Fowl Twins as a unit are very much finished with abiding by rules that we haven't had a hand in drafting. Everything about your little agreement was misguided, stupid, or wrong. If I could, I would press charges against, or indeed sue, the Fairy People. If it hadn't been for Beckett 'breaking your rules,' several thousand people would be dead, including myself, and where would the world be then? Bereft, that's where."

"Beckett and Specialist Heitz would also be dead," Holly pointed out.

"That is true. And many people would be devastated, including myself. But if I died, the world would be denied my genius and would end several centuries ahead of schedule as a result. All because of your little 'agreement.'"

Lazuli glared at Myles, willing him to stop talking or at least be a little less like himself. The only way she could avoid demotion or outright expulsion from the LEP would be if Myles backed off from the not-so-veiled threats.

Many people would be amused by a twelve-year-old making outlandish claims about his own future legacy, but Holly Short was not one of them. She had been involved in enough Fowl shenanigans to know better.

"Myles, you know we're being watched," she said, a gentle warning in her tone. "There is a shuttle with an entire squadron of LEPtactical directly above us. We could mind-wipe you before you could so much as blink, then all this rhetoric would be forgotten. Perhaps we already have erased certain details from your brain."

Beckett laughed. "Sorry, Holly. You should know that you can't outthink Myles. If anyone has been mind-wiped, it's probably you."

This throwaway statement gave Holly pause. It would seem impossible, on the face of it, for Myles to turn fairy technology back on the fairies themselves, but the impossible was everyday for a Fowl.

"Myles," she said. "You wouldn't."

Myles placed his fedora on the table and took a long drink from his Fowltini. "No," he said. "I wouldn't, because it's a barbaric procedure that could have a permanent effect on the subject. So I have decided that if the People ever attempt to mind-wipe Beckett or myself, there will be consequences."

"It sounds very much as though you are threatening us," said Holly evenly. "That is hardly the basis for a friendly debriefing."

Myles had to laugh. "Friendly debriefing? I know from your own files that Foaly is working on a remote mind-wiping unit. So maybe your technicians are tuning into my brainwaves even now."

Directly overhead, a gnome technician paused the brain-wave scanner.

"Let me tell you what happens if you initiate that procedure," said Myles. "Usually a magician never gives away his secrets, but in this case, there is nothing you can do about it, so I hope you're recording this."

Holly nodded. They both knew she was recording.

"When a mind-wipe is activated, it elicits a very specific Theta wave pattern. If NANNI detects this pattern in my brain, or Beckett's brain, that in turn will trigger an info dump of everything I know about the Fairy People to every major news outlet in the world."

Lazuli was horrified. "Myles, do you know what you're saying? You're declaring yourself an enemy of the People."

Myles disagreed. "No, Lazuli. I am being up-front, which is more than your comrades in the LEP are doing."

"But we're friends, Myles," said Lazuli.

"We *are* friends," conceded Myles. "We three. And Commodore Short is friends with my brother. And yet here she is, prepared to mind-wipe us. This is all politics. And sadly, politics usually takes precedence over friendship."

Holly knew this to be true, though it was certainly not always to her liking, but the further up the ladder she climbed, the more necessary politics became.

Perhaps I should climb back down the ladder, she thought. To a simpler time when it was just Artemis and me against the world.

That was exactly the rung on which Lazuli now stood.

Perhaps we do need the Fowl Twins, Holly realized. Myles is our ace in the hole, and Beckett is our wild card.

"So, what are your demands, Myles?" she asked the suited twin. "You wouldn't be a Fowl if you didn't have demands."

Myles opened his hands to demonstrate they were empty. "No demands. I simply wish you to do what you have just this second decided to do. Let things continue as they are. We keep our memories and our ambassador. You can continue spying on us if it makes you feel better, but in my opinion, it's a waste of a surveillance team's time."

Holly nodded slowly while she considered. "I will run this past the council and get back to you."

"Through our ambassador?"

"Precisely, boys," said Holly, standing. "Through your ambassador."

"Excellent, Commodore," said Myles, also rising to his feet. "And please tell Foaly that I fully expect him to start thinking about a Theta workaround. I have begun work on version two-point-oh, so I'll be ready for him. In fact, it should be fun."

Holly suppressed a groan. The boy was right. Foaly would enjoy having a new Fowl to joust with.

"I'll tell him," she said, and to Lazuli, "I'll leave the actual debriefing to you, shall I, Specialist?"

"Yes, Commodore," said Lazuli, smiling because she had managed to hang on to her rank. "Thank you, Commodore."

"Don't thank me, Specialist," said Holly as her suit began shimmering. "I just made you responsible for the Fowl Twins."

Holly disappeared from regular view, and Lazuli stopped smiling as she realized the implications of what her boss had said.

I just made you responsible for the Fowl Twins.

It would be considerably less challenging to be responsible for the elements.

She stopped worrying when Myles lifted his hug embargo, and Beckett in turn lifted Lazuli bodily from the boards, swinging her for several revolutions while humming the tune to the Regrettables' theme song. This pirouetting lasted fully a half minute and left both parties exhausted on the deck.

Myles gave Lazuli a few seconds to recover, then asked his first question. "Was Gveld's body recovered?"

"No," said Lazuli. "They didn't find Gundred, either."

"And the gold?"

"The LEP recovered every bar. Apparently, Gundred wanted nothing to do with it."

"I imagine it will go back to the rightful owners?"

"The family just has to file a claim," said Lazuli. "It shouldn't take more than a few weeks."

"So General Horteknut recovered the hoard after all."

"I suppose she did, although the remaining Reclaimers will end up incarcerated."

It didn't take long for Myles to absorb this information, because Lazuli was really only confirming what he had already surmised.

Lazuli had a question of her own. "Do your parents know you're on board the yacht?"

"Of course," said Beckett. "They're belowdecks in the state room, doing trance-yoga. It helps them relax after we've had one of our incidents."

Lazuli had to smile at Myles's sheer gall, scheduling a debriefing while his parents were exercising downstairs.

"Mother and Father are far too predictable," said Myles. "Though I suspect my brother and I will be under the microscope from now on."

"I suspect that, too," said Lazuli. "An electron microscope."

"What we need to do in order to placate our superiors is find a mission that will benefit all parties, human and fairy."

Lazuli sat in the chair facing Myles. Her LEP uniform cast a sparkle that reached her eyes. "And I bet you have a suggestion, Myles."

"Actually, Specialist Heitz, I do."

Lazuli looked out over the shimmering sea for a moment and wondered how many millions of gold credits Myles's *suggestion* would cost. She wondered how many times her magic would be initiated by *imminent death*. She wondered if Whistle Blower would ever lose his mistrust of the LEP officers who had been trying to tag him all his life. She wondered whether Myles would ever grow smart enough to realize that smarts weren't everything and that he would be lost without Beckett, who would in turn be in deep trouble without herself.

So many questions in a life she wouldn't trade for anything.

"Tell me your suggestion," she said to Myles, who knew his pixel ally was hooked.

He smiled and said, "Well, Specialist Heitz, I would very much like to know where General Horteknut got her hands on a clone of me. Not a particularly well put together clone, but put together nonetheless."

"That is a very good question, Heitz," said Holly's voice in Lazuli's earpiece. "Permission to pull on that thread is granted. And just to annoy Myles, tell him that, technically, it was a copy, not a clone."

"Of course, technically, it was a copy, not a clone," continued Myles. "I am trying to keep it simple for people listening who might not know the difference."

"Do you mean me?" said Beckett, who seemed to be trying to rip up one of the decking boards. "Are you keeping things simple for me?"

"No, Beck," said Myles. "You run on instinct, and instinct is the evolution of intelligence, which means you are the smartest person on, or indeed above, this boat."

Beck abandoned his destructive efforts. "Finally Myles says something right. That deserves a wrist bump."

Myles held out his wrist and Beckett rushed to bump it.

"Laz, come on," Beckett said. "Regrettables' salute. You're a Regrettable."

Lazuli wasn't sure she should join in until Myles commented, "Oh, for goodness' sake, dear brother, do not involve the specialist in our immature practices."

Which Lazuli was perfectly aware was a form of reverse psychology, and also Myles's way of welcoming her into the inner circle without appearing overly sentimental.

"That," she said, raising her wrist for a triple bump, "is the nicest thing you've ever said to me."

Myles did not dispute the comment, which was tantamount to accepting it. The three Regrettables bumped wrists, and Lazuli felt that in spite of being the Fowls' fairy liaison, she was also part of this group of adventurers.

She also could have sworn she felt a tiny electrical zap at the point of contact.

"*The Regrettables, the Regrettables,*" Beckett sang, and the other two joined in:

> "*We're completely unforgettable,*
> *We love our fruits and vegetables,*
> *That's cuz we're Regrettables.*"

Which was obviously the Regrettables' theme song.

Oh dear, thought Myles. That *fruits and vegetables* line really must go. Such a lazy rhyme.

But he said nothing and sang along with the repeat.

EPILOGUE POSTSCRIPT

Childerblaine House, St. George Island

Some five hundred miles directly south of the Regrettables' reunion sing-along, there was a man in a brass tub who was less than happy with how the entire Horteknut-hoard affair had worked out. Lord Teddy Bleedham-Drye, the Duke of Scilly, reclined in his saltwater bath of electric eels and read from a thin strip of paper tape that ran through a ticker machine that had originally transmitted stock price information over telegraph lines. The duke had adapted it as a low-tech way of receiving secret messages from Ishi Myishi, his friend and collaborator. The ticker-tape message was coded in twentieth-century stock-market terminology so as to appear utterly harmless, but it didn't really matter, because there was not an intelligence agency in the world that monitored telegraph lines. And just to make entirely certain that his secret messages were not somehow leaked,

Lord Teddy shredded the tape as he read, feeding the scraps of paper to his eels.

Sometimes the old ways are best, Teddy, the duke often told himself.

But today, as the trained electric eels tightened his epidermis with low-voltage shocks, Teddy was not so much enamored by the machine as angered by the message it conveyed.

The blasted Fowl Twins have survived. How is this possible?

Of course, such is the reserve of the British royal family that Teddy's fury showed only in a curling of his toes, which were modestly hidden underwater.

"I don't know why you're surprised, Teddy old man," the duke told himself. "Those infernal twins have more lives than a bag of cats."

Teddy switched off his machine and considered.

"Never send a copy to do a clone's work," he declared after a moment's thought.

For he himself was a clone, as his original body had been cooked inside a ball of cellophane, thanks to little Myles Fowl and his twisty schemes (see LEP file: *The Fowl Twins*). The new body was taking some getting used to—there was a certain deterioration between thought and action—but he was getting there, and Teddy had heard rumors of a magical rite performed in India that might speed up the process.

Six months, Teddy thought. Half a year and I will be tip-top and ready to exact bloody and prolonged revenge.

But then he corrected himself. *No. Not prolonged. A fellow does not toy with the Fowl Twins. When my chance comes, I will take it immediately.*

This notion calmed Teddy considerably, and so he lay back in his tub, uncurled his toes, and began to plot. . . .